MW01515069

THE WOMEN
OF
HARVARD SQUARE

ALSO BY MIKE LIEBERMAN

FICTION
Never Surrender—Never Retreat
The Lobsterman's Daughter

POETRY
Praising with My Body
A History of the Sweetness of the World
Sojourn at Elmhurst
Remnant
Far-From-Equilibrium Conditions
Bonfire of the Verities

THE WOMEN OF HARVARD SQUARE

A NOVEL IN SHORT STORIES

MICHAEL LIEBERMAN

Texas Review Press
Huntsville, Texas

Copyright © 2014 by Michael Lieberman
All rights reserved
Printed in the United States of America

FIRST EDITION

Requests for permission to acknowledge material from this work should be sent to:

Permissions
Texas Review Press
English Department
Sam Houston State University
Huntsville, TX 77341-2146

This novel is a work of fiction, and all characters, names, places, and events are either products of the author's imagination or are used fictionally. Any resemblance to actual people or events is coincidental and unintended.

Acknowledgements:
I am grateful to Carolyn Florek, Lucia Woodruff, and Paul Woodruff for reading early drafts of individual stories and to Scott Webber who helped liberate the women of Harvard Square from my ham-fisted grasp. I thank Seth Shulman and Susan Abel Lieberman for their careful readings of the manuscript. Their many thoughtful comments greatly improved the novel. I thank Ruth Irvin for copy editing and managing the production of this book and Alec Brewster for editorial assistance. The book would be much diminished without them. Seth Lieberman, Julie Wingerter, Jonathan Lieberman, and Soyan Lieberman filled in details about greater Boston and updated my anachronisms. Thanks to them the book is a far better read.

Learn more about Michael Lieberman and his work at his website:
www.michaellieberman.com
Contact him: poet@lieberman.net
Facebook: www.facebook.com/michaelliebermanpoetwriter
Tumblr: www.michaelwlieberman.tumblr.com

Cover Design and Oil Painting: Nancy Parsons, Graphic Design Group

Library of Congress Cataloging-in-Publication Data

Lieberman, Michael, 1941- author.
  The women of Harvard Square : a novel in short stories / Michael Lieberman. ~ First edition.
    pages cm
  ISBN 978-1-937875-85-5 (pbk. : alk. paper)
  1. Women authors, American~Massachusetts~Cambridge~Fiction. 2. Mothers and daughters~Massachusetts~Cambridge~Fiction. 3. Sisters~Massachusetts~Cambridge~Fiction. 4. Femininity~Fiction. 5. Harvard Square (Cambridge, Mass.)~Fiction. I. Title.
  PS3562.I434W66 2014
  813'.54~dc23
                          2014036610

For Susan, as always

Contents

Guide for Readers and Book Clubs

What the women of Harvard Square are saying about Mike Lieberman

Agnes Lubeck: Being in these stories is way cool. I totally loved it. It's not often that a budding neuroscientist gets to express her kinky side with impunity—no, with encouragement. Mike Lieberman is a master.

Diana Endicott: It was fun watching Lieberman deal with my material. I'm an aspiring playwright. I've only had my plays produced locally. So I held my breath as he incorporated my plays into the stories and later portrayed my blue funk. I'm on board with what he has done. This guy gets it.

Adriana Lubeck: At first I was a little uncomfortable being put under the microscope this way, but it all ended for the good. Even my relationship with my daughter Agnes improved because of this book. Lieberman helped me through a difficult patch in my life, and now, thanks to him, I'm seeing a fair bit of Norman.

Olympia Breathwaite: I'll be honest. I felt a bit of competition with Lieberman. We're both novelists, and he had the upper hand. What can I say? It is his book. I am a little disappointed though. No, let's call it what it is. I'm bitter. Both my stories are dark. One is creepy, and I loathed my part. In the other stories, I was a supporting actress who never found love. He'll get his in my next novel.

Beverly Ardmore: I've got a beef too. Lieberman eased Norman out of my life. I wanted him, and he gave him away to Diana and Adriana—both of them!

He's nothing but a pimp. It's all the more outrageous because we're both Texans.

Abigail Lubeck: That man was more than generous to me although he made me wait till almost the end of the book. I thought I would be only an old person, Agnes's creaky grandmother. But he gave me a great role to play, and you know what? He threw in a vibrator as well. He knows how to honor older women.

Henrietta Markham: Mike Lieberman gave me more than I deserve. He gave me motive and opportunity as the crime folks say—and with them sex and, well . . . I'll let you read *The Women of Harvard Square*. And he brought me back to Boston with my special friend A.E. to do a cameo reading from *The Lobsterman's Daughter*. He didn't have to do that. He could have mentioned the book and shunted me aside. I loved being with Agnes and Diana. I'll never find deeper soul mates. I think maybe Mike and A.E. are in love with us.

THE WOMEN
OF
HARVARD SQUARE

I. Our Lady of the Bogs and Pitcher Plants

Diana was the talk of Adams House. And Agnes, like everyone else, was swept up by her mystery and beauty. Diana hung out with writers and literary types and was rumored to be working on a play. The title, House scuttle had it, was *Disraeli's Apricot Tree*—which led to endless speculation. People googled "Disraeli." The curious, meaning a large swath of the undergraduates in Adams including Agnes, had to know every last detail. The more enterprising got hold of an old British TV miniseries and watched it avidly for clues about the statesman. And everyone kept an eye out for Diana in the common rooms and the courtyard and walking along the Charles or on Plympton Street or Mass Ave. The dining hall was prime viewing. What would she be wearing? Who would be her dinner companions? Was she dating someone?

Diana had instant glamour. She was fine-boned and delicate without seeming frail. She could make the simplest top and pants look as if they had come from the most expensive boutique in Boston, and when she did walk in for dinner, she seemed to have stepped simultaneously out of the pages of *Vogue* and *The New York Review of Books*.

One night Agnes watched Diana cross the dining hall to a table where three attractive, young women sat. She carried bound copies of something—her play, Agnes surmised. A jolt of excitement surged through the voyeur—a play devoted to young women, perhaps exclusively devoted to their sensibilities, and certainly written by one with undeniable charisma. And Benjamin Disraeli? What was he doing in their company?

This was in the early spring of their junior year—Agnes remembered because the crocuses were just in bloom. Later, when the tulips were at their height, she saw a performance of *Disraeli's Apricot Tree*, and her fascination turned to longing.

With Maynard it was different. Agnes was taken with him before she met him.

Her mother Adriana Lubeck first put her on to him—as it happened, after the crocuses and before the tulips, that is, when the forsythia were at their height. Agnes was quite certain of the timing because one day she came to her mother's office and found a generous clutch of the brightly flowered branches in a vase. She also found her mother grousing about Maynard.

Not many people had the courage to stand up to the formidable Professor Lubeck. Maynard was one of these. Adriana was famous for her brilliant, if sometimes idiosyncratic scientific investigations. Maynard had come from Princeton expressly to work with her and brought with him the highest recommendations and very clear ideas of his own about his dissertation research.

"He was exceptional, and so I gave him what I think will be a showcase project. The rub is that he wants to work on cancer and the human genome. He dismissed my project, calling it 'trivial and derivative.' He pronounced it, 'not fit for high school students.'"

His chutzpa, his strength of character, his conviction, his self-confidence—Agnes didn't know what to call it—interested her.

"I was furious," Adriana continued.

"So what did you suggest that he balked at?"

"Well, I told him I wanted him to develop a rapid, generally applicable method to use DNA sequencing to survey the insects and spiders that the carnivorous pitcher plant traps in the fluid of its pitcher-shaped leaves."

"Honestly, Adriana"—Agnes always called her "Adriana," never "Mother" or "Mom"—"if I didn't know you so well, it would sound like a yawn to me too.

If that's all the information you gave him, what did you expect? My generation was raised on the hype around the human genome. Let me guess. He stood his ground."

"He did, damn it. I don't understand why he didn't get it. He is so very able."

"So what now?" Agnes asked.

"I have to say this for him, he marshals his arguments better than any student I remember."

"Come back to my question. What's he going to do?"

"Finally I had to say, 'Maynard, trust me. You can make rapid progress in an area that is almost unexplored, and with climate change and global warming this approach might become a major tool to study changes in the earth's ecosystems. It's a lot of fieldwork, a lot of time collecting specimens in hot, humid bogs, but in the end you will have something.' Eventually, he agreed but only provisionally."

Agnes was sucked in before she laid eyes on him. Her resolve was only strengthened by another vignette Adriana recounted. Early on she had told Maynard to think about how useful recent DNA sequencing data had been in sorting out the species and subspecies of finches that Darwin had found in the Galapagos. Maynard responded that doing the project she proposed would be like being sent to Darwin, Australia—to a nineteenth-century Australian penal colony never to be heard from again. That bit of moxie clinched it for Agnes.

Disraeli's Apricot Tree was performed as part of an undergraduate drama festival, and Agnes and many other undergraduates made the pilgrimage to see it. She came away enthralled and titillated by Diana's beauty and talent. In appraising her, Agnes drew in her breath with decisive force, and as she let it out, a compelling but loopy plan seized her. She would stalk the playwright—learn the most minute details of her life, her interests, her romantic involvements. Agnes could not get the idea out of her brain. Most of her understood that such behavior was twisted, but a small part of her pushed back. Was not information gathering an essential part of science—and maybe life too? Was she not a scientist? Then good sense prevailed, and Agnes swallowed hard and let go of the misadventure.

The set was minimal—an artificial apricot tree and three high stools on a bare stage. The play was not. Diana anticipated the confusion the title would cause and provided program notes. Disraeli was much more than a famous nineteenth-century British politician. He was a novelist, a raconteur, and a confidant of the queen. Diana focused on his literary interests. The notes were silent on the apricot tree.

The curtain was raised on three young women in apricot colored bodysuits sitting on the stools under the apricot tree. They took turns speculating on what Benjamin Disraeli thought about Dostoyevsky's *The Brothers Karamazov*. It began with the deplorable state of the serfs in Czarist Russian and morphed to the fanatic reverence in which they held the church.

Agnes could not see where the play was going. She kept shifting back and forth in her seat waiting for something to happen. It felt like a dry academic debate, not a play. "Stasis" was the word that came to the young biologist's mind. Surely this can't be the whole play. Someone as smart and beautiful as Diana must be up to something more.

Then the actors began to talk about the conflicts between Fyodor Karamazov and his son Dmitri. They turned angrily toward one another. Spittle-mouthed, they hissed and snarled. "Ivan is the family patriarch. Disraeli respected legitimate authority." "He's a controlling despot. That's why Disraeli secretly admired him." "The son's an ingrate, a degenerate." "He's only trying to escape the overweening control of his father." Off their stools, the actors stalked one another, crouching and shaking their fists. It looked as if they were about to savage each other. "You apologist for hate, get off the stage." For an instant it seemed that the biggest of the women would push one of the others into the audience. "You don't know what hate is. It's the way men love."

Diana introduced a certain Grushenka. "This beauty has no right to be here," one actor said. "She does. She is Dostoyevsky's desirable, elusive woman. We need to hear what Disraeli thought," was the counter. "Surely we can all love beauty." Slowly the roughness gave way to conciliation. The three women began touching one another—very discreetly at first—and kissing in a restrained, almost demure manner. As they portrayed Disraeli's imagined disapproval of the competing lust of father and son, they were seized with the need to fondle each other and to kiss passionately. Soon a *ménage-à-trois* theme took over the play. Disraeli's imagination was no match for three young women in apricot-colored bodysuits.

Agnes sat transfixed watching the erotic forays of three women whose dress simulated nakedness. Her thoughts turned to Diana. She couldn't help herself. She was attracted to the beautiful woman who could conceive such a bold idea and carry it off. Was this an unconscious invitation on Diana's part? Maybe, but not to her specifically. The two had only met in passing. Was it a more general call to which she might respond? Possibly. What would it be like to sleep with a woman? What would it be like to sleep with Diana? What would it be like to sleep with Diana and Maynard together? Forget about Grushenka and the rivalry between father and son for her favors. Forget about the three women in body suits. How about getting it on with Diana and Maynard?

Agnes was too shy to approach Diana, yet alone to act on her fantasy. But the spell Diana cast was so strong that Agnes did manage a conversation before the school year ended. Agnes ran into her one day as she exited the Adams House Library and blurted out a "thank you." Diana's imaginative vision had broadened her horizons, she said. By now Diana was used to such abrupt openings, and at this point in her life she was still in her warm, gracious phase. She thanked Agnes and said that she was glad the play had "touched someone who was in science and not just another literary type like me. If you're really interested, maybe sometime we can have lunch or something. Maybe in the fall."

"Hold on. How do you know I am in science?"

"I know these things. It is the business of playwrights to know about people."

"Where are you going to be this summer?" Agnes said.

"I'm moving in with my boyfriend Maynard. The rent is free, and he's good company. Besides, he'll be gone all day at the lab, and I'll be able to write."

The conversation stopped. "Which Maynard? . . . Maynard Dresden?"

"Yes, why?"

"He is working in Adriana Lubeck's lab, my mother's lab."

"Oh, I see. I should have connected the dots. Well, we almost have something in common," she smiled.

They most certainly did. Agnes's heart raced.

"Agnes, you okay? You had this funny look for a second."

"Totally okay."

As she finished her junior year, Agnes was sick of undergraduate life. People like Diana and Maynard had broken out of academe's cloistered walls. Agnes dreaded another year of the Adams House dining hall and sitting around the common rooms with simpering pre-meds.

Diana's news was riveting. Basically she was living with Maynard—sleeping with him. One didn't have to live confined to quarters. Like the three women in Diana's play, Agnes could explore. And living off campus her senior year was a ticket to, well, to anywhere she pleased, even if she wasn't sure at the moment where that was. When Agnes raised the idea with her mother, Adriana liked it. She wanted to foster what she termed her daughter's "fructifying eccentricity." She agreed to help with the extra cost— which explains why, instead of moving back home for the summer, Agnes found an apartment on a quiet street a few blocks off Harvard Square. It was in an old, almost charming, red brick building with cement lintels above the entries and windows.

A week later Adriana called her daughter who had just begun to work in Vladimir Rajewsky's neuroscience lab for the summer. "Come by for a chat this afternoon. I have a proposal you can't refuse."

She sat in front of her mother's desk. "So, what's up? I've got to get back soon. I'm doing some single neuron recording."

"Maynard came in again to see me. I think he is secure in doing the project, but he is a little overwhelmed by the sheer volume of the work. It's a huge job to collect so much material over such a wide area. I took a liberty of asking him if he needed a little help and if he would like me to speak to you."

"Really, since when did you start procuring for me?" Agnes sat poker-faced.

"Stop it, Agnes. I'm not procuring for you. I'm simply providing a possible opportunity."

"You know I'm interested in neuroscience. I've never even met this dilettante of the fens and bogs."

"Look, Agnes, do you want me to lay this out for you or not? Let me know. Because if you want to go back to being just one more undergraduate plugged into some massive research project, some data slave collecting bits and pieces of Rajewsky's megaproject, let me know. I'll back off."

"Okay, tell me."

"I have no intention of dissuading you from neuroscience. It's a wonderful choice for a young person, but I really believe this is a unique opportunity. Remember we are talking about the summer, not your life. We are at the beginning of a major rethinking of the way ecology should be done. And Maynard has the right mix of ability, fire, and perseverance. Don't be snide. He's not a dilettante. I think you would learn a lot, and I am sure that by late fall we will have enough data to write a very good paper. And I know there will be a piece of this you can carve out as your own for your honors thesis. I won't go through the ins and outs of the scientific details with you again."

"Adriana, you know perfectly well I can't do my honors thesis in your lab. You are my mother."

"Some days I need reminding," she smiled. "We'll figure a way around this. Maybe Gladys Shumsky will sponsor you."

Agnes could no more resist Adriana than Maynard could. Besides she didn't want to. She liked the idea of being the sidekick of a buckaroo like Maynard—a fantasy she burbled to herself after Adriana mentioned that late one afternoon after working in the field all day, he showed up with a red bandana around his forehead. "Deal me in," she said.

And that is how less than a week later and after confronting a very red-faced Vladimir Rajewsky—"You vill never virk in neuroscience in this unifersity. I am promising you"—Agnes found herself standing at the edge of Henley Bog. How this snippet of a girl-woman with a single thick, black braid separating her shoulder blades came to confound and captivate Maynard Dresden.

The two stood near a stand of tamarack that gave way to blueberries. It was a cloudy day, not too hot, a good day for collecting.

"Wow, this is way cool. Amazing in fact." What Agnes found amazing in fact was a broad slightly depressed marshy area covered with spongy sphagnum moss through which poked occasional lichen-covered rocks and pitcher plants. She noted a scattering of sundews as well and at the far end more conifers, which she could not identify at this distance—swamp spruce, perhaps.

She watched Maynard wade in and look back at her. "Come on."

"Just a second, I need to tie my shoe." Facing the marsh, she went down in a fluid, genuflecting motion to one knee, looked up briefly, and bowed her head over her right sneaker for an instant. "Okay, ready."

The collecting went well enough. Two meticulous young people culling the arthropods—insects and spiders—from pitcher plants in a bog in south central New England were bound to make good progress, so much progress that they quit early. They had run out of collecting vials.

Agnes pulled out a point and shoot. "I want to take some pictures while it's cloudy. They might be good for my honors thesis."

They rode back in silence listening to the local classical music station. "It's Mendelssohn," she said. "*The Resurrection Symphony*. He's quoting Bach, if it matters."

Maynard let out a noncommittal "I know it. It's nice."

"You religious?"

"Not really."

"That was my guess. Adriana raised me Lutheran. I didn't understand why since even then it was clear she was a non-believer. Later I realized she wanted to give me something to rebel against. So, *Ein feste Burg, A Mighty Fortress is Our God* and all of Bach's sacred music got drilled into me early. But I've moved away from that."

Her eyes were shining. She glanced over at Maynard, who was focused on the road, and swallowed. The steady forward motion of the car, the Bach, the presence of this man with his Red Sox cap and the shaving nick below his sideburn were soothing and lulled her into a feline contentment.

After a moment he said, "To where? You've moved away from that to where?"

It was her turn to pause. He definitely wants to know more about me was her take. "I'm not sure—on different days to different places, but who can really know where they are traveling until they have arrived?" She backed off the intensity, no sense in distancing her new work partner—and eventually maybe something more. She might have shimmied herself a bit closer were it not for the bucket seats and center console. "So what are you interested in, besides science I mean?"

"Actually, that's my main intellectual interest. I love sports, mostly baseball, and I like mountain biking. I wouldn't say I'm an inveterate biker, but I like it."

"Maybe Adriana and I are too narrow. We seem to be all-work-and-no-play girls, or, to put it another way, our work is our play."

"So I have an idea. If you're not doing anything tonight, come by and watch the Red Sox Game with me."

"I understand you have a girlfriend—Diana, the playwright."

"So, where to begin. Well, we are living together, but at the moment she is out of town—in New Haven looking at Yale Drama School. Besides, I was inviting you over to see a Red Sox game, and I was going to order a pizza, that's all. Except for the salad, I mean."

She laughed. "Okay, the salad seals the deal. What time?"

"Yeah, so come by at, say, seven. I'll text you the address."

Agnes studied him from the safety of her bucket seat. It was not hard to spot a flirt. It was not quite come over and see my etchings, but one didn't need any special powers to understand this was Maynard's way of deepening the relationship and her opportunity, provided she eased into it and did not startle her prey, to help him do so. Was he not as committed to Diana as he seemed or was he just horny? She discarded the latter possibility. He would not use her. That would alienate Adriana, and she knew he could not take the chance. Play your cards right and you will be out of this bucket seat and sitting in his lap.

A man's apartment, definitely a man's apartment, she thought—*spare and tidy but lacking in nice touches.* A mountain bike leaned against the wall. There were no prints or pictures. No placemats on the counter, and she knew instinctively the drawers contained none. The cutting board was plastic. Other than a vase of purple irises on the kitchen table there was no sign of Diana. They were fresh, and she guessed that Diana could not have been gone long. The bedroom door was closed. Surely she had left her mark there. Later when Agnes used the bathroom, she found a container of cotton balls and two packets of hypoallergenic face wipes. She checked the medicine cabinet—one toothbrush, Maynard's she assumed. No cuticle scissors. No hair dryer. It and her makeup must have gone with her.

She came out of the bathroom and looked around the room and then at the small flat panel TV. A hefty, young Black woman with a major do was halfway through "The Star Spangled Banner." Yes, a man's apartment—a stack of *Sports Illustrated*s on the bookcase and a taller stack of *Science* magazines next to it. He was behind in his reading. The same biology, chemistry and physics texts she was using filled the shelves. And what's this?

"Hey, what are these doing here? Poetry books? Who are Paul Muldoon and C.K. Williams?"

"I took a creative writing course at Princeton, and they were two of my teachers. I thought I'd read what they wrote, so I bought them."

The doorbell rang, and a lanky teenager in a ridiculous delivery uniform appeared with the pizza. Agnes watched Maynard take pity on him and tip the boy an extra buck. She found the right cabinet, took down two plates and two bowls for salad, removed the vase of irises from the table, and taking the pizza from him, centered it—effectively exiling Diana from the apartment. Her lips moved into a silent purr as she deftly slipped the first slice onto Maynard's plate. The ballgame played in the background.

"You seem right at home here," she said.

"Yeah, it's all right. It's comfortable, and anyway, most of the time I'm either out collecting or in the lab."

Amazing, she thought, *here is this really smart guy, and he did things like mountain bike and watch baseball.* Normal things, things that were all but foreign to the Lubeck household. Baseball. His interest intrigued her.

They settled in on the couch to watch the game.

"Ouch, that's David Ortiz, the cleanup hitter, Boston's number four batter, and he has just struck out again."

Agnes murmured, but she wasn't really listening.

She was thinking how much she liked sitting there next to him. This might have been Diana's seat, but as far as Agnes was concerned, Diana didn't have season tickets. She moved a little closer and took in his smell—warm, clean, masculine—the smell of soap and Maynard.

"Okay, here's Youklas, Kevin Youklas, the Youk." Youklas took a strike and then fouled off the next three pitches. "Yes," Maynard shouted when the Youk poked a single to the leftfield side of second base. "Look at that. Did you see that swing? How does this guy do it? His swing looks like a broken mainspring uncoiling."

He leaped from the couch in enthusiasm, and when he flopped back down, Agnes made sure that his jeans and hers were snuggled together like two plump spears of asparagus. Maynard seemed oblivious, lost in the game. *The bright, beautiful Diana*, Agnes thought, *would have to take care of herself.* Easy does it, not too much more, not now. Let touch and scent do the heavy lifting. Anything more obvious might spook him.

When Drew popped up to second and ended the inning, he said, "Sorry I got a little distracted there. I should have been explaining how it works, how baseball works. Anyway the Sox are headed down the tube tonight."

"It's okay. I'm beginning to get the flavor of why it's so addictive. You seem to like it a lot. Did you ever play?"

"Oh, some. In high school in Cincinnati. I loved it, but I never was very good."

The conversation wound down. In the background the announcers were recapping the game. She could not push the evening any further. She needed to envelop him, and any move toward sex on her part might secure him in a way that would preclude her— she paused searching for the right word, "obtaining"— obtaining him. She thought of the pitcher plants and how slowly, slowly, bit-by-bit without any motion on their part they lured their prey—hapless insects and spiders, which functioned effectively in the world—

into their deep funneled selves, obtaining and slowly devouring them.

She was relieved when he stood and pulled her from the couch. "Thanks for coming over. It was fun. This was a nice thing to do. Maybe I can find some cheap tickets, and the three of us can go to Fenway to see a game."

"That would be nice." *Yes, very nice*, Agnes found herself thinking. At the door, she said, "Thanks for having me over. I really liked it. See you tomorrow."

She resisted her impulse to touch the shaving nick with her fingertips.

She walked down the block to her car. How would that work, the three of us at a baseball game? A glamorous playwright on his arm and me. People would know, they would simply know that I was there as a courtesy, a kindness. That cannot happen. What is he tying to tell me? Does he even know? She tried to recover his deep, clean, masculine smell.

"Hi, Maynard," she said as she got in the car the next morning to head out to Henley Bog. "Thanks for last night. It was fun. I'm surprised, but I liked watching baseball. Okay, I'll be honest. I like the idea of watching baseball. Maybe it will grow on me."

"Glad you enjoyed yourself. Thanks for coming over. It was a, well, a nice evening."

"You don't sound so chipper this morning. Your voice sounds a little, I don't know. Something wrong?"

"No, I'm good."

"Maynard, we work together almost every day. And you are not good. What's wrong?"

"Nothing."

They drove in silence.

"Stop being so glum and tell me what's wrong. And don't say 'nothing.'"

"Well, the shit hit the fan last night. In a very low-key but pointed way."

"Diana called," Agnes guessed.

"Yes. She told me all about her day in New Haven with Mario Adolfo Martinetti, you know, the playwright. He is famous. Well, he liked the video of *Disraeli's Apricot Tree*. Diana was very exited. She said they all but promised her a spot for two years from this fall. 'Finish your senior year and take a year off to write if that's what you want, and we'll hold a spot for you,' they told her."

"That's terrific. I'm really happy for her. For you too. So what's the problem?"

"So here's the rest. She has another day of meetings and informal interviews tomorrow. Then she asked what was up with me. I said 'nothing,' that I was collecting specimens as usual and getting organized to start the DNA sequencing. I mentioned that we had talked and you had asked me about my interests. I said that I had invited you over for pizza and to watch a Red Sox's game. She was very polite, but you could tell her antennae were up. She was a little miffed, I think. Maybe, more than a little."

"How so? I mean what did she say?"

"That she couldn't understand why I waited for her to be out of town to invite you over. The two of you knew each other a little from Adams House, and it would have been okay to have you over if she was there. She would have liked that. She said she wanted to get to know you. I said it was innocent. It just came up in the course of conversation."

"It was innocent," Agnes said.

"Of course it was. She was suspicious. She never said so, but it was obvious."

"So then what happened?"

"I said, 'Diana, it's you I care about. I would be thrilled if you ended up in New Haven instead of LA or even New York.' But you could hear in her voice that she was still upset."

"And?"

"I offered to take the train down and drive around New Haven with her to get a feel for the place and then drive up the coast and back to Boston with her."

"What did she say?"

"She was very cordial and at the same time a little cool. No, she said she would look around on her own and be back the day after tomorrow."

"Maynard, I'm sorry I got you into this. I should never have agreed to come over." She put her hand on his bare forearm.

"Don't be silly. It's not your fault."

"Would you like me to call Diana or have lunch with her when she gets back? I could explain how last minute it was, not planned at all. That it was a Red Sox game. That's all it was. It was about what you enjoyed besides science."

Maynard looked over at her. He hesitated. "No, she'll be home soon, and then I can talk to her. It's crazy that it should be this way, but in retrospect it wasn't the best idea in the world to invite you over. No matter what my intentions."

She wanted to call Diana, but she let it rest. He was right, or at least he was entitled to have his wishes honored. Less than a week later the two women practically ran into each other at the Harvard Square T stop.

"Whoa, this is crazy. I was just thinking about you. I was wondering how you were doing," Agnes said.

"Actually, me too. I had wanted to call you, but . . ."

"Had lunch? How about ABP?"

"I've eaten, but let's get coffee at Starbucks and catch up."

They found a table upstairs near a window and settled in.

"So, I've been wanting to clear the air a bit and apologize," Agnes said.

"For what? Everything's okay as far as I'm concerned."

"Well, for the record, I'm sorry I was with Maynard that evening when you were in New Haven."

"No need. I really am okay with it. I was out of line. I could tell from what Maynard said that he had painted me as, well, possessive or maybe jealous. Sorry. Maybe I was. You know how irrational and crazy people can be. I spend most days trying to get that kind of stuff down on paper."

"You're very gracious, Diana." She reached across the table, and reflexively she touched Diana's forearm in the same spot she had touched Maynard's.

"Life is too short for this crap. Let's give it up and wipe the slate clean." Diana said. "I suppose we can share Maynard. In a good way, I mean. I'm happy with your being the daytime woman. I'll be the nighttime woman, and things should work out. He'll be happy and we'll be happy."

Agnes had wanted to say, Are you sure? Do you understand what you're saying? Instead she simply said, "You sure?"

"Positive, I like you. Besides how else can it be? You seem like a really good person, and I'd like to see more of you. I haven't forgotten your kind remarks about my play." Diana stood up, came around the table and hugged Agnes. "Thank you, you were very kind to apologize and very sensible. I was out of line. So if I sit back down and promise to give up any residue of sulkiness, can we just go forward?"

"That's totally cool with me," Agnes said.

"So tell me about you. How's the summer going, and what are you thinking about next year?"

Agnes said she had made good progress in planning her honors project and had decided to work with the data she and Maynard were collecting and use it for her thesis. "But, after I graduate, I want to do a Ph.D. in neuroscience somewhere. I hope at MIT."

"Sounds like a great career move. And personally, I mean, how are you?"

"I'm good. I'd like to be in a relationship, but who wouldn't? Anyway, I'm good."

Diana reached across the table and took Agnes's hand in both of hers. "I would like that for you too. Agnes, I think you are an exceptional person. You have the kind of penetrating intelligence that is very attractive. Honestly the word is 'sexy.'"

"Forgive me, Diana, I'm not in your league. You turn every head in the room when you walk in."

"But you, and I hope this doesn't sound too personal, you turn every heart when you walk in. There's a big difference."

"You don't know," Agnes said.

"I do. I've lived in Adams House same as you. I've seen people's reactions."

Agnes looked directly at her and smiled. "Speaking of Adams, I decided to live off campus next year. I've found a place not too far from here. Once I'm a bit more organized I'd like to have you over. You and Maynard."

"I'd like to come."

"There's a side to me you don't know," Agnes said.

"Come clean."

"I'll invite you over and you'll see."

"Well, if you've seen my play, you know a lot about me. Playwrights may make it up, but it all comes from up here." She put her fingertips on her temples. "Of course, it's not all in one play, so I have a few secrets of my own. And I'm not quite ready to come clean either, but I'd love to come over with Maynard when you're ready."

The two young women stood and embraced again and maybe even clung to each other for an instant.

"See, ya."

"This has been great. See, ya."

After Labor Day there was less collecting to do, and when undergraduate classes started again, Agnes was in the lab afternoons to help with the DNA sequencing and data analysis. Her appearance had changed, well, not exactly changed, but enlarged. She wore a fine gold chain around her neck. What dangled from it was a mystery. It fell beneath the second button of her white blouse, another change from the summer's T-shirts. When he asked her about it, she hoisted up the object, which turned out to be a small, plain gold cross, one too tiny even for the delicate chain. It was as if Agnes were trying out faith, making a tentative commitment.

"You always surprise me. I never figured a scientist could be, ah, observant."

"Science is all about observation," she said.

"Don't dodge the question. You know what I'm asking."

"I'm going to see where this road leads. What most people don't realize is that for every Saul of Tarsus who has a vision on the road to Damascus, there are hundreds, no thousands, who see only lightning and hear only thunder and take refuge in the nearest inn. I don't know which I am."

"Okay, but while you're figuring it out, I have a problem of my own, or maybe I should say we have a problem of our own."

"How's that?"

She listened while Maynard explained that Dr. Lubeck, as he always referred to her in front of her daughter, had seen the preliminary data and liked it. She suggested that he write up the findings and that he and Dr. Lubeck submit a manuscript for publication.

"So why do *we* have a problem?"

"We've got more than one. The reason it is 'we' is that I told Dr. Lubeck that you should also be an author since you have contributed so much. And she agreed."

Agnes smiled. "Thank you, Maynard. You didn't have to do that."

"I wanted to. Why the smile?"

"Oh, nothing. Just sometimes Adriana's clairvoyance amazes me. Anyway, I don't see how that leaves us with a problem."

"She wants more data. She wants late season data, from like now, before we get a frost."

"I can get away Thursday. I'll cut my physical chemistry class. Or better, over the weekend. And what other problem?"

"That would be great. So that's the smaller of the issues. The bigger issue is that I'd like a little help, you know, someone to bounce ideas off as I draft the manuscript. You up for that?"

"Yeah, it'll be interesting. I'm game. I'm in."

The bog was dreary that Saturday. By midday the temperature was not yet fifty, and a gray blanket of grunge hung over the marsh and the nearby land that was once Henley farm and had now gone back to wild. They couldn't be more than a week or two away from a frost and maybe a hard freeze. They had struggled all morning to find specimens, and now it was three o'clock and the light was threatening to fade. She and Maynard put the partially filled Igloo coolers in the trunk.

"Well, it wasn't much of a day, but I guess you can only do as well as you can do. Next week we'll sequence what we've got," he said.

"Maynard, look. Do you see? Now that the colors in the bog are fading, the pitcher plants really stand out. They are amazing. I don't know what they are like. I've never seen anything like this. You know what? They are like a pipe organ, all those pitchers. They are God's pipe organ. Can you imagine this bog as Leipzig and that Bach is composing a Sunday cantata to be played here in this bog on this organ?"

"I never thought about it that way. It's a different take. I'll say that."

"Hey, friend, try to be a little sympathetic. It's a perfectly good way to look at things. It doesn't negate the science we're doing. It enriches it. Okay?"

"Yeah, nice. Okay. As I said, you just always surprise me, that's all."

She liked surprising him—that was how it would work. At once a strange field of attraction was emanating from his body, pulling her closer. And then his scent tugged even harder.

Later that fall the two sat in a corner of the lab holding printouts of a draft of the article. They worked their way through each section, tweaking the language so that it accurately represented their findings, squeezing out the hyperbole, which might provoke derision from other investigators, staking out their claims in a modest but assertive way.

Agnes liked working with Maynard. *This is sexy*, she thought. She leaned forward a bit and pointed to a sentence on his copy. She loved the closeness, and then there was his scent again. It sent a sharp jab to her solar plexus. She sucked her breath in for a second. *Focus, Agnes, focus. You're working on a manuscript too.* They went back through the draft again wringing out verbiage and tightening the language.

When they were finished, he said, "Thank you, Agnes. You're a great colleague." Agnes took in his smile, which gave off desire more than gratitude. She wondered what he might have said in place of "colleague" had he given free reign to his thoughts. He put his hand on her arm, and she put hers on top of his.

"Thank you," he repeated.

She moved her chair back a bit and looked at him. No time like the present. "So, I have a bit of an invita . . . an invitation, actually, for, well, you and Diana." She flushed a bit.

"What's that?"

"Well, I'm expecting a couple to come over Saturday night. I hope you can come and bring Diana. You know I loved her play. It was very clever, well, way more than clever. It moved me. You know, it surprised me—all the kissing, the erotica grafted onto Disraeli's imagined thoughts about Dostoyevsky. Very ingenious."

"She would probably like to come . . . ."

"Why the pause?"

"I'm not sure the chemistry would work, with the three of us I mean," he said.

"Of course it will. So invite her."

"Okay, but . . ."

"Bet she kisses well."

"What am I missing?"

"Nothing," she said. "The two of you should show up at seven."

"Great, I'd like to come. Sounds good. Let me check and make sure Diana's free."

As she stood to leave, he stood too. She smiled, as she always did, and was about to walk to the elevator. But she paused, stepped forward, drew him to her and hugged him. As she disengaged, she made sure her hand strayed across his butt.

Agnes looked down on the street and watched

Maynard and Diana arrive. She hoped the evening would be worthy of a scene Diana might write. Agnes had put her hair up, the dweebie black braid replaced by a stylish chignon. She was covered head to toe in a white muslin caftan on which the tiny gold cross was displayed. There were no other guests. Maynard asked her when the others would be coming. She looked at him mischievously and explained that they, he and Diana, were the couple of guests she was expecting.

Her living room was lit only by small candles set out in arrays. The couch and living room chairs were covered in white sheets. The door to the bedroom was ajar, and her bed too had been stripped to only a white bottom sheet. By her closet door stood three massive candles—the entire illumination of the bedroom.

She caught in Diana's face a knowing, or at least an anticipatory look. *Maynard*, she thought, *was sucking wind and trailing a good ways back. It's okay.* She would bring him along when she was ready. Diana's the one with the sense of theater. Agnes smiled and put a finger to her lips and motioned them to the couch. She went to the kitchen and returned with a small tray and three wine glasses half full with a golden liquid.

She raised her glass, looked at the visitors, and said, "To her who has protected us, nourished us, and brought us to this occasion. Don't ask, Diana, you can go to the internet in the morning. Hint, think *Shehecheyanu.*" Diana looked puzzled. "Just guess. Spell it phonetically, and it will come up."

"Agnes, who's the 'her'?" Maynard said.

"All will be revealed in its proper time. But for now, enjoy the libation. Just chill. It's not as weird as you think." Agnes tried to read him. What? Does he think I've flipped out or gone off the deep end? Maybe he thinks this is the real me, the only me, and he's been hanging around with a closet lunatic. Or does he think the whole idea is plain stupid? What she hoped she saw was at least open-mindedness, but she couldn't be sure.

"Agnes, what happened to the no nonsense, no frills, attractive woman I work with everyday?"

"What are you saying, Maynard?" Diana said.

"Well, I'm sorry, but she is. Agnes, what is this, ah, pageantry? This is a side of you I haven't seen before."

"And that, my brother, is why I am revealing it to you and our sister now. I'm going to ask you to pray with me."

"I'm a little rusty. It's been a while."

"Agnes, me too," Diana said. "But I don't see why not. We can try, can't we, Brother Maynard."

"Sure."

"Dear Lord, who made the world and all therein in six days and rested on the seventh, we are grateful for your gifts to us, your bounty, and the humanity you have given us. We would be nothing without you. Again, I offer up the fruit of the vine to you." Agnes motioned with her glass to the others and drained it. Brother Maynard looked at Diana, who had downed hers as well, and followed suit.

Agnes put her finger to her lips again and went into the kitchen and returned with a decanter filled with the golden liquid. She poured another round. "As I was saying, Lord, long before you offered us your only begotten son as our Savior, you created the fruit of the vine and gave it to the Hebrews and then to us for communion. I lift my glass to you." And she did. Then she tossed down her drink like a pro and nodded toward the others. Diana took a sip. Maynard gulped his down in one large swallow.

"Strong stuff," Diana said.

"Yes, strong for the task of honoring the Lord. It is Benedictine and Brandy, the preferred communion drink of the über faithful."

"I thought that was Grey Goose."

"Shush, Maynard," Diana said. "Go on, go on, Sister."

Agnes listed slightly to her left and raised her glass, "Dear Lord, as I am Agnes, I thank you for your work of the Eighth Day of Creation, and may those who have expunged its knowledge from the accepted canon burn in Hell." She finished off another glass.

"Amen, Sister."

Diana poked Maynard hard in the ribs.
"For on the Eighth Day, God created the Americas
and decreed that the ten lost tribes of Israel would
migrate here and prosper, and he created, and this
is the important point, the bogs and fens of New
England. The cradle of the science I do with my
Maynard." She refilled her glass and took a swallow.

"Agnes, don't you think the Lord can hear you
without more B&B?" Diana said.

"No way," Maynard said.

Agnes finished what was left in her glass. "We
should go on. Please rise." And they did. "Now follow
me."

Agnes headed for the bedroom, putting one foot
in front of the other as if walking a tightrope. She
almost succeeded. Only once did Diana have to reach
forward to steady her. At the closet door she stopped
and flung it open so hard it bounded back off the
wall. Diana caught it on the rebound. There in front
of them on the closet floor was a diorama of the bog
she and Maynard had worked all summer. She had
blown up her photos into a 180-degree panorama,
and you could see the blueberries that edged the bog
and in the center distance a few swamp maple. In the
foreground just beyond the blueberries, there were
clusters of pitcher plants.

"This is the vineyard of our labors." She knelt on
both knees, raised her arms, and spread them as if
to offer the priestly benediction. "Holy Mary, Mother
of God, pray for us now and at the hour of our death.
We ask you to intercede with the Holy Name for us
and our study, You, Our Lady of the Bogs and Pitcher
Plants."

She was about to tip over. Diana reached down,
steadied her with a hand on her shoulder, and helped
her to her feet. Agnes turned toward her, her eyes
radiant with the light of the possessed, and kissed
her long and hard on the mouth. She sent Maynard
an inviting smile, which seemed to apologize for the
prohibitive distance between them.

Diana wiped her mouth in surprise. "Nice . . .
very nice. I'll call you. We have a lot to talk about. I

want to hear about Bach and the pitcher plants. That could be an idea for another play, but I'll need your help. We could collaborate. And I've got something delightful I can offer in return. And Maynard does too. Don't you Maynard? Let's see how it goes."

"Under the aegis of Our Lady and with a little attention on our part, our enterprise will prosper." Agnes did not elaborate.

II. Adriana's Gift

It was a terse email to her old Radcliffe roommate. "Can we have lunch? I need to talk about a *situation*," is the way Adriana Lubeck phrased her problem. Which explains why she and the noted novelist Olympia Breathwaite found themselves sitting over two almost identical soup and sandwich combinations in a mediocre restaurant a few blocks from Harvard Square. The slight variance—Adriana's decision to forgo the provolone on her half turkey sandwich—was a concession to her never-ending struggle with her weight. It was the only concession the Harvard biology professor was prepared to make that day.

Long ago Olympia realized that Adriana's oblique, almost abrupt style resulted in equal measure from her no-nonsense approach to life and her vulnerability. Olympia did not try to parse the message further other than to recognize it for what it was—a cry for help. Adriana's succinct style had been part of her for as long as the two had been friends, which reached back to one autumn in the mid-seventies when two hesitant, awkward girls arrived at Radcliffe with battered suitcases and the wrong clothes. The insecurities they brought with those suitcases that fall remained—hidden by success and the personae of Harvard professors. But today a family crisis unmasked Adriana.

Lunch was the way the two women stayed in touch, shared gossip and reconnaissance, and solidified their connectedness. They were each other's closest friends. Many years ago when it appeared that Olympia's committee might not accept her dissertation on Faulkner and thus prevent her from receiving her doctorate, Adriana and her incisive intelligence were there helping recast arguments and tightening the introduction and conclusion sections. Her intervention had allowed Olympia to clarify her thinking about fiction and its role in society. The result was an exceptional dissertation that eventually became her first book.

How did it happen that a biology graduate student knew anything about Faulkner, much less anything useful enough to help Olympia? Adriana had no firsthand experience with Yoknapatawpha County, Mississippi, or any other rural setting, but Hans and Abigail Lubeck were unusual parents. They ran Lubeck's Books in Cambridge and had particular views on education—both were refugees, he from Nazi Germany and she from the Brahmin world of Beacon Hill. They sent their daughter to a progressive private school, which, even before Faulkner won the Nobel Prize, had incorporated his books into its curriculum. Analytically gifted and generously empathic, Adriana intuited the yearnings and failures of the characters who peopled Faulkner's world.

The friendship worked both ways. Some years later Adriana's marriage fell apart, and as a struggling assistant professor of biology, she became a single parent, the mother of Agnes, a precocious five year old. It was Aunt Olympia who helped by taking her daughter some Saturday nights so that Adriana could have a social life. Several times when there was a grant application deadline and Adriana was caught up in a frenzy of chaotic detail as she tried to finish on time, the novelist kept Agnes for a day or two. Olympia was often in the middle of a writing project and had her own classes to teach, but she never complained.

Today Adriana was hurting. She needed lunch to go beyond sharing gossip and staying connected.

"I've brought you a little something," she said and pulled out a box of handmade thank you notes.

Olympia hesitated but only for a second and then smiled. "What on earth are these for? That's very kind. Oh, I get it. You're in some kind of pickle."

"It's the *situation* I mentioned in my email. I really need your help, and a little bribery between friends never hurts."

To Adriana the broad outline of the problem was simple—her briskly intelligent daughter Agnes was driving her bonkers. The mother needed Olympia's novelistic perspective. Wasn't that the job of novelists—to explore the psyche, to understand the human condition? And Olympia's latest book, *The Delicacy of Clocks*, Adriana remembered, had been praised in the *New York Times* Sunday Book Review as a probing inquiry into obsession—though obsession was only a small part of the *situation.*

"You know how much I love my daughter and how exasperating she can be. I'm about at my wit's end. These days I want to strangle her."

They always chose to meet at modest places for lunch or coffee, and both agreed that this particular eatery was distinctly average. It was the total lack of pretension of the restaurant that attracted them. It helped them stay centered in themselves and in each other's orbit. The near shabbiness of the place allowed them to escape, at least temporarily, to a more grounded place. It also took them back to a time when, as students, such places were a temporary refuge from the withering atmosphere of the Radcliffe-Harvard world. Adriana felt it was this period in her own life that she needed to recover to come to terms with Agnes's choices.

Adriana was a self-made woman. Actually, self-made is too strong—she was a self-constructed woman. And occasionally, as she was the first to admit, she had set aside her warmth for her career. She went to Radcliffe as a National Merit Scholar—though between the bookstore and her mother Abigail's trust fund she received no financial help. Through sheer intelligence, focus, and strategic choices, which sometimes bordered on the injudicious, she had become a distinguished professor of biology there. One of these lapses concerned Agnes. Her marriage had been rocky from the first, and during one particularly difficult period,

Adriana had had several brief dalliances. Soon she found herself pregnant, and she could not say with any precision who had fathered the baby. It was an issue she had never discussed with Agnes. After the divorce Adriana took her maiden name again and legally changed Agnes's as well.

Adriana's practical, one-foot-in-front-of-the-other approach to life made it difficult for her to understand her freewheeling daughter. She hoped Olympia could help her today. Now the two sat over their untouched food. Adriana leaned forward. Best not to have others hear what she was about to discuss.

Before Adriana could nudge the conversation toward the *situation*, Olympia said, "How's your daughter doing?"

"Fine. Well, not fine, not completely fine. That's what I need help with. She's liking the neuroscience program at MIT and doing well, but of course she's just started graduate school. Her personal life is what I would call a bit, what's the right word here?, confused, alternative, maybe whacked out. I don't know if she is living with a man or a woman or both."

"Agnes, really? I'm surprised. I would have thought she was more grounded. Besides, don't I remember that she and that hotshot graduate student of yours are a number?"

"Yes, she's seeing Maynard, but she may also be seeing Maynard's former girlfriend, or maybe both of them together. It's not clear. She gave up her apartment. Well, she actually still has it, but she's not living in it."

"The one you were helping her with?"

"Yes, and she and Maynard and his old girl friend, or maybe she is the present girl friend too, along with Agnes, or maybe she's his past girl friend. Or. Oh, damn it all, I don't know, but the three of them are sharing the second floor apartment in an old house in Brookline."

"And you've visited? Have you been invited for dinner?"

"Of course not. I, the mother? I, the graduate

student's advisor? I, the mother of the other woman? The three rolled into one. They would sooner invite the Boston Strangler."

Olympia smiled. "What am I doing writing another novel? I should just drop by and take notes. I could write a nonfiction piece, maybe reuse an old Henry James title. How about *The Turn of the Screw*?"

"This is nothing to joke about. Honestly, I don't care whether Agnes is gay or strait or bi, but I do care about relationships. Maybe I'm even open to considering a little experimentation, a brief *ménage-à -trois*. Look, an evening is one thing, but a permanent living arrangement is another. There is bound to be an odd man, an odd person, out with three young people when the music stops. I don't want it to be Agnes."

"I think you're making too much of this. Don't flinch when I tell you this. I read a recent article somewhere that in Utah and Idaho some Mormon families even today live happily, though clandestinely, in multi-partner relationships. It can work long term."

"We're not talking about Utah, for Christ's sake. What planet are you living on? The subject is my daughter in Brookline, on Beals Street to be exact."

"Okay, sorry. I was a little off base." Olympia sent a sympathetic look her way.

"I don't want to see my daughter hurt. Sooner or later there's going to be a blowup. The mix of energy, ambition, and sex in that apartment is going to ignite, and someone is going to get burned in the ensuing fire."

"You think they are using?"

"My honest guess is not. I don't think Agnes is into hard stuff. They may smoke a little dope, but they spend too much time in class and the lab—at least Agnes and Maynard do."

"And the other one again. What does she do?"

"You may know her. Her name's Diana Endecott. She's trying to be a playwright."

"Oh, I do. Yes. She wrote, *Disraeli's Apricot Tree.* Last year it caused quite a stir among her classmates.

I didn't see it, but I gather it was an attention grabber. So she lives with your daughter and this guy, ah, Maynard? That must be complicated."

"Damn it, Olympia, that's what I've been trying to tell you. Sorry, I'm sounding testy. It's just that all of this has been very difficult."

"What are you going to do?"

"Nothing. I'm stuck. What can I do? They are adults in their twenties. I can't take my daughter aside and lecture her about relationships . . . ."

"Why not? You love her, and she's your daughter."

"Because she'd be offended. She would tell me to get lost or worse. And maybe she would be right. And as for Maynard, he's a graduate student in my lab. We may work together closely, but I can't get in the middle of his personal life, especially when he is involved or partially involved or whatever it is with my daughter. So how well do you know Diana? She's quite striking."

"We're not close, but I know her. The word around the English Department is that she is not going to work on a Ph.D. She is hanging around this year, that's the way people put it, writing and trying to decide whether she wants film school or drama school next year. So maybe the problem is time-limited. Next fall she's off to a new adventure, and the three musketeers become two."

"Agnes said her first choice is Yale or NYU," Adriana said. "Then she'd be only a few hours away by car or train, not very far. I guess I should pray for Los Angeles. I'm sorry, Olympia, I don't mean to monopolize the conversation. Tell me about you. How's the new novel coming?"

"Before we leave the subject, have you heard about Diana's new play? A student group is going to mount a production. There are notices up all over the English Department. It's called *Bach Among the Pitcher Plants*—odd title if you ask me. I know next to nothing about pitcher plants. We should go and get a sense of what's going on. Maybe it will help."

"Dear God, I'll tell you what's going on. Maynard's

project involves studying pitcher plants in nearby bogs. I think I told you that last year Agnes worked with him and used part of their initial findings for her honors thesis. And of course Diana and Maynard were involved with each other, so Diana has a wealth of detail at her disposal. I hope the play is not some sort of lightly fictionalized kiss and tell. Or maybe each pitcher plant will be an erect phallus. Something crazy. Please, can we change the subject? I started to ask about your novel."

"I'm not making much progress. I don't have writer's block, but I've been preoccupied. Normally, even when I teach during the school year, I have some time to write. You know, as I told you the last time we had lunch, this summer and fall have not been very productive. And it's not gotten any better."

"Oh, I'm sorry. Remind me of the details. It had to do with your former student."

"So a year or two ago I supervised the under-graduate honors thesis of a woman named Henrietta Markham. It was a piece of fiction, a short novel, which was quite good. She finished it, the committee liked it, and she graduated. And that was that, or at least I thought it was. You know how it is. Young people come and go. Many of them are bright and motivated, but one blurs into the next. But not Henrietta Markham. As I said, it was an interesting piece of fiction, which purported to tell her family's story. The piece was slightly macabre and bordered on fantasy. But it was good.

"Anyway, she graduated and left. I never expected to hear from her again. But last spring—you remember, I told you—I received a revised manuscript in the mail. It was an expanded version that added a long memoir type piece at the end. I had no way to contact her—she made sure of that. All I know is that it came from Barcelona. When I read the new version, it was stunning, a mature piece of work that most established writers would have been proud of. In her letter she asked that I try to get it published as a record of her family's sins and her atonement for her own. It still seemed like fantasy or maybe internal psychodrama, but I liked it. The piece haunted me, really obsessed me. So I've spent a good part of the summer and fall working with my agent trying to find her a publisher. I'm hoping someone will publish a novel by an unknown writer—a tall order. I'm not quite there, but I'm close. So I'm crossing my fingers. It's been chewing up my time and energies. I only had to do one thing with it. I changed the title. The one she chose gave too much away. I've called it *The Lobsterman's Daughter*. Okay, enough. I want hear about your love life."

"You know, Olympia, about like yours— nonexistent—though there is a new guy in the department. He moved here from St. Louis, brilliant I'm told. Actually, I know, I heard his faculty seminar. He's a molecular biologist and works on the protein chemistry of blood clotting."

"Not exactly a show-stopper of a topic."

"No, it's not, unless you are hemorrhaging at surgery or are in an auto accident. Or you're in Afghanistan. Anyway, his name is Norman Penderevski."

"And you've met him?"

"No, but I liked the way he handled himself at his seminar. You can tell a lot about people by the way they answer questions after a talk. He's kind and self-effacing with a sly sense of humor."

"And?"

"And nothing. I can't just throw myself at him. I'm trying to figure out an approach. Besides, the gossip is that he may already be seeing someone. Who knows?"

"Listen, Adriana, at our age there are not a lot of fish in the sea. And there are a lot of fisherwomen."

"Brilliant. If you wrote something like that in one of your novels, people would return the book in droves."

"All right, it was a little lame. Anyway, I have to run. I've got a creative writing workshop at two. Who knows when the next Saul Bellow or Alice Munro will appear? I'll call you about the play. Sorry, I couldn't be more help with Agnes." She put money on the table—her estimate of half the check and a tip—and left.

Adriana sat for a few minutes trying to collect herself. Olympia was right. She had not been much help. There was no easy way to understand the complicated circuitry that wired the three young people together. She was stymied. For the moment there was nothing to be done. It was rare that Adriana found herself without recourse to action. She was used to taking charge and fixing whatever was broken. She hated not being in control. She picked up the check and inspected it.

From across the restaurant she heard, "Hi, Adriana," followed by laughter. She looked up to see Agnes and Diana coming toward her. Their joined hands were swinging wildly to and fro. "What are you doing here?"

"What are you doing here?" was her mother's rejoinder.

"We came to get some lunch. We're celebrating. Can we sit down for a minute?"

"I think you'd better. What's going on?"

"We just came from the dress rehearsal of Diana's new play, and it went great."

Diana and Agnes looked at each other and broke into guffaws.

"You want to explain how you two are celebrating at two on a Thursday afternoon?"

"Mom, lighten up. Be light on your feet like us." The two young women were now chortling. Agnes started to stand to demonstrate how light on her feet she could be, but Diana pulled her down.

"Oh, for Pete's sake, Agnes, you're smoking dope in the middle of the day. I thought you were in graduate school. Is that what they do at MIT?"

"Cut us some slack. It's a celebration. I don't have any classes today, and I'm doing this dumb-ass rotation in this dorky guy's lab. The Michelangelo made us do it," and the two young women wailed with laughter. People were now looking.

"What in the world are you taking about?"

"You don't know about him, about the most powerful man in the world, about Michelangelo? It's all in Diana's play."

"For Chrissake, Agnes, lower your voice."

"You should see the play, Dr. Lubeck. You'll find out why the women come and go. Even T.S. Eliot didn't know what they thought about Michelangelo." The young women snickered and then heaved with laughter.

Adriana shot a withering look their way.

"If you aren't going to be open minded, then I'm going to have tea with Granny Abigail and tell her everything."

"Please don't. Your grandmother is too old for your antics. You'll only upset her."

"I will. I'm going to. Diana, let's swing to and fro with a hidiho. And here we go!"

"That's enough. Both of you. Agnes, when you come to your senses, maybe you can call and tell me what's going on." And without waiting for a reply, Adriana Lubeck, Professor of Biology at Harvard University, added money to Olympia's, stood up, glared at the two of them, and left.

After dinner Adriana finished the chocolate almond brittle in the living room candy dish and opened a pint of rum raisin ice cream. Once done, she ran her fingers around the inside of the container to recover any liquid her spoon had missed. What the hell am I doing dismissing my daughter like that? she muttered to herself. You keep this up and you'll have no relationship with her. She called Olympia. "You're not going to believe what happened." And she told her the whole story and closed by saying, "You know what? They were holding hands the whole time."

"And you think they are lesbians and sleeping together?"

"Something like that."

"Adriana, I'll give you the pot, okay. You know what it does. The fact that they were holding hands and waving their arms around extravagantly means that they were high. And that's all. You think that when Hansel and Gretel are holding hands in the forest, they are in an incestuous relationship? You don't have any evidence of anything. And besides, you said it was all right if your daughter was gay."

"What in the world am I going to do?" Adriana was sobbing softly into the phone.

"First you're going to try to get ahold of yourself. Take a step back and calm down. And then you're going to love your daughter. And even if the three of them are into it together, you are going to wait it out. And if it turns out that it's permanent, you have no choice. You are going to suck it up and love your daughter. In the meantime I have a suggestion."

"What's that?"

"It's what I mentioned about the play. We'll go see it. We can gather a little information. Maybe find out something about what's going on. The tickets are on sale in the English Department Office. I'll pick up a pair. And if I hug you when I see you, it doesn't mean that I am going to sleep with you."

"Sorry, I got it. You're right, I suppose. There is one more thing I didn't understand. They went on about Michelangelo and T.S. Eliot. They thought it was wildly funny. I only vaguely remember the poem from high school."

"Most kids don't get out of Freshman English here or even in some high schools, like yours, without reading T.S. Eliot's 'The Love Song of J. Alfred Prufrock.' There's a refrain in the poem about the women coming and going and talking about Michelangelo. It's supposed to represent the tedious boredom and superficiality of English upper class life in Eliot's time."

"Yes, it's coming back, but what's so hilariously funny about that?"

"I don't know. We'll have to wait and see the play."

Bach Among the Pitcher Plants was staged off campus over two weekends. Someone had helped the group, which in self-mockery dubbed itself the Gay and Thespian Alliance, find and rent a nearby fraternal hall. The venue worked only because Diana's staging was portable and minimal. The entire set consisted of eight gigantic, pitcher plants, each of which would accommodate a concealed actor. The set designer had made no attempt to catch the natural look of the plants. Rather they were covered in brightly colored patches of paint that owed something to the statues of Jean Dubuffet. At the edge was a keyboard and speakers. There was no curtain, so the director had all the actors in place before the doors were opened to the audience.

On the last Saturday night Adriana and Olympia arrived a little late and were at the end of the line as the audience filed in. Adriana did the math. Even with the reduced cost of tickets for undergraduates, and, say, one hundred and fifty people, she guessed they would be in the black.

The two women ended up toward the back, which worked well for both of them. Who wanted to be seen at a play, an advertisement for which began, "If you're over forty, you'll blush out loud. If you're younger, you'll enjoy it"? Adriana looked around. A few of her graduate students were there, friends of Maynard's she supposed. Thankfully Agnes and Maynard were nowhere to be seen. They had probably attended last weekend, but she spotted Diana standing to the left. She smiled, and the young woman blew her a kiss. There were other young people from the department she recognized—students who had rotated through her lab or she had taught in class. She waved to Regis and Sally Geldhammer who had been friends for years. And there were the Fitzwaters and Anna Malpensa from political science.

A young man in a black turtleneck and black jeans came to the front. "Good evening. I'm Gabe Bergson, the director of *Bach Among the Pitcher Plants*. You're in for a really great evening. The reception so far has been fantastic. I just wanted to let you know we will be a few minutes late in starting. We've had a minor technical problem that we are in the process of fixing. So thanks for understanding."

Adriana poked Olympia. "It's him, it's Norman,

the scientist from the department I was telling you about. He's standing up front near the end on the right." Next to him was a very tall blonde. She removed her coat, revealing a lime green linen blazer and well-fitted black slacks.

"She's too tall for him," Olympia said. "You still have a shot."

"Maybe, maybe not." Adriana's heart stopped beating. How was a pudgy woman like her going to compete with that? She tried to imagine taking off her clothes with him and cursed her binges. She resolved to throw out the box of caramel turtles in the freezer. Christ, the woman has a head start. She's already seeing him. To change the subject, she said, "So tell me, what's new with you. You look more relaxed than at lunch the other day."

"Well, I was wrought up then, but I am relaxed now. Something amazing has happened. I am back writing again. I feel so much better—like a great load is off my shoulders. I've solved the problem with that young woman's manuscript. Unbelievable. I got an email from a man in Texas who runs a small press and is going to publish it. He said it was 'startlingly original.' Just like that. You have no idea how amazing this is. To have some stranger like a piece of fiction that your agent sent him cold and then to agree to publish it. It really is like winning the lottery."

"Congratulations, I know you're thrilled, and you're right. I don't really understand how difficult it is. I can't even guess. So why? I mean, nothing just happens. There must have been something."

"Incredible dumb luck. It seems Henrietta, my former student, had returned from Spain and decided to go to Mexico. She stopped in Houston on her way and met a writer—a guy called A.E.—in a bar and decided to shack up with him. He has a friend who runs the small press. One thing led to another, and A.E. introduced Henrietta to him at a party. It was perfect timing. Completely by chance Henrietta's manuscript arrived within days of the meeting."

"I guess I'm glad to see you looking so happy and relieved and able to go back to your own writing."

Suddenly the lights were cut, and *Bach Among the Pitcher Plants* began. The stage was unilluminated save for a single penlight suspended from the ceiling. The eight large pitcher plants stood hulk-like, almost forlorn in the half darkness. The keyboardist began a slow, darkly muffled rendition of "Jesu, Joy of Man's Desiring." After he played it through, eight heads—four men and four women—almost invisible in the minimal light, materialized from the pitchers and began hum along. Diana had neatly achieved a marvelous balance of joy and darkness. An air of anticipatory mystery hung over the room.

The lights came up, and the actors unzipped their pitchers and stepped out—all eight in black turtlenecks and leotards. Almost inaudibly the keyboardist played Bach's "Sheep May Safely Graze." Over the music the eight took turns reciting texts that Diana had written—one on the importance of the natural world and our obligation to preserve it, another on the joy of discovery and science, others with similar themes. At this point the play felt liked a staged reading. It was interesting, but it was losing energy by the minute. The keyboardist switched to a moderately paced version of "The Goldberg Variations." Without warning, Diana danced onto the stage, pirouetting as she moved around the actors. It appeared that she was in one of the apricot-colored body suits from *Disraeli's Apricot Tree*. Someone gasped, and then there were murmurs as the audience realized she was naked as the day she was born.

Adriana leaned over and whispered to Olympia, "God, she's beautiful."

Like an apparition she was gone, her movements replaced by those of the eight actors who danced in and out of each others' embraces in a graceful, though technically imprecise way. The keyboardist picked up the pace as if Glenn Gould were playing in overdrive. The actors moved at an ever-dizzying speed and then fell in a heap. A man rose and intoned what he said was a hymn to Isis, who, he explained, was the Egyptian mother goddess and patron of nature. At the end a women climbed from the heap, stepped behind him, and embraced him. The mood turned from celebratory back to sexual. The actors in turn performed a series of readings, each more suggestive than the last, as the others danced in the background. By the end the dancing had given way to writhing. The undergraduates loved it. The older crowd was puzzled but indulgent.

Next Diana's script broke the all-Bach theme. Her muse called for a keyboard arrangement of the Triumphal March from *Aida*. Then one of the men stepped forward and proclaimed himself Rademes. The keyboard introduced "Celeste Aida." "In English it's 'Heavenly Aida,'" he explained. Rather than entrusting a Verdi aria to an untrained singer, Diana had him chant a hymn of praise to Michelangelo against a pianissimo rendition of the music. The student's squealed with delight. The adults hummed along.

The play moved toward a finale as the actors joined hands and began to chant a poem with a Bach prelude in the background.

> More than Jesu is man's desiring,
> Michelangelo's gift is awe-inspiring.
> T.S. Eliot was way off base,
> he hardly knew desire's face.
> Embrace the booty, tender maid,
> Accept the offer, don't be afraid.
> The pitcher plant: vagina, phallus?
> Either way, a pleasure palace.
> The Michelangelo is nature's boon,
> guarantied to lift your gloom.
> It's tender as a lover's face,
> a modern toy that knows its place . . .

The audience under thirty was on its feet. Their wild cheers drowned out the rest of the actors' lines. The older members of the audience sat silently, not sure what the message was. Gabe Bergson signaled the musician who began to play Busoni's keyboard arrangement of a Bach chaconne that was by turns contemplative, lively, and prefiguring. The house lights came up to more cheering.

Adriana and Olympia funneled toward the exit and found themselves face to face with Norman and his friend. How dare he date her? was Adriana's reaction. Against all rationality Adriana looked at her green linen jacket and labeled Norman a turncoat for not dating another scientist. It was an act of betrayal. Adriana recognized this judgment for what it was—preposterously ludicrous. Still she could not help herself. She hardly knew the man, and she was jealous of his date.

There were introductions, and the four chatted awkwardly as the line move slowly toward the exit. There followed an uncomfortable silence. No one was willing to venture an opinion of the play. The material was too blatantly sexual, and the message too indecipherable—especially the business about Michelangelo, which Adriana was sure the others found as impenetrable as she did. Up close Adriana determined that the woman was older. In fact as she thought about it, she decided she was age appropriate for Norman. This irked her all the more. And knowing her name—Beverly Ardmore—was useless. Who was this opportunist, this interloper?

Olympia drove Adriana home.

"What did you think of the play? After all, you're the writer."

"No, you first. Give me your take."

Adriana began tentatively. "I'm no expert, but it sure seemed disjointed to me. A little of this and a little of that, all glued together with a superficial knowledge of Bach. And Diana never explained why Bach should be among the pitcher plants. You and I may know because we have insider information, but not most people."

"I agree. It's not first rate work. She'll have to do much better if she's going to make it."

"You know, I'm the scientist, but my guess is that she doesn't have it. She's going to fold and end up teaching drama somewhere. Which is okay, but probably not what she's thinking."

"It's way too soon to tell with kids that age. Some mature and grow into accomplished writers. Others lose momentum and fade. I think she has a good shot at succeeding. She is driven and bright."

"And good looking," Adriana said.

"What am I hearing? That's the second time tonight you've mentioned it. You envy her looks don't you? Maybe her youth too."

"How could you not?"

"Oh, honey, you have a bad case of the I'm-feeling-old-and-unattractive blues."

"I guess I do. And seeing Norman with that tall blonde didn't help."

"I know it sucks. But hang in there. You can never tell what will happen."

"There's one thing more I didn't get about the play. Again, you're the writer. I'm still stuck with the business about Michelangelo. What am I missing? The kids seemed to find it very funny. It's clearly something sexual. But I can't seem to figure it out."

"Me neither. But I'll ask the women in my undergraduate fiction writing class. They are wired into everything going on." She pulled up in front of Adriana's. "Okay, Professor Lubeck, I have one assignment and you have one. Mine's to find out about Michelangelo, and yours is to buck up. Moping around like a doe in heat is not going to help. You need a more active strategy for your social life. Anyway, I'll be in touch when I know more."

A few days later Adriana emailed. "Any news about project M? I'm still curious. By the way, I ran into Norman Penderevski in the department office. At first he seemed distant. Then I realized he's a little shy. In the end he was very cordial. If you hear anything, let me know. And please use my personal email. Adriana."

Toward the end of the week Olympia emailed back. "Okay, I've got the information. Can we meet for a drink after work tomorrow? And Adriana, I'm your friend. Listen to me. Stop pining and start planning. It's clear with this guy you're going to have to make the first move. Olympia."

Adriana's first move was to sink into a deep funk. Her second was to the freezer.

*   *   *

When they met over two chardonnays, Olympia launched in. "You're going to be amazed, I promise. I was stunned and then, well, at first I was incredulous, and then I laughed and laughed. It almost feels as if Diana's play was crowd-sourced. The women in the writing workshop think the Michelangelo is, as they used to say, the answer to the maiden's prayers. But let me back up some."

"That would be a good idea. You're not making a lot of sense."

"It started as a joke, morphed into a literary allusion, and became a reality."

"That's helpful. What joke and what reality?"

"Well, the students were red-faced when I asked about Michelangelo, but finally Lynn Michiko Yamamoto, who is originally from Kyoto . . . never mind, too much information. Anyway, she said that someone had bought a vibrator at a sex shop not two blocks from where we sit. And liked it. Really liked it. It was special. I was surprised I got that much out of Lynn Michiko. She is usually so shy. And so this young woman, the one who discovered the vibrator, talked to some of her friends, and they bought them and liked them. It spread like an epidemic. Eventually word got to Diana, and she began to use the same model. It's a little unclear who said what to whom because by this time a number of women were involved. But someone noted what generations of art historians have remarked on—that Michelangelo's big, strapping 'David' is, well, underendowed. That caused some tittering, and someone suggested that they should nickname the vibrator they all liked 'the Michelangelo' as a sort of compensation.

"And let me guess. I don't know Diana well, but I can imagine, especially after seeing Agnes with her at lunch. Diana latched on to the idea, and then it began to take over her play."

"I think you have it about right," Olympia said. "The other women were encouraging, and according to my sources, Diana felt emboldened. She told some of them that by pure chance she remembered an old art history professor talking about Michelangelo and mentioned an old novel by Irving Stone *The Agony and the Ecstasy*. The women from my seminar said that Diana started to laugh and mentioned something to the effect that some unknown spirit was instructing her. She was going to develop the idea further. She put great stock in the chance revelation. She stuck with the vibrator's nickname in her play because, as Lynn Michiko tells it, Diana said, 'first there was agony and then there was ecstasy.' The end product of all these chance occurrences and her embellishments is what we saw Saturday night."

Adriana smiled and screwed up her face into a look of disapproval. "All I can say is that it helps to have insider information. The whole thing falls flat without it. Not a good strategy for a playwright. Anyway, what's the business about T.S. Eliot and the women got to do with it?"

"I don't think much of anything. It was simply a gratuitous addition to the play. Unless there is some pun on the women coming."

"To a scientist, all of this sounds pretty far fetched and disorganized. My guess is she doesn't have a bright future in your racket."

"There is one more piece to the story. After a rehearsal one day, Diana and Gabe Bergson, the director, went to the sex shop and convinced the owner to repackage the vibrator and sell it as the Michelangelo. They thought it would boost ticket sales."

"Well for me, this turns out to be not nearly as interesting as I thought," Adriana said. "It's basically some bright, young cutups being clever."

"As I said, there is one additional bit. I bought one."

"You did? No way."

"You use a vibrator?" Olympia said.

"Come on, you know the answer to that."

"You didn't ask, but I'm going to tell you. The girls were right. It really is fantastic."

"Olympia . . ."

"Lighten up, Adriana. It's the twenty-first century. And while you're trying to work up your courage to engage Norman, I've got a little something for you." And she reached into her briefcase and pulled out a package wrapped in plain brown paper.

A sly, unreadable look came over Adriana's face. "I don't know if you remember, but when my parents ran Lubeck's Books, they used to stock art books, so I am more than familiar with Michelangelo's statue and his renderings of human anatomy. Thank you, Olympia, I think I'll take my lead from you, my friend."

III. Beverly Ardmore's Secret Life

I have always believed there are certain passions in life which one does not easily or ever share with others. They are needs too intimate and personal for polite discussion and cravings too deep to fathom. They stir a part of the self which often feels essential for wholeness. At other times one may be engaged by pursuits which may seem alternative, ludicrous, or even zany. These may make no sense on their surface, but they allow one's self to settle into a necessary cohesiveness. It is not that such escapades, as I choose to call them, are necessarily shameful—although in some cases they certainly are. Yet they may befuddle others, especially when a new relationship is developing.

Do not to judge me harshly for a bit of evasiveness. Deceit on a woman's part, especially in the realm of relationships with men, dates to Eve and is crucial for attracting and holding a man's attention. Eventually though one can be trapped by lies, find oneself in a relationship built on concealment, and have no way to extricate oneself. That's what happened with Norman. As my affection for him grew, my lie caught me as if I were a finger in a Chinese finger trap. The more I tried to pull myself out, the firmer it encased me.

I have asked myself honestly if something as simple as lipstick or blush or even mascara is not a form of deceit or at least misrepresentation—the accretion of unearned allure. There may be beauties in this world so blessed that their gifts rival Aphrodite's, but for the rest of us, queens and Jezebels alike, the Greeks and Egyptians developed cosmetics. Should I fault myself for eyeliner or dying my hair to recapture its original blonde color? It is a misrepresentation to pluck my eyebrows? At base life is a lie. The only thing I can say on my behalf is that men like to be lied to—or at least up to a point they do. They love the excitement of the eternal feminine and hate the idea of, and here is the point, emotional misrepresentation.

I believe that what I did to Norman was not a misrepresentation of anything—only a warm-hearted evasion that heightened my mystery and settled us into a happy relationship.

It began several months ago. The first time I saw him, I was totally without pretense. How could it be otherwise? I was standing at the vestibule of my brownstone, the rain sheeting off my umbrella, my hair reduced to matted spaniel. I clutched bunches of sunflowers and gladiolas to my raincoat with my umbrella arm. My other hand grasped a shopping bag overstuffed with groceries. I tried to think how I could get to the keys in my shoulder bag without putting down the umbrella or setting the already soaked grocery bag on the puddled concrete and risking its dissolution.

"Excuse me. May I help?" And there at the bottom of the steps of my brownstone was a pudgy professorial type. His raincoat and beret soaked as if they had been fished from the Charles. He held a wind-ravaged umbrella aloft and clutched an ancient leather briefcase. It didn't seem he was in a position to offer anyone assistance.

I was startled, but he had a kindly face, the type that comes from long experience in helping others. Without any evidence I sensed his intentions were generous. If he wanted to rob me or assault me, he was the most ill-prepared assailant imaginable. And I must have I looked a sight. There could not have been any chance of my feminine wiles entering into his calculation.

He did not wait for an answer. Without another word he walked up the steps, put down his briefcase and umbrella, and took the overheaped grocery bag from me.

"Thank you so much. You're very kind."

I fumbled through my bag—it seemed to take forever to find my house key. He held the groceries uncomplainingly. I got the vestibule door open, and we stood inside, sopping wet looking at each other. His face was relaxed, but you could imagine that at times he could set his jaw resolutely. And he was short—I'd say at least four inches shorter than I am.

"I'm very glad you offered your help," I said. "'It's the kindness of strangers,' I suppose—something we don't have enough of in this world." I had a crazy thought, well, maybe not so crazy given his appearance, but the kind you're not supposed to have. I burst out laughing. "It looks as if we have showered together with our clothes on." I wiped the hair from my eyes.

"Of course," he said. "I wouldn't want to be too forward."

"I like men with a sense of humor. Look, would you like to come in and dry off? I'll make some tea."

"If it wouldn't be too much trouble. I live close by, but It's is pretty nasty out there."

I opened the house door and we walked in. I stood looking at a bedraggled Don Quixote on my front hall rug. "Here, give me your hat and coat, and stay right there."

I returned in a minute with a man's sport shirt and slacks and a pair of dress socks. "My son-in-law's. The powder room is there."

I went to the kitchen, put the kettle on, and promptly lost my courage. You don't know this man. Hitler, Napoleon, Mussolini—they were all short. The world is full of stories of apparently mild mannered men who turned out to be murderers. Get ahold of yourself. He is a pudgy middle-aged man with a briefcase and a nice smile. Joseph Goebbels was a little man with a briefcase. I let out a laugh. Let's go see if he is the butcher of Riga.

I had just set a tea tray on the coffee table when he emerged in stocking feet, his sleeves and pants rolled up.

"Not exactly Armani, but you look fine," I said.

"That's okay. Professors, even Harvard professors, or maybe especially Harvard professors, who grew up in South Philadelphia don't wear Armani suits. So, I'm Norman Penderevski."

"And I'm Beverly Ardmore, and no Texas girl, if she can help it, would ever greet visitors with hair like this. Sorry, I ran a comb through it in the kitchen, but it didn't do much good. So we're neighbors. And you're a Harvard professor. Just what do you profess, Norman?"

"I'd have to know you better to tell all, but it's not the black arts or alchemy. I'm a molecular biologist. I've been in Boston about three years, though I'm new to the neighborhood."

"Where did you come from?"

"St. Louis. The St. Louis Zoo and Washington University."

"Oh, the zoo. Very nice. What did you do at the Zoo, my non-professing professor?"

"Go easy, actually zoos do a lot of important research. It's not all the monkey house and penguins."

"I'll bet they do."

"So, I study snake venom proteins. Many snake venom proteins are anticoagulants—they prevent the blood from clotting—so they are very important in medicine. They can help prevent heart attacks or lessen the effects of strokes. Anyway, I made a few discoveries and characterized some of these proteins, and Harvard made me an offer I couldn't refuse— more lab space, a good research package, and the Fanny and Albert Snifter Chair. Sorry, I guess I'm a little defensive. I'll stop. I don't want to sound too full of myself. I hate it when men go on and on about themselves. Tell me about you. It's always more interesting to hear about others than to tell one's own story."

"You're kind to ask. I'll tell you, but first, more tea?" He nodded. "Well, to make a long story short, I'm from Texas, but I have lived in Boston for many years. After a degree in English here at Harvard, I got an entry-level job in publishing in New York. I loved the energy, but after Texas, New York was claustrophobic. Concrete and more concrete. I decided to come back to Boston, and I found a position with Jamaica Atlantic Publishing. I did well. I was promoted to editor and began to work with some moderately famous people. I edited Sally Osternagel's debut comic novel *Lichtenstein Writ Large* and Bryce David Horner's collection of short stories, *When the Devil Won't Tell.* Then the bubble burst—Jamaica Atlantic was acquired. In the consolidation I lost my job. I also got married and divorced along the way. He was a classmate, also an English major, whose passion for a dissertation on Robert Graves and the White Goddess was greater than for me."

So you said, "'A farewell to all that' and left."

"Something like that. How do you know about Robert Graves?"

"I've got an interest in a lot of things that are not molecular biology or protein chemistry."

We made small talk about the neighborhood and the nearby shops on Newbury Street. It turned out that he had done well for a professor. He was part of a startup that went public and made a little money. He could actually afford an Armani suit, I surmised, though you could hear a trace of South Philadelphia in his voice. I guessed he was a Joseph A. Bank man. I was a little evasive. I didn't mention what my family did in Texas or the house in Wellfleet. Finally I glanced at my watch and stood up. I told him to wear my son-in-law's clothes home—he could bring them by sometime.

"May I return the hospitality and take you to dinner Saturday night?"

I explained that I was busy. That was all he needed to know for now.

"How about Saturday during the day. Perhaps we could walk in the Boston Garden and the Common or along the Charles and then go for coffee."

Of course I agreed. I liked what I had seen at tea. I towered over him, but it didn't matter. He was smart and charming in a slightly smart-ass way. And he had a great smile.

My height has always made me an outlier. And

my looks and academic gifts too. I take no credit for them. They are completely unearned blessings. They have always set me apart. In my twenties I was striking. The room stopped when I walked in. In heels I'm six two or three. I did a little modeling in college. I didn't need to, but I paid for my education out of my earnings. Now my height is not so much a problem as an inconvenience. I've had to make some adjustments, and occasionally when men, say Norman's size, would feel a bit uncomfortable dating me, I would say, Look, if someone my height is going out with you, people will know instantly that you have something on the ball.

Good fortune shone on our walk that Saturday—it was a warm, clear day—not impossible for late October in Boston, but not altogether usual either. We strolled past the shops on Newbury Street and into the Garden and the Common. Norman had a penchant for detail, and he noted the contrasting beauty of dark green conifers and the scarlet blaze of the fall maples. It was very different from St. Louis, he said, where the silver maples were candle orange, and reds were absent except for the occasional sweetgums.

"Texas is the same way," I said, "though I've lived here so long, I take it for granted."

We nursed the relationship along, content in each other's company, making chitchat and looking at the young couples pushing babies and the old ladies feeding the pigeons from the benches. To me it seemed very companionable, though we must have looked the odd couple. It was not only the difference in our heights, but our clothes—our entire styles—were mismatched. I wore make up, a favorite camel's hair coat, and an elegant scarf at my neck. I had recently refrosted my hair—I always allowed just a bit of gray to show through. Its presence reflected the tension between raw truth and illusion—or if you hold me to my words, the "misrepresentation" we spoke of earlier. As for Norman, thank goodness he left the beret at home. He wore a Red Sox cap, jeans and a zip-up black jacket that bunched about his middle. None of this mattered—he was arrestingly good company. And when he laughed, which was often, he had laugh lines about his eyes and mouth.

Eventually we found ourselves at the Faneuil Hall Farmer's market and, as I now remember, at Angelo Cosetti's vegetable stand. It was there in front of a mountain of broccoli—where it came from at this time of year is anybody's guess—that Norman asked if he could take me to lunch.

"Fine," I said. "More than fine. That would be nice. But I have to be back by four. I've got to take a nap before tonight." Again I offered no further information. He said nothing. I took pleasure in the slight puzzlement that came over his face.

"That's okay. We'll get a bite, and you'll be back in plenty of time to rest up for your mysterious evening."

"Who said anything about mysterious? It's just an evening with friends."

We ate inside. He had the shepherd's pie and peas with a beer, and I ordered a Cobb salad and a glass of chardonnay. Conversation was sparse. We tried to keep things general and not too personal.

Finally, less out of curiosity than a desire not to let the afternoon die, I said, "Tell me again about you're work. What do you actually do in the lab?"

"So here's the fifty-cent answer. My team recently isolated a new protein from a rare Indian cobra. We're busy trying to characterize it. I'm hopeful from what we now know that it will be a powerful anticoagulant and medicinally useful. As I mentioned when we had tea, the goal is to develop new drugs that will save lives and make others better. In a nutshell, that's it."

"Thanks, interesting, and just about the right level for me. I think I understand. It sounds like detailed and complicated work. Good work, actually. Important work."

He paid the check and we walked toward my house. At the door, he smiled. In it there was a slight, almost undetectable flicker of indecision. I recognized the problem immediately. I put my index finger to my lips, kissed it, and placed it on his. "Next time. I had a great day. Thank you. Please call me soon."

That night when the three of them—Lester, Joe,

and Jorge—picked me up, I told them the story as we drove. Lester laughed. "Go ahead and take the initiative. He'll like that."

I took his advice. I invited Norman to an opening the next Thursday at the Institute for Contemporary Art. When he came to pick me up, I saw that he had double-parked—he had become a Bostonian—and we hustled down the steps and into his Camry. I remember having to push back the passenger seat for extra legroom. I had planned ahead a bit and scoured Boston for a pair of peach Cuban pumps to match my dress. It was the best I could do—I won't deny that in spite of all my attempts at liberation from convention, I was still a little self-conscious about the disparity in our heights.

The opening was a bust—the show consisted of installations of machines whose parts were painted in flat rainbow colors and moved randomly. Old black and white TVs were mounted on some of the longer arms and displayed changing test patterns. Later we went back to my place. On impulse, I decided to salvage the evening and level the playing field in my bedroom. When a girl kicks off her pumps and gives herself over to love, there is no telling what can happen.

The rub came the next morning over coffee. Could he take me to dinner Saturday night?

"Oh, Norman, you know I've become fond of you, but I'm doing something with friends. I have a sort of standing commitment."

"What kind of thing? The movies? Drinks with the girls? Dinner?"

"I am not seeing anyone if that's what you're trying to ask. It's just something silly that I enjoy and I'm committed to. And frankly, a little embarrassed by. So for now let's let it go at that." I could see he was unhappy.

"After last night why are you keeping your distance?"

"I'm not keeping my distance. I like you, Norman. I enjoy your company. And last night was nice, but it was last night. Look, let's pick another time."

As he left, he said that he would call soon. It was a half-hearted gesture. I thought eventually I would hear from him but not soon.

He was upset. Men sometimes get that way. You could tell he felt excluded just when we were developing a closeness. But I wasn't ready for so much intimacy. I was afraid if I shared my Saturday night deal with him, he would dismiss me as frivolous. Norman had a great sense of humor, but he was also mired in seriousness. I worried that he wouldn't get it. I imagined I could slowly wean him from this misplaced earnestness, and when the time was right, reveal my, what?, my vulgar side, my coarse side, perhaps my common side. He grew up in South Philadelphia. Maybe he would take my kickback Saturday nights in stride, but I had to wait until I knew him a little better—until I was sure he would cut me some slack.

Then I got a surprise. Funny how people's actions reveal their character. Lester and the boys picked me up in his old Buick at seven the next Saturday. I dressed in black leather pants, black spike heels, and a white silk blouse. I put on a black wig, replaced my diamond studs with hoops, and walked out the door in my Camel hair coat. It was a drizzly night, and visibility was bad. As we drove, we chitchatted. The roads were bad. I did not want to distract Lester, so I talked mostly to Jorge and Joe, actually to Joe. I love Jorge, but he's not very interesting. His talents are elsewhere.

"Well, Sergeant, what's up with the Cambridge Police?" I said to Joe.

"Not much. The usual—stolen cars, stolen bikes, break-ins, domestic violence. The faces changes, the cars change, and the stories remain the same."

"Come on, Joe. Lester's an accountant and I am unemployed. We never do anything interesting from one Saturday night to the next. We want to hear a story, don't we, Jorge."

"Yeah, come on, Martinez, what's up?"

"Okay, here it comes, by popular request. But

I have to be a little circumspect. I'm cooked at work if any of this gets out. So there was a little narcotics action at one of the boathouses near the Harvard Campus. The vice squad needed extra hands for the raid, and I got assigned. So there I am in a flak jacket with an assault rife at two in the morning at a boathouse on the Charles. We creep up, surround the place, and a dozen police rush in. I was assigned as backup cover. When they broke the door down, they found more than shells and oars. They brought out four young people, all Harvard undergraduates, and sealed off the building. They estimate the pot and drugs they found are worth a million dollars on the street."

I said I didn't remember reading about it or hearing anything through the grapevine. "Why was there nothing on television or in the *Globe*?"

"The chief kept the whole thing under raps. It seems one of the guys is a congressman's son. The chief worried about publicity and fallout."

"You're not going to believe this," Lester said, "But I think we're being followed."

"Can't be," Joe said. "No one is going to carjack us for a ten year old Buick. You sure? It's a rainy night and everything looks the same."

"Maybe, but this guy has been hanging back almost since downtown. I'm gonna get off the road here onto a side street and see what happens."

He did and the guy stayed with us.

"What do we do now?" Lester said.

"Don't stop. If it's for real, the last thing you want is a confrontation," Joe said. "Let me take a look. Slow down a bit." He turned and wiped the fog from the back window. "Okay, get back on a major street." He picked up his cell. "I'm going to put you on speaker phone." He dialed.

"Cambridge Police. How may I direct your call?"

"Hi, Janice, this is Joe, Joe Martinez."

"Hi, Joe, what's up. I thought you were off tonight."

"I am, but I need someone to run a license plate check."

"I'll give you Denny. Just a sec."

Denny came on and Joe said, "It's a late model Toyota Camry. I can't tell the color—it's hard to see. It's a Mass plate and I only have the first three letters.

A moment later Denny said, "It's a vanity plate that some nut owns. The whole thing is VENOM1."

"Who's it registered to?"

"It's a 2009 Camry. The owner is a Norman C. Penderevski from Boston."

"He have any record?"

"No, the car's been in the state about three years now."

"Damn it," I said. "Thank Denny and hang up. I know who this is. It's Norman, the Harvard professor I was telling you about. I knew he was jealous of my Saturdays, but I didn't think he would actually follow us. Funny, I was clear that I was not seeing anyone else. I guess he's more curious about me than I realized.

"You mean he's spying on you," Jorge said.

"He may be a stalker. I think we should call Boston PD. What kind of guy puts VENOM1 on a plate?" Joe said.

There was a long back and forth in which I explained that he was harmless and a nice guy, just a little overzealous. Joe disagreed. He had seen too many nice guys beat their wives and girlfriends. He was for what he termed a "vigorous response." In the end I prevailed. I convinced them to forget Norman and drive to Chico's. Norman would check out the place from the street and be too timid to come in.

I admit I was a little shaken. Of course, Norman was not a stalker. You hear all kinds of stories. Love and desire can bring out the worst in people. But I was betting Norman was mostly hurt or jealous, and if I came clean, his errant behavior would evaporate. I hoped I was right.

It turned out that Norman did not come in. The night left me in a quandary. Suppose I was wrong or that he was a normal guy, the person I thought he was, but he had become temporarily crazed and dangerous.

I decided not to answer my phone or my cell for a few days. And just in case, I slipped away to my place in Wellfleet. No matter what the reason, I like to spend time there, especially at this time of year. It's a good time to walk. Usually the weather has not turned bitter and no one's around. Also I had chores. The guesthouse on my property needed a new vanity in the bathroom, so I called ahead to my plumber. But mostly I took advantage of the time to walk and think. The only interruptions were the twice-daily calls from Norman, which of course went unanswered.

"Hi, Beverly. Are you okay? I haven't heard from you. Please call me back. I worry."

Who was the real Norman I wondered—the intense researcher who knew about Robert Graves and drove a Camry? The ardent lover with whom I had spent the night? The frumpy, plump guy in the bunched zipper jacket? The amateur sleuth, who could possibly be, if not a stalker, then too possessive for me? VENOM1? And he probably had an edge since he grew up in South Philly. The holder of an endowed chair? All of these images swarmed about me, competing for my attention and asserting their credibility. There was no real Norman, I realized. There were many. Like the rest of us, men and women alike, he was a composite. As I struggled with what the various Normans would think of me, I wondered what an heiress and sometime model with a Harvard degree and a background in publishing was doing at Chico's with three Latinos? ¡Caramba! I also wondered what this same woman was doing sleeping with a guy she had only seen twice before?

There was no answer to any of these questions. A sensible woman would have picked up one of his calls, made a date for coffee and explained everything. She would have kissed him on the mouth in public and suggested that they head immediately back to her place. I was not one of those women.

Instead I was taken over by devilment. I tried to imagine how much Norman actually knew. He must have seen me get into an old car and perhaps knew it contained three men. He certainly had to wonder why we cut through a neighborhood and then headed on our way again. Of course, it's impossible to know what he made of this. Then we ended up in a dilapidated Hispanic neighborhood. He had seen me get out in front of Chico's with two men and the car pull away. Most of the signage was in Spanish, but he certainly would have deduced that Chico's was a bar. What about the instrument cases that Joe and Jorge lugged from the trunk. Of course, speaking Spanish and being from Texas, I had seen "El Mariachi." I knew what a guitar case could conceal. Growing up in South Philly, he must have had similar thoughts.

When a tall woman wears a black wig, gets into a car with some men and drives to a bar in the barrio, what can that mean? Norman may have thought I was turning tricks. You know, rich girl gets a thrill from adventure. Doesn't need the money but loves the high. It's true I am old for that sort of thing, but I've seen the way men still look at me. I have always imagined that because of my size, a certain type of man has fantasies about dominating me. It is possible that Norman thought the same thing. Or drugs. He may have thought I was buying or selling. What kind of innocent explanation could have crossed his mind? It was hard to say. These Walter Mitty types long for adventure. And here was a chance to experience it vicariously.

It is not strictly accurate to call Norman a Walter Mitty type. He was adventurous in his own way. He grew up in a tough part of Philadelphia and had achieved escape velocity. He had risen to the top ranks of his field and held an endowed chair. He was certainly no namby pamby milk toast. But neither was he a hardened man. Maybe his brother Jan came closer. Norman had mentioned him. Jan had stayed in South Philly and now ran what Norman termed "a notions and novelties business" there. He was reticent, but it seemed from the context and Norman's careful phrasing that Jan was involved in some illicit activity or other. Maybe Norman's background was not so vanilla. Maybe Norman had a few mysteries of his own. I wondered how this unknown side of Norman colored his take on me.

The odd thing was, in spite of the scenarios he may have imagined, he was still attracted to me. He had an alternative side to him. His frontal lobes registered sex and drugs and gave me a pass. "Go for it, Norman," they must have said.

My goal in all of this was to have a little fun, give Norman a view of my behavior, and in the end solidify our relationship. Easier said that done. I wanted to sting the mark but in a nonlethal way. Just enough venom to paralyze his critical faculties but not so much that he became, well, I'm not going to censure my thought here, that he became impotent, or impotent with me. I suddenly realized that the distance from South Philadelphia to River Oaks where I grew up in Houston is less than a millimeter. I wouldn't go as far as to say that my craziness was his, but if he was who I thought he was, our bizarre takes on the world were first cousins.

Slowly a plan emerged. I called him back and explained that he couldn't reach me because I was on the Cape, that I had gone there to have some alone time, no not from him, but from the gloom of Boston in early November. I invited him for dinner on Thursday, and to make sure he understood that I was not calling to have things out, I said, "Bring a toothbrush."

The evening went well, a small rack of lamb, a bottle of red, a joint, and no mention of the Chico's episode. I wasn't going to say anything. I had no interest in blowing my cover. And he, I think, seeing that I was trying to mollify him, did not raise the issue.

I couldn't allow us to live a lie, not if we were going to go forward, so the next morning at breakfast I said, "You've been very good about not intruding on my Saturday nights. I enjoy being with you, and I don't want this to come between us."

"You're quite an amazing woman, Beverly, wonderful, in fact. I've never met anyone quite like you before. I would be lying if I said I wasn't curious. Tell me what you're thinking."

"Come by my house about seven on Saturday.

Dress casually. You'll get a firsthand look, and all will be revealed." I smiled. Of course I knew that "all" didn't have to be revealed, that part of it was already revealed. He had seen the site of the action—Chico's. It was fun knowing more about what he knew than I let on.

I got ahold of the guys and clued them in. "In the car, no English, only Spanish," I said.

Lester said that his Spanish was pretty rusty. "Just stick to *buenas noches* and let Joe and Jorge talk." I was startled when Norman appeared. In five-inch heels I was eight or nine inches taller than he was. I knew that when our relationship came out later at Chico's every stubby guy from Matamoros to Tierra del Fuego was going to die of lust. It was not hard to imagine what they were thinking on a normal night, but to confront a successful rival in the flesh, and one their size, was going to drive them up a wall.

I bent down and kissed Norman briefly. "This is Lester and Joe and Jorge. Norman, Norman Penderevski," I said.

In return we got three versions of "*Buenas noches, señor, mucho gusto.*"

"Nice to meet you," I clarified.

As we drove, I translated. The guys evaded Norman's questions, and I smoothed things in my renderings. Once or twice I thought I heard Joe snickering in the front seat, but his amusement didn't blow my cover.

Norman cleared his throat. "So as best I can tell, the four of you have some business at a bar, at Chico's. Is that about right?"

Joe and Jorge spoke to each other in a slang I only partially understand, but I knew they were enjoying themselves.

"Pretty close," I said. "Just be patient."

I was loving the whole deal. It seemed all in good fun. In twenty minutes Norman would be in the know. He'd have a few margaritas and enjoy himself.

Lester dropped us off and went to park. When Joe, Jorge and I walked in with Norman, the bartender

Enrique did a double take. Before he could say a word, I asked him in Spanish to give Norman a margarita and to pretend he knew almost no English. "If he asks you anything about us, feign incomprehension. And whatever you do, don't tell him that you're a college professor too."

It was early, but there was already a good crowd. Lester walked in lugging his *bajo sexto*, his Mexican bass guitar, in a large case, and as the four of us disappeared, people clapped and whistled enthusiastically. I don't know what was going through Norman's mind. At some point he certainly cottoned on to what was going on, but I am sure he had just enough lingering doubt and lack of experience in Mexican dives to be uncertain of the details. I still held out hope that he thought I was going to do a little lap dancing.

We came on stage, and I looked at Norman straddling a bar stool in the back. He smiled uncertainly at me. He looked tense. Of course, he now realized that I was a singer and the three guys were the band. I could tell, though, he was a bit uncomfortable on foreign turf.

"*Buenas noches*, y'all," I said with a Mexican Spanish accent that slid to a Texas drawl. "I'm going to say a few words in English tonight first."

"*Ándale, muchacha*," some guy shouted from the side. "You go, girl!"

"I'm dedicating the first number to my good friend Normandito who is here tonight," and I pointed toward the bar. The crowd clapped and whistled. "We're going to do this song in English. For those of you who don't know it, it's called 'You Are My Sunshine.' Here it comes, *Cariño*."

After the first set I went back to see how he was doing.

"I'll be damned," he said. "I thought I had seen everything, but this is amazing. You are one foxy bitch."

"I'm not used to such profanity from Harvard professors." I gave him an arch smile.

"I'm having to adjust a bit," he laughed. "I didn't

know I was dating Boston's, no New England's, tallest, female, Mexican vocalist. While you were backstage getting ready to go on, I read the chalkboard. Now I know who Beverly Cienfuegos is. And Enrique spilled the beans a bit, Miss Hundred Fires."

IV. Olympia Loved Charlemagne

The day after Thanksgiving Charlemagne died. The death of Olympia's poodle was a blow. The novelist lived alone, and she doted on the dog. She silently joked that he was her man. In fact three years earlier when she bought him, she made the decision not to have him fixed. Such dismemberment, as she referred to it, violated some spiritual command, a covenant with the earth. And besides she was self-aware enough from the beginning to understand that she was in a relationship with the dog. Not a physical relationship— she would provide for his intimate needs in a most unusual way—but in an emotional one.

She had decided to call the puppy Charlemagne. She had no idea where the name came from. It had burst into her consciousness geyser-like from below. What part of her deeper self clamored for attention was hard to say. Did the poodle represent some undefined possibility she longed for or some void she felt a Charlemagne could fill? Certainly a dog with any name could—no, would—be faithful and loving and, yes, loyal.

In a reflective moment she recognized it was the largeness of the ruler's vision she sought. She hoped that in some magical way the Holy Roman Emperor would enlarge her vision as a writer. And maybe too it was about power, that she wanted a companion who could, at least in a symbolic way, stand up to her, prevent the extravagant arpeggios that plagued her early drafts. He would take her in hand, compel her to edit out excess. She was in no way abstemious. She imagined Charles the Great would assure that her writing had a modicum restraint.

She had thought about other names. Nietzsche or Rilke would not do. She might want to read them but not live with them. She could call a dog Wallace Stevens but that bordered on the creepy, and besides she would not want to live with him either. Then in a wine-fueled, madcap moment she wondered about Ezra Pound. Yes, that was it. She could call her animal Dog Pound. Or instead of Charlemagne, how about Napoleon? Or instead of Nietzsche what about Husserl? Spinoza? Augustine? Finally she had had enough of invention, and she settled back and finished her wine.

She tried to sort through why she had chosen a poodle. She was certain a German shepherd would have been the wrong choice. In her view these animals lacked the finesse and warmth she was looking for. They were certainly strong, masculine authority figures, but she feared their ferociousness would dominate her—intimidate her in an unpleasant, physical way. She had begun by reading about different breeds. The job was exhausting, and many of the descriptions seemed abstract. It was hard to imagine how these would translate into a dog's actual behavior. She knew instinctively that a big, warm, slobbery mastiff was not right. Labs and retrievers were not edgy enough. After discarding bulldogs and cocker spaniels, she hit on the idea of a poodle. They were masculine dogs, bred for a variety of practical tasks, but the right grooming and cut might bring out their feminine side. She was confident this androgynous quality would help her writing.

Was she in a relationship?

Can a woman love her dog? Perhaps not in the sense in which the term is usually employed, but she could have a fantasy life centered on him. Olympia Breathwaite understood the emotional niceties that enabled and limited her canine tryst. She was an insightful thinker and grounded enough to realize that Charlemagne was a dog. Period. Yet as in any relationship, an attentive lover provides for the needs of the other. Like a character in one of her novels, she tried to get inside Charlemagne's head.

Practically speaking, her devotion led to three decisions. It might have been simple projection, but since she herself loved food, she attributed her preoccupation to him and served him gourmet meals and treats. She knew poodles were active dogs and could not be confined to a house, so she fenced her large yard and gave him free reign to run and root.

Whether her third act was a matter of projection or simple recognition of the needs of male animals is impossible to say, but she even provided for his rutting. She found a veterinarian in Somerville, not her regular vet who would soon necropsy her poor Charlemagne, but one who offered a unique service. He maintained a number of bitches in artificial heat with hormones, and once a month—for a fee a john would find steep—she arranged a conjugal visit for her companion.

The visitation room was equipped with a one-way mirror. At first, she dismissed as disgusting the possibility of watching Charlemagne *in flagrante delicto*. It was perverse even to imagine it, but bit-by-bit the possibility of observing him grew on her. She couldn't believe what she was thinking—she wanted to watch the Holy Roman Emperor get his rocks off. She knew she was not supposed to find the sex life of her dog interesting, but she couldn't help herself. One day she succumbed. What she saw fascinated and stunned her—somehow in her girlhood she had never seen two dogs together in the street. At once she was overcome by shame—shame at what she had done, for she felt she had violated Charlemagne's privacy. And shame at finding the process titillating.

She made a conscious decision not to explore the genesis of this voyeurism. She was careful not to let her salacious eccentricity and her rich fantasy life enter directly into her novels. These were literary—meant to appeal to academics, students in creative writing programs, and former English majors who set high reading standards for themselves. No bodice was ever ripped in one of her stories. And unfortunately it had been a while since anyone had caressed her, yet alone ripped her bodice.

*   *   *

A few weeks before Thanksgiving Olympia had confidently exhorted her friend Adriana to pursue Norman Penderevski. Olympia was direct with her friend, "Just get started, one way or another, and, you'll see, things will take the proper course." In truth, Olympia was a genius at moving men and women in and out of relationships in her novels but seldom so assertive or successful in her personal life. Maybe that is why she was so deeply attached to Charlemagne.

Thanksgiving week began as it usually did for the novelist. Her writer persona disappeared, and a more domestic woman emerged. She picked up a fresh turkey at a local specialty store along with sweet potatoes, broccoli, and green beans. Oh, and cranberries for her mother Portia, the self-appointed queen mother of cranberry sauce. She bought a bag of Pepperidge Farm stuffing mix, which she supplemented with bread cubes she had made from dried seven-grain bread. And canned pumpkin for the inevitable pumpkin pie. The author was as attentive to detail in these preparations as she was to character development in her novels.

The week was always a family affair, which meant that her brother Chandler arrived the Sunday before from Tucson. He too had stepped out of his professional persona, what she called his stargazing, and flew in. It had taken her a long time to get used to the idea that one could be a successful astrophysicist and not work at Harvard or MIT. Chandler had explained that theorists like him enjoyed working in close proximity to experimentalists, and experimental astrophysicists needed access to the night sky. Yet even after many years and no firsthand knowledge, she considered the University of Arizona a barely adequate oasis in the academic desert of the southwest.

He was here now and could help, not with the preparations so much as with Portia whose monopoly in the cranberry sauce business dated back half a century. She still lived independently in a brownstone near the Boston Common. Each morning Chandler would fetch her to join them in planning and preparing Thanksgiving dinner. By general agreement between mother and daughter, Portia went home each night. Neither had ever considered living with the other. The women loved each other, but too much Portia would kill Olympia's gift. And too much Olympia would kill Portia, who in her late eighties was still very much the family matriarch. Even Charlemagne had the good sense to behave. Portia had dubbed him Charlie Brown and dominated him the way Lucy did.

It was a predictable collection of characters who were to assemble at four Thanksgiving afternoon. Portia, Chandler, and Olympia would be joined by George Morrison from the English Department and his partner Gregory from the mayor's office, Millicent and Hermann Hofnagel—she a photographer in Olympia's book club and he an attorney—and Jillian and Giles Ramsey, on sabbatical for the year from the other Cambridge. Olympia was also good about including stray undergraduate writing students trapped in Boston over the holiday—this year Lynn Michiko Yamamoto would come.

And there were some unanticipated, but not unwelcome additions.

Henrietta Markham, Olympia's former student, called a few days beforehand to say that she was back in Boston visiting family over Thanksgiving. Could they have coffee? No, the week was too busy, but how about coming to Thanksgiving dinner? As soon as the invitation slipped out of her mouth, she regretted it. Olympia intuited from Henrietta's fiction that her family life was complicated, and her invitation might force Henrietta into a difficult choice.

Then Adriana called. "Do you have room for one more, two more actually? The three crazies are at it again. As of yesterday, my daughter Agnes was supposed to bring Maynard and their girlfriend Diana over. And Abigail and I were going to have Thanksgiving dinner with them. I have been taking your advice and trying to be more open and accepting of Agnes. But yesterday, for God's sake, the Wednesday before Thanksgiving if you can believe it, I get a call from her. I'm sure she had been smoking. They weren't coming. They had bought a turducken and were going to eat as a threesome. And get this— she said that they were going to find out who was the turkey, who was the sitting duck and who was the chicken. I was angry, really angry for the last minute change. 'What about Granny Abigail?' I asked. 'She'll be very disappointed.' She ignored the question. I told her to do what she damn well pleased and hung up. So I'm at loose ends."

"Come, and of course bring your mother. Portia will be here, but I think it will be okay in a large group."

"If I can impose, that would be lovely," Adriana said.

"It's not an imposition. I'd love to have you both. You'll know almost everyone, but there are two interesting additions. One is Lynn Michiko Yamamoto, you remember, the one who spilled the beans about the Michelangelo. The other is the young woman I was telling you about, Henrietta Markham, the one who wrote the strange little novel, *The Lobsterman's Daughter.*"

"Thanks, I need to come. It's not only my mother and what to do with her at Thanksgiving, but I'm feeling pretty vulnerable right now. Besides Agnes, I'm down about Norman. He and that blonde have become a number."

"Just come and enjoy yourself."

What to do with the Charlemagne? Olympia knew that he could be high strung around a large group, but she decided not to exile him to the yard Thanksgiving afternoon. Let him roam, and if he gets rambunctious, that would be the time to send him packing.

Henrietta arrived early. Olympia greeted her and slipped back into the kitchen, leaving Chandler and Portia to chat with her.

"Are you from here?" Portia said.

"Yes, I am, and I'm glad to be back for a few days."

"Well, dear, why are you not spending today with your family?"

Henrietta reached down and ran her fingers through Charlemagne's curly hair. "There's a good dog. It's complicated. My father's not around. I'd rather not go into that. And my mother's a mess. I needed to escape her and my brothers."

"In any case, my dear, we are happy to have you. You must tell me what you think of my cranberry sauce."

The doorbell rang and in walked Lynn Michiko and the Brits, Jillian and Giles. People shook hands all around and began to look for connections. It turned out that both Chandler and Lynn Michiko had spent time in the other Cambridge—he as a postdoctoral fellow in astrophysics at the University and she when her father was on special assignment from the Japanese government. They stood in a loose circle, and to keep the conversation going, Chandler asked Giles about next year's prospects at the Henley Regatta. Henrietta insinuated herself between Chandler and Lynn Michiko and listened.

"Right, well, you know what happened this year. You Yanks, some Californians, won the men's Grand Challenge Cup, and Harvard won the Ladies' Challenge Cup. The odd thing about rowing in Cambridge, that is, our Cambridge, is that . . ." Giles was saying, but Henrietta was otherwise occupied. She edged toward Chandler and managed in the gentlest way to rub the lateral aspect of her thigh against his. The touch was so slight that if caught, she could apologize and claim it was an accidental consequence of close quarters and nothing more. It is not certain if Chandler noticed and was enjoying himself or was indifferent or even oblivious. Giles continued to explain that Cambridge rowing was on hard times, and Henrietta, who had a brief attention span for athletics, reached down to pet Charlemagne.

Henrietta was not the only one scouting the territory. At dinner, Adriana took stock and reached the same conclusion. Chandler was available. When you eliminated the gay couple and the married men, who were a no-no for her, it left only Chandler. She had known him forever. He was two years ahead of her at Harvard and, for an astrophysicist, not uninteresting. At once she came to her senses. Tucson was on the other side of the moon, much too far for a relationship.

Finding common ground for conversation over a seventy-year age span and three continents was hard work, and everyone struggled. What passed for interaction was a series of opinions, stated more or less dogmatically, but politely. They were broadcast into a vacuum with little expectation of any meaningful response. As the wine flowed, opinions became pontifications—mostly male—and at times bordered on filibusters.

Portia insisted on collecting individual opinions about her cranberry sauce. She was hoping for glowing testimonials but was happy with the guests' polite and kind comments. Henrietta got under her skin a bit when she asked Portia how she thought Charlemagne liked "her concoction."

Mostly, however, the dinner was dominated by precious observations and bon mots of the kind almost unknown outside of the desiccated world of academe. Thus the adults became engaged in spirited haggling over whether Gary Wills's or Adam Gopnik's articles were more interesting.

Olympia favored Gopnik. "He has an amazing breadth of knowledge, and his writing can animate a pharaoh. I grant you he is not a scholar in the usual sense, but his articles are . . . I guess you could say 'learned.'"

"Yes," chimed in George Morrison, her colleague from the English Department, "As an expository writer with a gift for relaxed style, he is exceptional."

Chandler took the opposite view. "No one is smarter or more knowledgeable than Gary Wills. His articles are like papal encyclicals. They are the last word."

"But you know he is a Catholic," Portia said as if a Back Bay matron from the twenties were excoriating the Boston Irish.

"Thank you, Mom, but I don't think that enters into it," Olympia said.

"Really, if you analyze what everyone is talking about, it's the difference between *The New York Review of Books* and *The New Yorker.*" Who was this speaking? Then someone realized it was Henrietta. "There's is no comparison," she continued. "Isn't that right, Charlemagne? What do you ever see in *The New Yorker* that is anything like the collaboration and insightful writing of Tony Judt and Timothy Snyder? Nothing, you have to admit. Isn't that right, Charlemagne." It was as if Henrietta had no interest in what the humans thought. The final arbiter of conversation would be a poodle. She slipped the dog a slab of dark meat from a drumstick. Charlemagne curled at her feet for the duration.

"And our colleague Louis Menand, he writes for *The New Yorker.* What would you do with him?" George said.

"Read him," Henrietta said a bit too quickly and glibly for the adults.

And that's how it went from the first sip of Chardonnay to the last sliver of pumpkin pie. Chandler passed around cognac and port.

Jillian wanted to talk about the Man-Booker prize. She looked at Olympia and George and asked who they thought would win next year's prize.

"Hilary Mantel won this year's prize," Lynn Michiko said.

"Thank you. We can all read the papers," Henrietta said. "For the coming year, it's way too early to tell. If the field looks weak, you can count on publishers to rush books into print."

"In my day, children did not speak before adults," Portia said.

"It's okay, Mom. They can participate," Olympia said. "I'm proud of them. They are my students. And Henrietta has a book of her own that is just coming out."

All of the adults but Chandler smiled indulgently. "Well, young lady, that's quite an accomplishment," he said.

"Your sister was a big help. It would not have happened without her."

"You seem well read," Chandler said. "Who do young people find interesting these days?"

"In my day it was D.H. Lawrence and Henry Miller," Abigail chimed in.

"My word, Abigail. What are you thinking?" Portia said.

"Well, Chandler," Henrietta said, "I don't know about other young people, but I have been following William Levy. I'm wondering what others think of him."

Hermann Hofnagel finally said something. "The author? The guy who wrote *When Will Burma Be Free?*"

"No. I meant the famous one," Henrietta said.

Blank stares around the table.

"Oh, yeah, the Latino heart throb," Chandler said.

"But he must be Jewish," Portia said. "How can he be Latino? They're the rye bread people from New York."

"Mom, just hang in there. These kids weren't born when those commercials aired." Chandler winked at Henrietta. "In Tucson I see him all the time on Hispanic television, on Univisión."

"He's Cuban American, but in Mexico—and here—he is all the rage," Henrietta said.

The guests looked uneasily at Henrietta. Most were trying to decide how much to indulge her edgy behavior. Everyone but Chandler, that is, who was wondering if he might indulge himself.

Two other facets of this gathering are worth noting. No one had the slightest interest in playing touch football. Perhaps Olympia could have called the event for two, and the guests could have played before dinner. But age, focus, gender, and of course the Brits' total lack of knowledge made choosing up sides an unlikely scenario.

The other was that the television was silent in Olympia's house—yes, the novelist owned one and liked WGBS, the Boston PBS affiliate. But not sports. Unlike millions of others who saw the Detroit Lions play the Texans on Thanksgiving or tuned in to find out the final score, everyone but Henrietta was oblivious. She had flown in from Houston a few days ago, and A.E., her friend-lover-sugar daddy-mentor-mark-keeper-victim-john was a football fan.

Out of mischief she asked if they should turn on the TV to find out the score.

"What on earth for, child?" Portia asked. "The score of what?"

"Don't be so condescending, Portia," Abigail said.

"The football game. Detroit is playing Houston," Henrietta said.

"My, my. Is that what they do in Houston on Thanksgiving?" It was Portia pressing a point.

"Mom, it's okay. Many people are interested in sports," Chandler said. "In fact almost everybody but us. In Tucson you can't go anywhere, not even to the physics department without hearing the constant banter."

No one else seemed interested in indulging Henrietta's curiosity.

"Maybe Henrietta can tell us a little about her novel," Olympia suggested.

"I'd rather not. I don't want to spoil it other than to say it's about five generations of murder and deceit in a Maine family."

"Oh, come on, surely you can say a little more without spilling the beans," Lynn Michiko said.

Henrietta glared at the young woman as if she had taken a fork full of turkey off her plate. "I really don't think that's appropriate. It's about murder and deceit. You can read the rest when it's out."

"Good Heavens, young lady, how do you know about such things?" Portia said.

"Mother, it doesn't matter. She knows. That's what writers do. That's what I do. We make up stories. Okay, enough. Chandler is coming around to refill everyone's glass one last time. As most of you know, this is pitch-in time. Jillian, will you take the empty wine glasses to the bar sink and wash them? I don't like to put them in the dishwasher. And Chandler and Giles, bundle up all the trash and put it outside in the can. Henrietta, make yourself useful and let poor Charlemagne out back to do his business. The rest of you can clear. I'll put the dishes in the dishwasher. Lynn Michiko after the table is clear, put the tablecloth in a heap by the door so I can take it to the cleaners in the morning. And fold the pads and put them in the back closet. That should get us started."

"Come on, pooch, let's get you outside," Henrietta said. The dog trotted after her to the back door and bounded down the steps. He raced out into the darkness and made periodic loops back toward her. She picked up a stick and threw it. It landed somewhere in the void, and in a moment he returned it. The game became more and more intense, and soon Henrietta wandered beyond the lights. She would throw the stick out into the darkness, and Charlemagne would return it to the now invisible Henrietta. She petted his flanks and rubbed his back. She kissed his head. Then he lay at her feet and rolled around on his back. She reached down and stroked his flank and tummy. She was as frisky as the dog. She went down on her knees hugging the dog and romping with him. As Chandler came down the steps toting a large plastic trash bag, he heard a yelp that sounded like pain.

"Is everything okay? Yoo-hoo, anybody out there?" he said.

"Yeah, we're fine. I'm giving King Charlemagne some run around time. We're over here by the garage."

"Well, come on into the light where I can see you."

She walked toward him, the poodle trailing slowly behind.

"Looks like you gave him an real workout. He's so tired he's practically licking his wounds."

"Not really. I just wore him out. So that was pretty fast footwork at dinner, Chandler. You picked right up on William Levy. Not bad for an astrophysicist."

"You know, when you move away from the groves of East Coast Academe, there's a whole world out there. Lots of interesting things and people with different priorities. You must have seen it in Houston."

"For sure." She watched him lift the trash bin lid and drop the garbage bag in.

"I wonder if you would like to have coffee tomorrow. I am curious to find out more about your novel and what you've been doing since graduation."

"Only if you promise to give me a primer on astronomy."

"How about life in Tucson? For most people it's a little more interesting than the stuff I do at work. Give me your cell number, and I'll call you in the morning. Failing that, let's meet in front of Out Of Town News . . . by the T stop at ten."

He smiled, touched her shoulder lightly, and headed back up and inside.

A few minutes later, Henrietta and Charlemagne clambered haltingly up the steps.

"Looks like everybody's gone," she said.

"Everybody, but me, dear. Chandler is going to drive me home in a few minutes," Portia said.

Chandler smiled.

"Where's Olympia?"

At that moment she appeared. Henrietta thanked her for the invitation and dinner, kissed her on the cheek, smiled at Chandler and Portia, and made a brisk exit.

"That young woman certainly is energetic," Chandler said.

"Yes, a little too energetic sometimes," Olympia noted. "She was very unusual when I had her in class. I had forgotten, but it certainly came out tonight. There is something strange about her. Her book is strange, but after all it's fiction. Tonight though, it felt as if I were meeting a character from a novel she might have written. There is an unappealing side to her that I can't quite place."

"Nonsense, she's a very vivacious young woman who likes to live," Chandler said.

"Well, if you ask me, she's a bit uppity. Young people need to listen when the grownups talk," Portia added.

Olympia surveyed the damage. The powder room needed a good cleaning. The living room rug needed vacuuming. And the kitchen was still grimy. It could all wait until morning.

"Mom, Chandler's ready to take you home. I'm bushed. I'll call you in the morning. Chandler, thanks, just turn on the coffee if you come down first," and without waiting for them to leave, she climbed the stairs, stopping at the landing to be sure Charlemagne was in tow.

"You're as bushed as I am, pooch. Look at you. Come on, baby, up we go."

As he did every night, Charlemagne followed her into the bedroom. She bushed her teeth, combed out her hair, peed, and slipped into bed.

"What's this, honey, aren't you going to come into bed to give mommy a good night snuggle? Come on."

The dog looked up and whimpered, but he did not come. He curled on the floor at the foot of the bed and lay there.

"What's wrong, friend?"

The frisky three-year old lay slumped on the floor. Olympia got out of bed and switched on the overhead light to get a better look. To her he seemed listless, and his eyes glassy. His normal slobber had all but dried up.

"Poor baby, you're not doing well. Too much food and then too much running around on a full stomach. In the morning I'm going to call the vet. We'll get you tuned up again. I don't like to see you this way."

He looked up and then dropped his head on a paw. Exhausted, Olympia slept deeply.

A garbage truck working its way down the street and the noisy grinding as its mechanical arm hoisted trashcans woke her. She made her way to the bathroom. When she emerged, she let out a moan. Charlemagne was splayed across the floor in the same spot she had left him. "What is wrong with you, honey?" She bent over the dog and nudged him. He didn't move. He didn't seem to be breathing. She went to the bathroom and brought back a mirror. She held it to his mouth and nose. It didn't fog. She screamed. "Chandler, Chandler, I need you."

He was there in a second. "What's wrong?"

"It's my dog. It's Charlemagne. It's terrible. I don't think he's breathing."

After a moment he said, "You're right, he isn't breathing. And he's cold. He's got no pulse." He pushed the dog gently, then harder. There was no response. "I'm sorry, Olympia, so sorry. He's dead."

She stood, then dropped to her knees again and clung to the dog. She sobbed—her ratchety gasps punctuated by short piecing wails. After a moment she got ahold of herself. "This is silly. I know it is only a dog, but I loved him. He was a joy in my life. If you don't own a dog, you can't understand. I loved him like family. What am I going to do?"

"We need to call the vet," Chandler said. "I don't think you can save him, but we should try."

She got the answering service. The clinic was closed until Saturday morning. She explained that her dog had died, and it was urgent that she reach Dr. Modrakis.

Fifteen minutes later the phone rang. "Hi, Olympia, it's George Modrakis. The answering service said you had a problem with your dog, with Charlemagne. Tell me what happened."

When she had finished, he said, "So he was sluggish last night after running around the yard for a while and unresponsive this morning."

"That's right."

"And he's cold and not breathing?"

"No, both my brother and I tried to rouse him. We couldn't. Chandler says he has no pulse."

"I'm sorry, Olympia. You must feel terrible. We come to love our animal companions very deeply. In cases like this there is really nothing we can do. We can't bring Charlemagne back. I know your next question will be why. Well, it could be a lot of things even though he's young. Maybe a cardiac problem. Or maybe he had an unrecognized leukemia, and the severe exercise took him over the edge. If you want, I can do a necropsy."

"Yes, he meant a lot to me, and I'd like to know exactly why he died."

"Okay, I'm glad to, but I can't get to it until Monday afternoon."

"It's Friday morning," Olympia said.

"I know, but we are closed today. And Saturday my schedule is full. I have chemos to administer and some surgical cases. And I have to keep a few slots open for urgent walk-ins since we were closed Thanksgiving and today."

"Tell me what to do. I mean with Charlemagne."

"Bring him by in an hour. I'll arrange to have someone meet you. And we'll take it from there. We'll refrigerate the body until I can get to it. One more thing. Necropsies can get pricy depending on how much time I have to spend."

"It's okay. Please figure out how my Charlemagne died."

Chandler put the dog in the back of her SUV, covered the body with a blanket, and drove Olympia and the dog to the vet's. On the way home, he explained he had a meeting later and asked if he could borrow the SUV. Of course he could. When they were done, he dropped her off. He called Henrietta and apologized. He should have called earlier, but something had come up. Now he was free. They agreed to meet, as planned, in half an hour.

They walked to Café Algiers and settled in upstairs over two black coffees. For his part he found her attractive and vivacious. For hers, the idea of talking to an astrophysicist promised something exotic. His age didn't matter. After all she was living with A.E. in Houston. No, in fact it was an asset. Older men knew things younger men didn't. Besides she was dying to know what kind of astrophysicist knew about William Levy. And it was better than hanging around with her mother and her dorky brothers. Her only disappointment that morning was Chandler's total lack of sympathy for her interest in astrology. He found it silly and superstitious. She wondered if the stars might predict future events in a way that rational thought could not. They spent the rest of the morning together and the afternoon. Then they spent the night together. Who can say what whoopee a macabre young novelist and an astrophysicist who knew about William Levy made?

After Chandler had dropped her off that morning, Olympia went inside to make herself a cup of tea and tackle the kitchen. The phone rang. It was Adriana calling to thank her.

"A terrible thing happened this morning," Olympia said and explained that she and Chandler had found Charlemagne unresponsive. "Adriana, I don't know what I'm going to do. He's dead. I talked to the vet myself."

"Oh, no, I'm sorry. I know he meant a lot to you. Is there anything I can do? How did he die?"

Olympia went through the story. The necropsy results would not be available until late Monday or early Tuesday.

"How did you think it went last night?" Adriana said, hoping to take her mind off the poodle.

"Other than Charlemagne, fine."

The two combed through the evening and the guests.

When they got to Chandler, Adriana said, "Your brother is interested in that student of yours . . . Henrietta. You could see it in the attention he paid to her comments and his eye contact."

"I'm sure you're right. After we dropped off poor Charlemagne at the vets, he asked to borrow the car for a meeting that had materialized out of the blue. What else could it be other than meeting her? What do you make of her?"

"Hard to say, but after watching my daughter Agnes and Maynard and Diana . . . well, you were at Diana's play. You saw Diana on stage and what she had written. Henrietta is somewhere in that universe. Very smart and sure of herself. Smug, really. My instincts are not to trust her, but I can't tell you why."

"Maybe, but I'm not so sure," Olympia said. "It's true she showed up at my house and commandeered the conversation. I am her mentor, and she was completely uninterested in me and what I was doing. It was as if a stranger, not her thesis advisor, had invited her to dinner. But that has nothing to do with trust. That's simply discourteous behavior. I hadn't realized how self-centered and rude she can be, but as you picked up, it's more complicated. You're right, there is a darker side to her. How dark is the question.

"As you know, her novel obsessed me for much of the fall, and one of the reasons was its darkness. Then she breezes in for Thanksgiving dinner and breezes right out. Yet there is one thing I cannot deny—she has immense talent, and it needs to be nurtured. I owe her a start in spite of her, her, let's, well, sometimes I think she's satanic. I know that's extreme, but I really do. Well, that's more than enough about Henrietta and my problems. Tell me, did Agnes ever call to explain why she suddenly ducked out of Thanksgiving dinner?"

"Funny you should ask. I talked to her about an hour ago. She went to pieces on the phone. It seems that she and Maynard and Diana had a terrible row last night. Maynard sided with Diana, and the two headed for New York early this morning. My daughter is a basket case. She's coming by for a visit and I suspect to spend the night. She was very blue on the phone."

The traffic to Logan Airport was crazy that Sunday when Olympia dropped Chandler off. She could not face going home to an empty house. On impulse, she headed to the arboretum in Jamaica Plain. It was a cold, gray November afternoon for an older woman wearing only a cardigan to walk outdoors. She found herself almost as alone as she would have been in her living room. Everyone else was inside with family or helping them depart or getting organized to resume life Monday morning. It was bleak. The wind had come up and blew a fine grit into the air. The deciduous trees had shed their leaves, and the only marginally welcoming presence was the collection of conifers the arboretum had assembled from around the world. She spent an unpleasant twenty minutes walking into the wind and gave up.

At home she finished the last of her chores from the weekend. She left Charlemagne's food and water bowls untouched. She looked in the closet at the large bag of special poodle food, thought for an instant to dump it in the trash, and closed the door.

On Monday afternoon she went though the motions of her undergraduate fiction workshop and then waited at home for Dr. Modrakis's call. She paced and fidgeted until the phone rang at eight.

"Hello, Olympia, I know your are anxious to hear about Charlemagne, so I'll dispense with the pleasantries. I know how your dog died, but I don't know why. When I did the necropsy, his abdomen and the retroperitoneum, the space behind the abdomen, were filled with blood. So the short answer is that your dog died of internal bleeding. But the puzzle is the cause. When animals or people bleed to death, there is some underlying cause—maybe an aneurism or congenital malformation that burst, or perhaps trauma or a wound that tore a blood vessel, or possibly leukemia or a clotting problem. If Charlemagne wasn't making enough platelets, he could have bled to death. I don't have an answer for you right now."

"Bled to death? It makes no sense. He's always been a healthy animal, and he's relatively young. How can a dog be fine in the afternoon and dead of internal bleeding the next morning?"

"I've tried to rule some things out. There were no bruises on Charlemagne, and I could find no evidence of wounds or punctures. I did an X-ray and there are no broken bones. At necropsy I inspected all of his vessels—the major arteries and veins—and there were no aneurysms or malformations, no burst vessels that I could find. There are several additional possibilities. Sometimes bleeding disorders are the result of poisoning, either accidental or intentional. Could Charlemagne have been exposed to rat poison or any insecticides or toxins?"

"That doesn't seem likely. I don't keep anything like that around. And what I do use—any sprays or treatments—the gardener brings with him. And it's late November."

"Do you think your neighbors have a rodent problem and use rat poison?"

"Not that I know of. And before you ask, I don't think any of my guests deliberately poisoned my dog . . . but it's not impossible. Can you run toxicology tests on the blood or something?"

"Yes, I've already prepared the sample, but since there is an additional charge, I wanted to check before I sent it."

"I'd like to know. Just to be sure, so please send it off."

"Fine, we'll know in a couple of weeks. There is one more possibility that I mentioned earlier. I think it is unlikely that your dog has an inherited coagulation problem, but poodles are somewhat susceptible to something called Von Willebrand's disease. His symptoms don't really fit because the bleeding is confined to the abdomen and retroperitoneum. I could send a sample off for DNA analysis if you would like, but again, I don't want to run up your bill.

"I suppose it's silly to grasp at straws, but, yes, I would like to know."

"Olympia, I'm sorry to have to ask an indelicate question. What would you like to do with your poodle's remains? Are you thinking about burial or cremation, or do you need more time to decide?"

"I loved that dog, but I'm not sentimental. And no matter how much I cared for him, he is not a person. Please send him off for cremation. I don't need the ashes. Thank you, Dr. M., for all your help."

She knew not to wait for the toxicology results or the DNA testing. These would provide no answers. The vet had ruled out any foul play, accidental wounds, bruises or punctures. It was all so terribly inconclusive. There was nothing to do but mourn. And mourn silently. People were sympathetic when a family member died, but they would think she was, what was the word, "theatrical," maybe, if she mourned Charlemagne publicly. Even Adriana wouldn't understand.

The only real intervening circumstance that Olympia could remember was Charlemagne's romp with Henrietta outside after dinner. *He had left a vigorous animal and returned tired, too tired,* Olympia thought, *for the amount of activity.* She could not say why, but she felt Henrietta was somehow responsible for Charlemagne's death. What would be the reason Henrietta would do such a thing? Where was the motive? How could she have done it? Olympia did not know. At the end she was left with a question—was a young woman who could write a tale as chilling as *The Lobsterman's Daughter* capable of acting on her fantasies? Yet with no sign of physical violence, Olympia had no choice but to wait for the toxicology and wonder if Dr. Modrakis had missed something.

The novelist in Olympia knew that life was unlike fiction—that often there was no resolution, no answer to the questions circumstance or underhandedness or evil posed. Still, she longed for closure—she needed peace of mind. She instinctively sensed life would not be so obliging. She bit a corner of her lip, and her mouth resolved into a bitter smile. She sobbed. "She did it. She did it. I know it. I just don't know how."

V. The Goddess of Harvard Square

Diana's life went into free fall after *Bach Among the Pitcher Plants* was staged over two weekends. In accordance with the laws of physics the velocity of her descent increased rapidly.

The adulation of the Harvard students, which the young playwright craved desperately, arrived at once, and it quickly spread. At first it was exhilarating—the applause and cheers at the end of each performance, the warm congratulations of Maynard and Agnes, the praise of friends, instant recognition on the street with the inevitable greetings and enthusiastic words, a short note in *the Harvard Crimson*—"An amazing tour de force from a recent alumna, one of our own." Everyone knew her. People adored her. Practically overnight she had become the goddess of Harvard Square.

Then the character of the attention shifted. Admirers, often perfect strangers, assumed a familiarity that was unnerving. On the street people would recognize her and invite her for coffee. Several invited her for dinner. The sense of intimacy became intrusive. One man wanted to take her to Victoria's Secret and buy her "whatever she most desired." An older man asked her to spend the weekend at his house on the Vineyard. Text messages turned sleazy—undisguised invitations and come-ons from young men—and not a few young women. Acquaintances she barely knew became chummy and suggested their relationships were deeper than they were. Diana began to loathe the smiles of recognition from the baristas. What did they want of her? Even the panhandlers had gotten wind of her success (and had heard about the beauty's naked cameo). Many of their smiles seemed lurid, and a few licked their lips.

Everybody wanted a piece of her. She felt as if she were about to be dismembered and dispersed—that there would be nothing left.

She started to avoid people. Their attention was corrosive. The undisputed beauty, who as an undergraduate had written *Disraeli's Apricot Tree*, was becoming an unhappy recluse in the aftermath of *Bach*.

One afternoon she boiled over.

"Damn it, Maynard, what did you expect when you hooked up with me? I need a little space. This is who I am. I'm a writer, not some sex object. I write plays, for God's sake. I've got to write what feels true for now, for today. I need to be able to do that. I can't help it if you're upset that I danced naked in a play about a vibrator. I'm not going to write twentieth-century drivel. What do you want? Another rerun of 'Ozzie and Harriet' or 'Leave it to Beaver'?"

She was on a tear. "Earth to Maynard, turn off the TV. 'Cheers' is dated bullshit. You want something retro like the Pogues in two acts or the remake of 'Hawaii Five-O'? Get real. Life is messy, disjointed. Things don't fit together the way you would like. The plays I write take things apart and leave the pieces for the audience to pick up.

"Stop. Don't say a word. Think about that stupid mountain bike of yours—how I came in one night and found you bent over a thousand parts on the floor. Here's the difference. Your bike fit perfectly back together. People's lives don't, and so they can't in a play. The idea that *All's Well That Ends Well* is bullshit. Shakespeare pandered. Okay? *Shakespeare Pandered*—that could be a play in itself. You know what your trouble is? You've got your head up your pitcher plants."

The goddess marched back and forth in jeans and black over-the-knee boots. Maynard sat uncomfortably on the couch.

"Why is everything so dramatic with you, Diana? The boots, the pacing, the naked dancing, your kinky approach to screwing? It's not normal."

"You think you're so normal, Mr. Princeton Tiger? Normal? You liked all that stuff even if you didn't understand it. You had no gripes until my naked cameo in *Bach Among the Pitcher Plants*. Now that people are paying attention to me, you're jealous out of your tree. And you liked the sex plenty. You want to call it 'kinky,' fine. You chose to hang with me. You can't be Mr. Clean Cut. Actually, maybe you can. Maybe that's the problem. Every boy-man in every sports bar in America wants to hang with me. And once they do, they want out. Their desires are driving me nutso."

She paused. Maynard seemed at a loss. Did he not have anything to say about their relationship? She was locked in some private space that had nothing to do with the Beals Street apartment they shared with Agnes or their relationship or anything he had said or done. She was in emotional lockdown, jailed by her own demons. He sat, hardly breathing, perhaps, she imagined, hoping the storm would blow out to sea.

"What's the matter, Maynard, shame got your tongue? As soon as everything's not neat and tidy, as soon as you can't wrap things up with a bow, you go mute. You know what your problem is? You can't process anything that can't be reduced to a formula or an algorithm." She stopped. Her lower lip quivered. She looked down at her boots. "Oh, shit, Maynard, it's not your problem. Really, it's not. The world needs people like you. How could we feed ourselves or shelter ourselves without the yous of this world?"

He swallowed as if about to say something. She waited, but nothing came out.

"No, you're not ashamed of the kinky sex and how much you liked it. You're overwhelmed. I can't help it. I just can't help it. I have to be who I am"

She closed the apartment door deliberately. It was a firm, decisive click, and once down the stairs, she walked out into the Brookline neighborhood. Now she found living with Maynard and Agnes claustrophobic. At first been it had been fun to do things as threesome. There was no odd person out. It worked all the way around, both emotionally and sexually. But now nothing worked. She needed space. She needed out. She needed to recenter herself. Most of all she needed to be alone.

A month later she exploded again, and after excoriating Maynard for being "only a transducer of data from one form to another," and adding that he was "dumb as a circuit board," she stormed out for good. She found an apartment—little more than a studio, a room with a galley kitchen at one end and a tiny bedroom—not far from the heart of the Square. Here she would focus on her work without distraction—without the tiresome projections of men, the envy of women. Even the simple quotidian aspects of existence might be kept at bay.

Her life seemed more questions than answers. What are you about as a playwright? she asked herself. What are you doing? What are you trying to say? How had she allowed an object of pleasure, a vibrator, to become the central conceit of a play about Bach and nature? Was what she had done so terrible? Just as she had grasped the dramatic possibilities of pitcher plants being Bach's pipe organ, she had seen immediately that a vibrator called the Michelangelo could be an integral part of a play. She hoped her new freedom here in Cambridge would open up more paths to these illogical but exciting juxtapositions.

At the moment there was no way out of this labyrinth of questions. She languished in the twin limbos of self-flagellation and loneliness. Life was hermetic in a tiny apartment without friends or context. Her world was impoverished. She needed the sights and sounds, the smells of Cambridge.

Soon she took to going out again. She added a maroon cape to her jeans and a new pair of over-the-knee boots. Her hair flowed behind her as she strode through the streets with apparent purpose. She bought a stout walking stick at a secondhand store. She made it her business to frequent different coffee houses and cafés on a rotating basis, always with an open laptop in front of her. She wrote nothing, but people noticed her. It did not occur to her during this time of truancy that she had become a caricature of a writer. She rationalized her paralysis—it was a period of gestation, she assured herself.

Then she was spotted in front of Dickson Brothers Hardware with a young Irish setter. Was this her bodyguard? people wanted to know. A way of keeping the men at bay? Of deepening the mystery that enshrouded her? Of heightening her allure? No one knew for sure. But now she was impossible to miss—a good looking young woman with flowing hair in a maroon cape, wearing boots, accompanied by an Irish setter. No one saw the other side—the lonely soul who had no idea how to move her work or her life forward. She seemed so glamorous, so together. That she could be confused or plagued by doubt never crossed anyone's mind.

One day she decided her walk needed a little variety, and she drove over to her old Brookline neighborhood. She strode down Harvard Street in full regalia, walking stick and all, the Irish setter tugging her forward. She found her way to a crowded coffee shop in Coolidge Corner. It was one of those unfortunate days that had become more frequent in her isolation when the smallest slight provoked a torrent of anger wholly out of proportion to the perceived insult. As she gathered her coffee and walked toward the door, the setter, spooked by something, growled and lunged toward a table of texting young people. The four looked up from their lattes with a start. Diana pulled the dog back before she actually touched anyone.

Diana tried to move on, but one of the guys stopped her and said. "You should rein in that dog of yours. I think you need to apologize."

How dare he insult her or her dog? Did he know who she was? Did he not recognize that the setter was little more than a puppy? Where did he get off asking for an apology? Something snapped inside of her, "Get lost."

At this the young man stood. "Look, sister, you

are really out of line. I'm only asking for you to own your dog's problem. Is that so unreasonable?"

"You arrogant bastard, how dare you? She's done nothing. If you hadn't provoked her, nothing would have happened."

And before he could say another word, she swung her walking stick like a scythe and swept the table clear of cups and loose cell phones. "That will teach you."

She pushed the young man away and ran out the door before anyone realized what had happened.

Her luck was different in Harvard Square. She seemed to have no unpleasant encounters. In fact her reappearance excited another wave of texts and emails. Initially she deleted these. But she had to turn somewhere, and emotionally she was unable to reach out for help, to call Maynard or Agnes, or to seek out other friends for companionship. She began to read the texts and emails which earlier she had thought of as an intrusion on her solitude and a drain on her energies. Now in the absence of a creative direction, she scrutinized these attentively.

"Like 2 meet u. I write 2. Trained in philos @ H. Write sci fi. Salsa dance. Play marimba. Coffee? Drink? Wont disappoint," one guy wrote.

"Younger man seeks older woman. Play chess. All AP courses. Do dope. No hard stuff. Brown in fall. Want to mow yr lawn," came from a preppy.

"Speak to our LGBT group? 1st Tues @ the Matrix. Serious folks. Deal with issues. Great way to meet us. Its IN to be OUT," read another.

"I want 2 bite yr bit," an IT guy wrote.

None of these had the faintest appeal to her. These people had nothing to teach her. They would embroil her in their own needs and waste her time. Such weirdos could not provide diversion or aid her quest—though the real problem was that Diana had no vision and no idea how to find one. Then she decided, quite reasonably, that there might be many quests, many ways forward, all related and leading to, well, now she was into it, leading to, all she could think of was, another journey. She laughed out loud. *Really,* she thought, *speaking at the Matrix to serious folks, that was going to help?*

Maybe the way to look at her problem was to ask who could help—who were the enablers? Who were her muses, her mentors? Male writers, her classmates included, seemed to have muses—either actual identifiable individuals like Yeats and Maude Gonne or Berlioz and Harriet Smithson—or goddesses to whom these men owed fealty. Sometimes women, especially women like her, became the willing or unwilling objects of these men. For men, muses were as old as the troubadours and courtly love. Older. Did not Homer and Virgil invoke the muses? Where was the force of the "Song of Solomon" if not in the beloved as muse?

But women like her? Who were their muses? Who helped them create? It was hard to think of Emily Dickenson having a muse. But she must have had someone or something. As Diana thought of other women writers, she realized she knew too little about their lives to make any judgments. She allowed that some women might have male muses—the reciprocal of the female muse for the male, some man or god who obsessed them or to whom they were devoted, but she herself was not one of them. She looked to mentors—older men and women alike—who might help her. Homer, she remembered, had invented, or at least codified, the idea of the woman as mentor. The original Mentor was a trouser role for Athena in the Odyssey, she remembered.

It was with this cold calculation in mind that she returned to her email. Most people over thirty were not comfortable enough to act on their projections or fantasies and contact her. Yes, there were the occasional long emails from perverts of both sexes, but only a few. They were not the challenge. Strangely, the unsettling emails which held promise came from established, older men, mostly full professors. How to sort out potential mentor from opportunist?

"I know you are not going to believe that I'm writing to you, but some months back I saw your play *Bach, etc.*, and I was very moved. I am a linguistics professor at MIT, and I thought your use of language was exceptional. As you moved from subject to subject your word choice and syntax provided a unifying consistency. The counterpoint came from the music. And choosing Bach provided a serious and sacred context. The Verdi was brilliant. I was very impressed. I would like to propose that we have coffee and discuss how I see language anchoring your play. Please let me know if this is convenient. Sincerely, Winston Monsour, Ph.D."

She had nothing to lose. She checked. He was an eminent linguist at MIT. She was lonely. She recognized her isolation, and without Maynard and Agnes to fall back on, she worried that she would spiral into depression. Maybe she should write back. Have coffee. What harm? See where it went. It could be a come-on. But every call, every letter, every good morning in the street could be a come-on or simply a distraction which was bad enough. Did she want to spend the rest of her life alone writing in a tiny apartment that was too small for her, even forgetting her Irish setter?

She meant to email Professor Monsour, she really did, but somehow in her simmer over juvenile text messages, dog care, her self-imposed striding and posturings at the local cafés, her ducking into restaurants to be seen, shopping and window shopping, she never found the time. The idea of meeting Professor Monsour went cold.

When a mathematics graduate student texted, "I want 2 square yr Pi," she looked at her phone derisively and threw it across the room.

Gradually in some unexplainable, marvelous way, her psyche began to heal and restore her. At first it was no more than a trickle of good judgment about small things like opening the shades to let in the morning sun. Then the flow swelled. She put aside the persona of playwright and donned the sweatshirt and running shoes of working playwright. She was up early to take her clothes to the laundromat and walk her Irish setter when few people were on the street. She bought Folgers coffee in place of fair trade Sumatra. She began to daydream about scripts and kept a list of ideas on her iPhone. She found the focus to sit at her laptop and surf the web for ideas for a next play.

Maybe she did have a play in her called *Shakespeare Pandered* or perhaps she could choose a story from Greek mythology and adapt it. She imagined a play blending corporate greed and King Midas. Could she transform Thomas Mann's *Death in Venice* into a play involving an older woman who visits Hyannis or Chatham and is struck by the beauty of a teenage girl? Or should she do what Arthur Miller and Eugene O'Neill and August Wilson had done? Borrow from life. Disguise people she knew and write their story.

Suddenly there it was, a subject before her eyes. Agnes, the daughter, and Adriana, her mother. The tension between a famous mother and her brilliant daughter, who had a similar career goal, was worth exploring. The play could have as few as two characters and would be cheap to stage. A living room or a coffee shop where the two confront each other. Only one long act or two shorter ones with a change of scene and time for a different perspective. Had it been done? Probably in some form. But it didn't matter. She would put her own spin on it.

Then she got email from another professor.

"I'm sure this is not the only appreciative email you have received about *Bach Among the Pitcher Plants*, but I wanted to write to you even at this late date to tell you how much I enjoyed the play. I have to be honest; I didn't get everything in it. I'm a molecular biologist who moved here from St. Louis a few years ago, so forgive me if I didn't understand some of the allusions. I loved the music and the musings on saving the earth. I thought they and the others were very interesting, but of course I don't really know. Some of the Michelangelo business I got. The reference to "The Love Song of J. Alfred Prufrock" and the sexuality of Michelangelo came through, but not the specifics. I wonder if you would give me the pleasure of having coffee with me and explaining what I missed. Just to be clear, I'm an older man in a relationship. I'm looking to broaden myself a little. Sincerely, Norman Penderevski, Ph.D., The Fanny and Albert Snifter Chair in Biology."

The email was polite, almost quaint, she thought. It was touching. I'm glad someone can write a simple email without an angle, she said to herself. But it would be a waste of time. She could not see how it would help clarify her views or sharpen her skills. She set it aside and went back to making notes about Agnes and Adriana—every scrap of every conversation she could remember, all the postings about Adriana and her accomplishments she could find on the net. She went by the biology department to look at the bulletin boards and tried to talk to the students as they exited Adriana's freshman biology lectures. At MIT she poked around the neuroscience department to see what she could learn about Agnes.

She sucked it up and invited Maynard to coffee. She led him on a bit, implying that she had been too harsh and perhaps they might see each other again. When they met, she let her dog settle at her feet and placed her open shoulder bag with her iPhone set on record on the table. Maynard reached down and petted the dog, who looked at Diana.

"It's okay, Argo. He's a friend, a very good friend."

In the course of making nice, she sifted through his relationship with Agnes looking for new angles on Agnes's personality and fresh details of her upbringing. At the end Diana got up, hugged him to keep him available for return interviews, and smiled. There was no legitimate way for her to talk to

THE WOMEN OF HARVARD SQUARE~95

Adriana. She thought about sitting in the back of one of her lectures. But even in a large lecture hall, Adriana would spot her for sure.

Agnes was a different story. "Come over for coffee," she texted. "My place. Been too long. Let's talk." A few days later Diana pushed aside piles of books and papers on her table to make space for two mugs of coffee. Her Irish setter hopped up and sat alert between the two women. Agnes stroked the dog's neck and flanks.

"What's her name?

"Argo, I named her for one of Actaeon's bitches."

"Nothing is ever simple with you, Diana."

"This is easy. You remember the myth about Actaeon, the hunter, coming upon Artemis bathing and seeing her naked. She turned his own dogs against him, and they tore him to bits. One of Actaeon's bitches was named Argo."

"So?"

"So Artemis was the goddess's name in Greek. In Latin, it's Diana. It just seemed like fun. Enough literary trivia, catch me up."

Agnes thanked her for having coffee with Maynard and "starting the healing process." She went through her lab work in the neuroscience program at MIT. The details of functional magnetic resonance imaging—fMRI—and single neuron recording were lost on Diana, but she enjoyed hearing Agnes's take on graduate students and her adjustment to the new culture.

Diana probed a bit. How was it as a twosome? Now that she and Maynard were at different institutions did the relationship still work? She threw Agnes off by asking if they had found a third roommate to replace her. No, they hadn't, they liked living as a twosome.

"Of course if you want to come back or something, you would be welcome, at least as far as I'm concerned."

Were there doubts about Maynard? No, but Agnes hadn't actually talked to him about it.

Diana drew out Agnes for the iPhone recorder,

which she had hidden in one of the stacks of papers. At the end, she shooed Argo off the couch and moved a bit closer to Agnes. She stroked her cheek and followed this with a gentle hand on Agnes's thigh. Soon they were kissing. Diana was hungry. It had been a long dry spell since she moved away from Beals Street.

"Argo, you stay here." She led Agnes to the bedroom and closed the door. "You know the rules, Agnes. I want to be a virgin, technically speaking, when I marry. I'm serious. Nothing, well, to be a little indelicate, intrusive."

There is no telling which rules, if any, were violated, but both looked relaxed and happy an hour later when they emerged.

"Think about moving back with us," Agnes said as she kissed her goodbye.

Another email from this Norman Penderevski fellow arrived. It wondered if the first email had been lost. The new email included the old email pasted in the message. She read it and then read it again. What to do? Respond, delete it, save it and procrastinate? Yes, definitely procrastinate. But for what? What were the options? He was nice and boring. He was nice and boring and too old. He was nice and boring and too old and in a relationship. The relationship he had already mentioned. He was a pervert. It was a come-on.

The flip side was her chronic loneliness. She nodded and smiled at acquaintances on the street and maybe stopped to chat for a moment. But she wasn't up to meeting people for dinner or a concert or just to hang out. She had begun writing again, but she was still in recovery mode. If she had been living with Maynard and Agnes and had had some support, she might have been more resilient. She might have been able to shrug off the objectifying comments and lame, but sincere pitches in the texts and emails. But not alone. Not with Argo as her only dinner companion.

So when Agnes called one afternoon and wanted to stop by when she was done at the lab, Diana readily agreed. This time Diana opened a bottle of wine and left her iPhone recorder off. They chatted in an easy and familiar way. About what? About nothing. The peeling paint on the outside of the Beals Street house, the lousy service on MBTA buses, the weather, the saggy elastic in Maynard's briefs. It was good to have human contact. This time it was Agnes who motioned Diana to the bedroom. Argo roamed around sniffing.

Diana had begun to imagine the structure of a play but not without guilt. She was ripping off Agnes's and her mother's lives. Was this fair game? Fair use? Would they mind? Would they notice? The last question needed only a split second's deliberation. Of course they would notice, no matter where it was set and what the circumstances. She took the path many, perhaps most writers have taken—she pilfered their stories. This would be her truest work to date—a play that was not a far-fetched attempt to ask eccentric questions about arcane subjects. The play would deal with a real mother and a real daughter—it would be about love and conflict and its lack of resolution.

Now that she felt tracked in her writing life, she worried again about relationships. She sensed that moving back in with Maynard and Agnes was not a good idea, at least for the present. Love triangles, even with mutual consent, never worked. She thought about joining a writers group and then decided against that too—she was not sure she could stand the acid comments. It was in this frame of mind that she came upon Penderevski's second email as she was cleaning out her inbox. She read it again.

The crux seemed to be at the end: "I wonder if you would give me the pleasure of having coffee with me and explaining what I missed. Just to be clear, I'm an older man in a relationship. I'm looking to broaden myself a little." And he was the holder of an endowed chair. It seemed safe enough, and the email, she thought, revealed an engaging mind. She would invite him and his friend to coffee somewhere away from Harvard Square, say downtown by the waterfront. And she would bring Argo. She wrote back a polite email laying out her terms and proposing a small bistro she knew near the Marina. He would be delighted, he answered, but his friend had returned to Texas for a month to tend to family matters. She agreed to meet as a twosome the next Saturday at two.

She knew at once that the older, slightly plump man with the beret must be Norman Penderevski. She smiled as he came over to introduce himself. She remained seated, but Argo jumped up and sniffed.

"Argo, sit down. Now! Sorry, she does that. Nice to meet you Professor Penderevski." She smiled one of those glowing, irresistible Circean smiles that reduced men to swine. "Might we change the plan a little? It's such a nice day. We don't get that many sunny days in January. Do you think instead of tea we might walk?"

"Perhaps we might have a cup of tea first and then walk," he countered.

She agreed. He wasn't at all what she expected, except that he was exactly what she expected. Her fantasy was that he was younger, taller and better looking. She couldn't decide if the beret made him look authentic or ridiculous.

Penderevski smiled. "First, please call me Norman." He paused and searched for a way into the conversation. "I know you must have received many emails, and I thank you for agreeing to meet. Beverly and I saw the announcement for *Bach Among the Pitcher Plants*, and we, actually it was me, and we were very curious. I have no formal training in literature, but I try to read widely. I'm a molecular biologist interested in blood clotting though naturally I have an interest in many different biological systems. So when someone writes a play with 'Bach' and 'Pitcher Plants' in the title, one wonders how they fit together. Where did the idea for the title come from?"

Without mentioning names, she explained about Maynard's research on pitcher plants and Agnes's help with the project.

"Oh, I see," he said. "Yes, I'm beginning to understand. I have met your friend's advisor, Adriana Lubeck. We have been talking about a joint research project in protein structure. So you know these people, this graduate student and her daughter?"

What could she do? What she had imagined would be a discussion of dramatic principles and an amusing story about a vibrator that she had dubbed "the Michelangelo" had now turned personal. "Yes, Agnes is ah, ah, a friend, and I used to date Maynard."

To her relief he brought the focus back to the play. "So the idea was serendipitous?"

"You could say that. Originally the idea for the play came from Agnes's imagining pitcher plants as a pipe organ on which Bach could compose. I used that as a starting point."

"And the texts such as the one on the importance of science, where are they from?"

"My ideas and my lines. The music, of course, I borrowed from Bach and Verdi."

"Yes, I knew that could not be Bach. I thought it might be Verdi—then I placed it. It's famous, of course. Who would have thought to mix Bach and Verdi?"

The conversation went on in this fashion— Norman asking polite, but penetrating questions, and Diana explaining her intentions. He carefully avoided her naked cameo partway through the play. Not that he was indifferent to the bodies of beautiful young women, but to him it felt unseemly to raise the issue on a first encounter. Perhaps ever.

"The walk, let's walk," she said.

He paid the check, and they and the leashed Argo ended up walking past the aquarium, along the wharfs and Marina and then into Waterfront Park.

"Well, let's call it what it is—not the world's most beautiful or exciting walk. Sorry, Norman."

"No matter. Anyway, I want hear about this Michelangelo. I understand that it's something sexual. But how in the world did Michelangelo find his way into a play about Bach and, well, the environment? I've missed the connection. I don't understand it, and that evening of course neither Beverly nor I had any idea what was going on, though the young people seemed to enjoy it."

For a moment she paused and looked away. Of course, he didn't get it. No one could get it without inside information. However much fun it was to the initiated, the rest of the audience was left out in the cold. She had known that the premise of the play was weak, unsustainable in fact, but Norman's questioning was quietly devastating. Yes, the play had flaws, she did not deny that, but somehow Norman's discreet analysis brought them to her deepest attention. Years later she would remember this instant as the beginning of her transformation from wunderkind to playwright.

"Did I say something wrong, Diana? You look preoccupied."

"You, you're the problem," she smiled. "Or rather your comments are the problem. It's that your simple, logical probing is helping me to clarify how I write. So to your point about how a renaissance artist came to the play. Well, I guess fessing up is the best thing. The Michelangelo in the play is a vibrator. It's a long story. You really want to hear it?"

"Sure, I'm game. Tell me the story. We have time. There is still light. It's a nice afternoon to stroll."

She explained that some undergraduate women found a vibrator in a shop near Harvard Square and really liked it. She looked at Norman. He seemed unfazed. "They jokingly dubbed it 'the Michelangelo,' they said, as a compensation for the 'underendowment' of certain aspects of the anatomy of his statue of David."

Norman smiled. "So it's a gag."

"Yes, I guess you could say that. I picked up the idea and embellished it. I was so intrigued that I gave it free reign, and it took over the second half of the play."

"Forgive me, I don't want to press the point, but was your thought to include some, ah, let's say for lack of a better word, 'reality' in an otherwise cerebral play? Sort of drama *vérité*?"

"No one has ever put it quite like that. Well, yes and no. I mean that was certainly part of my motivation, but it wasn't exactly conscious. I just went with it."

"And you're pleased with the final product?" he said.

"It's a good effort, but I think I can do better."

"I do too. Well, I don't want to impose on you anymore. My I offer you and your dog Argo a lift somewhere."

"Oh, professor, Norman, you've given me quite a lift already by being such an attentive playgoer. I think I'll walk for a while."

"Very cute. So, thank you again for taking the time to talk to me."

She thought she detected a look of pleasure in his face. He shook her hand and turned to walk to his car. She watched. It was not a stride, not a command-and-control stride at all, but there was a confidence in his step. She wondered if it came from a life of solid accomplishment.

Like Norman she had enjoyed herself. That was a surprising thought for Diana. Not something that she could have anticipated a few hours before. Pleasure, genuine pleasure. And one thing more, her womanly intuition caught a hint of flirtation in his smile—muted and subtle, but a sign that he recognized that she was a beautiful woman as well as a playwright. She happily held onto this realization.

That evening, Saturday evening, she sat alone, her feet propped up on the table, drinking a glass of wine and feeling just the slightest bit sorry for herself. Right now she couldn't face working on her as yet untitled play. "Argo, tell me what you're thinking. What do you make of the professor?" The dog rubbed up against her affectionately. She laughed. "Oh, how I wish you were Mister Ed, the talking horse. But of course, you're not a horse," she paraphrased the reruns she had seen as a child. Argo whimpered in disapproval. "I don't know what to think either." He's probably older than my father. And so? So nothing. What about Charlie Chaplin and Eugene O'Neill's daughter Oona? She was thirty-six years younger than the actor. She googled "Woody Allen." Just as she remembered, a big gap. Thirty-five years separated Allen and Soon-Yi Previn.

What is wrong with me? What about getting your head screwed on straight? Don't let the heart, is that the right word?, get ahead of itself. No, don't let stupidity, vulnerability, and loneliness get ahead of themselves.

Each day she sat at her laptop working on her script—piecing together imaginary conversation and incidents for the still nameless daughter and mother. The setting was another problem. The only certain thing was that it could not be Boston. Agnes came by one afternoon to see her. The visit further blurred the distinction between reality and fiction. It made Diana uneasy. She did not want to repeat the mistake Professor, okay, Norman had so nimbly identified in *Bach*. She was feeling less self-conscious. It seemed more okay than ever to walk Argo in jeans and a sweatshirt. People took no notice of her, especially early. Just another young person with a dog.

A vague ache of disappointment hung over her. Somehow she thought Norman would email her on a pretext—an additional question or a suggestion—and they would meet again for coffee.

Nothing happened.

Should she write to him with a question of her own? Or propose another meeting to try out some of her new work? She didn't know. And there was no one to ask, not even Agnes, whom she now considered resurrected to friendship. Anyway, she couldn't call Agnes cold and say, "I've been wondering what you would think if I started a relationship with an older man."

So she worked at her play, she walked Argo, she shopped for groceries, and she waited for something to happen. She remembered Milton's line that "they also serve who only stand and wait." Her fear was that "all good things come to an end."

She had to force the issue. It was killing her. But how? She could not email him directly, but how about a sleight of hand? Suppose, just suppose that she pretended to send an email to Norman Samitz who had done the lighting for *Bach*, and by mistake it went to Norman Penderevski. Norman, her Norman as she was beginning to think of him, might write back out of courtesy to explain that her email had gone astray. She could then write to him to thank him and perhaps hint at something.

"Hi Norman, I hope everything is okay with you and Mandy. Look, I have a question. You did such a great job lighting *Bach Among the Pitcher Plants* in that dreadful hall. I was wondering if I could pick your brain a bit about a new play I'm working on. We are not nearly ready to think about staging, but I wanted to try some stuff out on you. I'll buy you a Jamba Juice if you'll let me. :) Diana."

And as planned it went only to Norman P.

"Diana, I received this email, which I imagine was intended for another Norman—the man who did the lighting for the play I saw. Sounds interesting, Norman, who is in the dark"

Well, well, well, the hook is in the tuna's mouth, she thought. How to reel him in with such light tackle? She reread the email she was about to send—*a little forward,* she thought, but she sent it anyway:

"Oh, sorry, Norman, your diagnosis is correct. I clicked on the wrong name. I don't know that you would be interested in such a small, preliminary detail when I don't even have a first draft. But I'd hate to keep anybody, especially you, in the dark. If you would like to hear about it, I would be pleased to have coffee again. Please let me know what works for you. :) Diana"

That evening: "Okay, Diana, coffee it is. I'd like to meet before Sunday when Beverly gets back. I'll be busier then. What if the wealthy professor buys the struggling playwright brunch Saturday morning? Does the rarified world in which you live include Jamaica Plain? How about Centre

Street Cafe at ten? Nine would be better for
getting a table, but I'll leave the choice to you.
Norman, the curious"

He's flirting. He is definitely flirting and using
Beverly as cover in case he has to deny it. Okay here
goes:

"What is so rare as a brunch in January? See
you at nine. Diana"

"I can't imagine a Whittier response. Thanks.
See you then. N"

Not bad for a molecular biologist or whatever
he is.

Diana hardly thought about what she would say
about the play when they met, but like her namesake
she spent a long time at her toilette trying to look as
if she had just thrown on her white turtleneck and
charcoal sweater. It was a cold morning, but she
chose a skirt and knee socks. With her long brown
hair spilling over the collar of her black car coat and a
hint of blush in her cheeks, she looked like a modern
version of a nineteen sixties coed. *It was like a play,*
she thought. *Good lines were essential, but costumes
were important too.*
   He already had a place in line outside when she
arrived at nine.
   He smiled. "You look wonderful this morning. I
guess it's another example of beauty and the beast."
   "Many days I feel like the beast," she said.
   "Nonsense. You'll tell me about it when we get a
table. Not too bad this morning. We should be seated
in a few minutes."
   "You sound like a regular."
   "Yeah, I like this place. I found it soon after I
moved here."
   "Do you live in JP?"
   "No, but it's worth the drive. I have a brownstone
off Newbury Street. And you?"

"I'm in a tiny, tiny place maybe twenty minutes from here near Harvard Square."

"So, Diana, last time, why did you suggest we meet near the Marina when you live in Cambridge?"

"The truth is, I wasn't sure what I was getting into. I didn't want to give too much away. Just in case. You know."

"So, my young friend, are you sure you know what you are getting into now?"

"Yes, I mean I think so. You seem like a good person, and I know you're very smart, very intuitive about drama for a scientist. Sorry, scratch that. You're very intuitive, full stop."

They were ushered to a corner table so small they both had to work at keeping their knees from bumping. When the French toast and the Huevos Mexicanos came, they were already well into the details of the new play. Diana explained that she imagined a mother and daughter sitting at a small plain kitchen table over tea discussing medicine. Sarah, the mother, was an academic internist at an unnamed medical school, and her daughter Samantha was a resident in the training program trying to decide between private practice and an academic career.

"I don't get why you need to know about the lighting when you are still in the process of developing the tension between the two protagonists," Norman said.

"Because if I have an idea of what the other Norman is thinking as a lighting person, it will help me with the mood I am trying to establish."

He paused and looked at her. It was not an avuncular look but the look men get when they are overcome with desire and see no way forward, the look that vacates everything else. Man overboard about to be swept out to sea without recourse.

"Okay, Diana, my turn." She gave him a puzzled look. "The play is over. What are we really doing here? Certainly not discussing a lighting problem for a nonexistent play, sorry, for a work in progress."

She looked down at her plate. "No, we are not.

Why do you have to be so damn perceptive about people's motivations?"

"It's easy, if they are the same as yours."

"Norman, am I so transparent?"

He swallowed and reached over and raised her chin so that she was looking at him. "No, not transparent. Beautiful. I shouldn't be attracted to someone so young."

"I'll bet you have children older than I am."

"I do. Does it matter?"

"No, not right now, at least. It's not important," she said. "Oh, I'm so terribly embarrassed. I should be interested in your ideas, and that's all. I've made a real mess of this."

"I don't think so. Hearts have a logic of their own. I understand that I know nothing about writing plays, but I'm sure that if a person can't be honest with herself, she'll never write well. So good for you."

She looked at him, then fished in her pocket for a tissue, and blew her nose and wiped her eyes.

"I must be a sight," she said.

"Not at all."

She pulled out a pen, wrote her address on a napkin and handed it to him. She stood up. She could not believe what she was about to do. She should have better judgment, better impulse control. Whether it was loneliness or feeling sorry for herself or the beginnings of love, she didn't know. How could you not feel something like love for someone, maybe the only one, who had such a deep appreciative understanding of your work and the gentleness to guide you back to a more grounded reality. Suddenly what had felt wrong an instant ago, now felt right. She kissed him on the forehead.

"If you see to the check, I'll head for my apartment. Give me about ten minutes and then come over."

She answered the door in a white terrycloth robe. "Well, you found it. Here, let me take your coat." Argo sat up and growled. "Stop that, Argo, you have met Norman. He's a friend. Come sit down. I've made some tea."

They sat on the couch at an angle, looking at each other, knees touching. They talked for a long time, so long that at one point Norman had to get up to pee.

She told him about her life as an undergraduate at Harvard, her interest in writing, how she had fallen in with Maynard and Agnes, and how her instant fame from the production of *Bach Among the Pitcher Plants* on the heels of *Disraeli's Apricot Tree* had caused her life to spiral downward. The only thing she left out was her physical relationship with Agnes. For some reason that felt like too much information.

She reached over and took his hand. "Thank you for coming over this morning. I am so pleased you came."

When it was his turn, he talked about his two sons and their girlfriends, his ex wife, their drifting apart and their divorce. He had been happy in St. Louis, but the Harvard offer was too good to turn down. And Beverly Ardmore, how he happened upon her in the rain one afternoon.

"Norman, tell me, if you are in a relationship and you like this woman, why did you agree to come back to the apartment?"

Before he could answer she picked up his hand again and kissed it gently.

He drew his breath in slowly, emitting a soft sound half way between a whistle and a purr, and searched for a way to begin. "What to say? Honestly, as I said at breakfast, the heart feels what it does without the strictures of the mind. I guess, simply put, you are a very intelligent, interesting, beautiful woman, and I am very taken with you. Is that so hard to understand?"

"No, not really. I know I have this power over men that is mostly the gifts I have been given—my intellectual abilities and my looks—and the ability to work hard. But many guys, especially guys my age, find my intelligence a turn off."

"Perhaps, but not with men who are sure of themselves. My interest in being with you is easy to understand. What is harder is why are you interested in a molecular biologist in late middle age who is not at all prepossessing in his appearance."

He smiled at her, and began to stroke her thigh lightly through the terrycloth robe. She placed her hand on his and squeezed it and put it under her robe.

"In the vernacular of my age group, I like being with you because you get me. Your intuitive sense of my work and the kindness with which you treat me and my work is, I guess since we are both being honest, sexy. You have a way of being direct and honest without being hurtful or judgmental. That counts for a lot. I'm comfortable enough with myself to take people as they are."

"Diana, that's lovely, but, well, the truth is, I'm not old, but I'm on my way."

"If I may steal a line from you, 'the play is over.'"

She took his hand from beneath her robe and kissed it. She removed his glasses and kissed him lightly, almost breezily. She stood and pulled him to his feet, stripped the belt from her robe, tossed it playfully over his head, and drew him toward her. "Now, I have you."

"Nice to be had, especially by you, Diana." They both laughed.

They looked tentatively at one another for an instant, and she kissed him again. It was not much more than a brush of his lips, but it seemed to ignite him. He kissed her passionately this time. She encircled his torso with her arms and drew tightly to her. His mouth was tough, firm against hers— insistent and probing. It was a long kiss, and when she drew back, she made a deep, throaty sound. She could feel him through his pants and reached down and stroked him.

Argo growled. "Shush, Argo. It's all right." She began kissing him again. "Oh, Argo, for God's sake, cut it out. Stay."

He turned her, clasped his arms around her belly and kissed the nape of her neck and nibbled at her ears. She put her hands on his and stroked them with her fingertips. She lifted them to her breasts and then pushed her robe apart. He slid his hands down over her naked belly and below. She let out a soft, ratchety cooing—plaintive and warm like a morning dove's. She could feel him hard against her buttocks and pushed back against him. Then they were in the bedroom, kissing as they went, she undressing him and both of them fondling each other.

He eased her onto the bed.

"Wait," she said. He looked at her quizzically. "Touch me, but don't enter me with your fingers. I've got this, ah, problem around, I don't know what to call it, 'purity,' I suppose. I want to be a virgin when I marry. Oh, screw it, come here, forget it."

He buried his face in her crotch. She whimpered and began to moan—softly at first and then more forcefully.

She lifted his face and gave him a long, imploring look—the look of an inviting but hesitant goddess welcoming a mortal at the gates of paradise. She touched his cheek and opened herself widely to him.

As he was about to enter her, her body stiffened. "No, no. Please, no. Stop, at once. Stop. I know what I said, but stop. Now!"

With a fencer's speed and precision, she slipped out from under him, turned on him, and bit his thigh. Norman let out a cry that was half surprise, half pain. Argo barked and sprang onto the bed.

"Are you crazy, Diana? What are you doing?"

"No, Argo, no. Get down, get out." She jumped up, shooed him from the bedroom, and slammed the door.

"What's wrong with you, Diana?" His tone was harsh.

She sat at the edge of the bed, her lithe body tilted forward, her face buried in her hands. "I don't know. I don't know. I'm so sorry. I didn't want to hurt you. I didn't mean to. Something came over me. Norman, please understand. Please, if you'll let me, I can make things better. Come here."

VI. Under My Skin

Olympia was already famous, or at least as famous as a novelist could be. Her previous novel, *The Delicacy of Clocks*, had been a *New York Times* notable book. National Public Radio had done a feature on it, and it had been nominated for a Pulitzer Prize. The recent release of *Under My Skin* showed every sign of making her rich as well. In only a few weeks it had risen high on the bestseller lists, and her agent was already negotiating a movie deal, which she promised would astound her. "If this goes through, Olympia, all the biotech start-up guys will beat their DNA sequencers into word processors."

Olympia was not so sure her scientific colleagues at Harvard would want to trade places with her—not after what she had been through. The posters at the Cambridge bookstores showed a handsome woman wearing a teal blue top with an elegant pearl choker— lent to her by her agent for the photo shoot. A closer look revealed disquietude in Olympia's face.

The photo was taken in the midst of what can only be called writer's remorse. Now she sat in a robe in her study, her jet-black hair stringy and unwashed, her eyes red from lack of sleep. Her rule of thumb for publishing something had been simple. Would you want your mother or your teenage daughter to know that you had written the piece? *Under My Skin* did not come close to passing the mother/daughter scrutiny test. Fortunately she had no teenage daughter, and Portia was sharp-tongued about everything she wrote. Of course, they were only a proxy for her own standards, and *Under My Skin* was lurid fiction, or at least that is the way she billed it—fiction.

* * *

It was not the novel she had set out to write. Her original idea was to do a psychological study of an investigative journalist she called Sarah Leswicki and a maritime lawyer who helped companies bend import rules. She abandoned Boston early as a venue and debated between New York and Los Angles. *No, she thought, there are hundreds of waterfront novels— crime novels, thrillers, detective novels, exposés, psychological studies like her planned novel, some contemporary, some historical—set in these cities.*

A sixth sense sent her elsewhere. Well, not actually a sixth sense, but her re-reading of Joseph Conrad's *Heart of Darkness*. What captured her attention was that one could view Conrad's novel as a story about trade and corruption on a river and at an isolated upriver trading post. It wasn't the plot or Conrad's story-within-a-story technique that interested her. It was, pure and simple, that there was a way to tell a maritime story on a river. After discarding everything on the Mississippi from New Orleans to Minneapolis and working her way north on the Ohio, she settled on Pittsburgh.

The city had never entered her thinking, yet it had the reputation of a Rust Belt city that had gotten its act together, a livable city that was attracting internet start-ups and biotech based on the University of Pittsburgh and Carnegie Mellon. More recently oil shale had driven a resurgence of the petroleum industry there. Sight unseen she thought Pittsburgh would be a great backdrop for a story about corruption: what got left in the corners when a place was swept clean. Her assessment was prescient, though it would turn out that Olympia Breathwaite and not Sarah Leswicki would experience the harsh underside of Pittsburgh.

What did Olympia know about Pittsburgh? her best friend Adriana asked her over lunch at ABP in Harvard Square.

"Nothing, absolutely nothing," the English

professor replied. Olympia shaded the truth a bit so as not to appear too cocky. "I've never been there and never imagined I'd ever get there." She could muster a few facts—the confluence of the Allegheny and Monongahela Rivers formed the Ohio there, and the city had two major universities, Pitt with its Cathedral of Learning and Carnegie Mellon, and, and well, nothing else but some sports trivia from her brother Chandler.

With the exception of Adriana, Olympia did not share ideas for her novels or work in progress until she had a firm draft and was ready for feedback. But as her oldest friend and former Radcliffe roommate, Adriana was in a special category. Besides the scientist had pulled Olympia's fat from the fire many years ago when she was struggling to complete her dissertation on Faulkner. So when Adriana asked Olympia what she thought she could accomplish by setting a maritime novel away from the coast, Olympia was silent for a moment.

"Well, I'm going with my gut. There is some reason to do this, but I'm not sure what. Maybe it's that it's a new slant, something that hasn't been done. My hunch is that when I get into it, I'll find that the people and problems are different there. It's not an international port city with the usual mix of longshoremen and organized labor and slightly disreputable foreign types trying to get their goods past customs."

"Well, at least you're honest about what you don't know. So what's your idea for the story?"

Olympia went through the parts Sarah Leswicki, her protagonist-heroine, and the maritime lawyer, unnamed at present, would play. "Actually, I'm not clear on what the major conflict is. I simply don't know enough about maritime law, and certainly not enough about the particularities of river law and interstate commerce to plot the lawyer's scheme. I don't know—drugs, falsified bills of lading, outsmarting the Feds by smuggling immigrants up river from New Orleans. Maybe violating safety standards with a subsequent disaster. Who knows? A scheme to rig salvage prices. But I'm making this up."

"They all sound good. It's just the plausibility I don't know about."

"That's one reason I need to visit Pittsburgh. I have to get a feel for the city and find out a little about how things work on the river."

"You seem to have your mind made up about this, but I think you should reconsider New York. It's close and easy to visit. Friends or friends of friends can put you in touch with people. You remember Francine O'Malley who lived down the hall from us one year? Well, she's deputy assistant something or other in the mayor's office. She would be a place to start."

"You're right, Adriana, but my mind's made up. I want to do Pittsburgh."

"Okay, tell me once more, why Pittsburgh."

"Adriana, you're exhausting me. Why? Because Sarah Leswicki needs me to go. She needs me to understand her life there. Does that make any sense to you?"

"If I did research the way you write novels, the National Institutes of Health wouldn't give me a dime."

"Nonsense. You have hunches all the time. You just dignify them by calling them hypotheses. You're going with your gut too. You try out a few things in the lab just the way I try out different plot ideas. When you get a little preliminary data, you choose that idea."

"At least I have data."

"Horse feathers, Adriana. Not when you start, you don't. When I get back from Pittsburgh, I'll have data too. I'll have a solid basis for imagining what happens to Sarah Leswicki. I'll be able to tell her story, just the way you tell the story of a gene."

"I give up. Go for it. I'm sure the novel will be a great success. But you're out there in Pittsburgh with no contacts and no context. I know it's not Siberia, but it's not exactly the Port of New York either."

Now stacks of *Under My Skin* sat in front of her image at Harvard Square bookstores. She saw the books everywhere—stopping for coffee in the morning, walking the dog, heading for class, driving to water aerobics. The cover was arresting—a black dust jacket with a sensuous forearm cutting diagonally across its face. The cream colored skin of its underside was both alluring and distancing at the same time. In the middle of the obviously feminine forearm and at a right angle to its long axis, a man's thumbnail pushed into the skin, making a slight indentation that suggested an impending breach and penetration. What the average prospective buyer made of this incipient intrusion is hard to say, but for her the image was devastating. It was a direct link to what had happened to her in Pittsburgh—between her physical person and the deeper layers of her Self, that Self which had been violated on her trip, the shame the visit had inflicted on her, and the further shame of treating her experience as fiction and not owning it forthrightly.

Her trip to Pittsburgh had started well enough. The taxi from the airport came through the Fort Pitt Tunnel and spread the downtown skyline, the three rivers, and the water plume of the fountain at The Point before her. She was stunned.

She fumbled for words and finally said, "Amazing, absolutely amazing. I've never seen anything appear so suddenly and so grandly."

"Yeah, that's what most people say, or something like that, when they see the Golden Triangle for the first time," the cabby said.

"You must feel lucky to live here."

"Not really."

"It seems very inviting."

"You can't tell first off what it's like here. And me, do I feel lucky? I'm pretty much dependent on the airport, you know, tourists and business people, for a living. It's not like before. In my father's day there was good money in the mills, even the Blacks did good. Now, that's all gone. They talk about service industries. You wanna make sandwiches at Subway or bus tables? Work for a cleaning service? Most of us are just getting by, unless you're an engineer or in computers. Maybe the medical center. One of my regulars from out of town got it right, 'There's a little software in what's still a hard scrapple town.'"

"I'm here to look. I guess I have a lot to learn."

"Lady, which hotel again?"

"The, ah, the Omni William Penn."

"Well, meaning no disrespect, that's not Pittsburgh. But, hey, if you're here on vacation, it's great."

"No, I'm here for work."

"What kind of work you do?"

"I'm a writer, actually. I'm writing a novel about Pittsburgh."

The cabby let out a low-pitched whistle. "Well, I'll be. Can you make a living at that? Sounds like a tough racket."

"There are a lot of people who try, and a lot of them are driving cabs. I'm luckier. I have a teaching job at a university. That pays the mortgage."

"Don't get me wrong. Driving's okay. It's just that you struggle every day to make it. Anyway, for what it's worth, you want to write about Pittsburgh? It's okay to stay there at the William Penn, but in Pittsburgh things happen in the neighborhoods. Like anywhere I expect. Don't let the clean air and the trees fool you. There is still some pretty edgy stuff going down here. There's still action. Things can get ugly here."

They pulled up at the hotel, and she paid the fare.

"I don't drive tomorrow. It's my day off, so if you want someone to take you around, Augie Carbone's your man. I'll bring my own car, and for a hundred dollars and, say, twenty for gas, I'll take you anywhere you want to go or I'll give you some ideas."

She thanked him and was about to say she'd think about it. Then she changed her mind. "Okay, you're on. This might be a good way to see things from the ground up. Come by at about nine-thirty, and we'll go."

Later she took a taxi from the hotel to a restaurant on Mt. Washington, the bluff overlooking downtown on the far side of the Monongahela River. She sat looking at the same view she had seen from the taxi coming in from the airport. But now it was even more spectacular. In the dark the lights of the skyline winked—evocatively, she thought. Adventure beckoned. It was thrilling. She was eating and alternately studying a city map, trying to decide where to ask the cabby to take her, and looking at downtown.

Then all at once there was a man at her elbow. He came from behind and startled her.

"Oh, sorry, didn't mean to sneak up on you, but I saw you looking at a map and out at the city, and I wondered if you were a visitor."

"Yes, yes I am." And she let her words hang, not sure what was coming next.

"Well, I'm Edvaldo Eichenbaum. I may be able to help you," and he gave her his card: Edvaldo Eichenbaum, M.C.P. *Planning and Drafting Consultants.* "Look, I'm a city planner, and I run a small business that services government agencies, nonprofits, and developers. I know a lot about the city."

She was unsure. He seemed okay, but he was big, very big, perhaps 6-5 or even 6-6, with a broad frame. He wore a black silk shirt, pressed jeans, and a beige, suede sports jacket. Gay? she wondered.

"What are you suggesting?" she said.

"Only that I join you for coffee and dessert, my treat, and see if I can help."

She looked at him again. There was an old scar above his left eye. She hoped it was from a fall or an athletic injury. He wore a big-faced watch with all sorts of wheels and dials—a chronograph, she remembered. "Okay. I could use a little help. Maybe you can give me some input for my project. I'm Olympia Breathwaite."

They settled in, and Olympia explained that she was a novelist from Harvard here to get her bearings. She needed to know how to use the city and its rivers to advantage. "I have only a few days, because I have to teach my writing seminar on Friday."

He smiled. "Well, I went to school just a little south of you in New Haven and then to Berkeley for a masters of city planning." Now she noticed that his English was slightly accented.

"Where are you from? Originally, I mean."

"Argentina. Buenos Aires. I came here for college and never went back."

"So here's the kind of stuff I need. I need, for example, to know where a lawyer, a maritime lawyer who might be living somewhat beyond his means, would live in Pittsburgh?"

"Depends on the angle, if he's in the social swim, Fox Chapel or Sewickley. If he wants to be out of circulation, he's got a big spread, maybe an old farm that he's converted, up near Mars or Zelienople. If he's trendy and doesn't want to spend all his money on real estate, he may have a place in the old Arsenal/ Strip District."

She had all sorts of questions like this. Where would he send his kids to school? Where were the courts? What was barge traffic like on the river? Where would a successful lawyer office? What were the important boards in town? Where did people gamble? Where was the seamy side of Pittsburgh?

To this last question he answered, "All over. Maybe not readily visible, but everywhere. I'll tell you, it's a lot like the Buenos Aires I remember. Beneath the sophistication and the money there is everything you can imagine and a lot you can't."

They talked for a while. She had no interest in him, no romantic interest, but he seemed to like her.

"Maybe I can show you a little more tomorrow," he said. "I'm tied up most of the day, but you could come by the office at, say, six. I have some large relief maps of the city and Allegheny Country. It might help orient you. Then I'll take you for dinner somewhere. I'll figure it out. In the meantime, can I give you a lift to your hotel?"

Best be prudent, she thought and explained she had already arranged for a car to take her back. "As for the dinner tomorrow, I have to see how much the day's schedule tires me out. I'll try to call and let you know."

The day with the cabby was busy. Augie seemed intent on leaving nothing out. Maybe he felt that the success of Olympia's book depended on the completeness of the information he provided. As they went, she snapped photos. That was the only way she could hope to remember anything. The detail was endless. The North Side with its casino and Heinz Field, then the Hill District ("the Blacks lived real bad here till the city renewed it"), a drive through Oakland to see Pitt and Carnegie Mellon, Squirrel Hill ("the Jews live here, it's safe"), Fox Chapel ("this place is great if you're rich and a blueblood—you can join one of those fancy country clubs"), the Highland Park Zoo ("in Pittsburgh most of the animals are not in the zoo"), Homewood ("don't come here at night, you're safer in Afghanistan").

From the backseat she took out her cell phone and Edvaldo's card and punched in his number. "Hi, it's Olympia. Can I take you up on your offer and meet you at your office at six? . . . Great, I look forward to it."

"What's that?" Augie said.

"Nothing, just an appointment I have."

"I'm not going to bother you with Penn Hills or Wilkinsburg. It's bad. It's more of the same. The only mill we still got is in Clairton. U.S. Steel. The rest of the Mon Valley, all the river towns are depressed. They're dead as Jimmy Hoffa. You know, it's like I said yesterday. There is gentrification. Lots of money coming in and being made. But for the rest of us, we're just hanging on. I'm gonna drive you through Shadyside. Walnut Street is the center of it. It's fancy schmancy, upscale wantabe, if you ask me.

"You asked about barges on the river. Yeah, there seem to be lots of them. Not like it was, but they're there. They run aground, they run into each other, they sink. I don't know what goes on. You can be sure it's not all sand and gravel, coal. But, if you want my guess, for your book you can just make stuff up. There is nothing too sleazy for people here. They got to get by. Your readers should believe anything you can imagine."

Back at the hotel she paid him and tipped him twenty dollars.

"Listen, you need a ride to the airport, just call. Augie's ready to serve you."

She was exhausted from a long, dizzying tour. With Augie it had been a case of too much information. Her head was spinning. It felt to her as though she had to memorize the entire contents of the British Museum in one pass. Oh, she was weary. What she needed was a long soak in a bath and room service. She wondered if she had the energy to absorb anything else. Perhaps she could call Edvaldo and cancel. *No*, she thought, *suck it up and learn what you can.*

It was a short walk to Edvaldo's office from her hotel. When she arrived, the staff—his secretary, the planners and draftsmen—had gone. It worried her to be alone with him there, but he welcomed her warmly. They sat for a moment as she recounted as best she could the places she had seen. "Actually, it's all a bit of a jumble. Everything is flying around in my head."

"I've got the perfect solution," he said. "I've laid out two large relief maps on our drafting tables. Let's take a look. We can start with the county map and then get more detail with the city map."

It was helpful to have him show her the physical relationships. She had not realized how the hills and rivers cut the city into natural divisions. Here, neighborhoods were not arbitrary. They had boundaries and character. Shadyside, Oakland, Point Breeze, and Squirrel Hill were physically separate, and each had a distinct feel.

He showed her the way Frankstown Avenue ran like a vein of despair out of Homewood, an ailing Black area, and Murray Avenue threaded down from Forbes Avenue toward the Monongahela River through a heavily Jewish area. On the other side, old ethnic neighborhoods—Morningside, Stanton Heights, Lawrenceville—flowed down toward the Allegheny. *There was plenty of room for the imagination here*, she thought. Augie, Edvaldo, the photos, the relief maps gave her the beginnings of what she needed. And she could always come back if she was unsure.

Now they stood at one of the drafting tables. She was expecting him to mention dinner, but a strange look had come over his face. Then suddenly without warning he grabbed her and pushed her flat on her back onto the table.

"What are you doing? Are you crazy? Stop."

One giant hand spread out over her breastbone and secured her thorax. It felt like a huge cement column was crushing her chest. At once he reached up under her skirt with the other and immobilized her with his palm on her pubic bone. She writhed like an insect pinned at two points on a board.

"Don't resist, and I won't hurt you."

She squirmed and thrashed all the more. She screamed.

"Don't bother. There are three doors between here and the hall. I'm not going to hurt you."

"How can you do this? Is this your style? To prey on vulnerable women?"

"Shut up."

"You're hurting me. Let me up."

"I said, shut up. I mean it."

Then she felt his fingers groping her. They were like four tines raking over and over her panties and pressing into her. They slithered across her private space like snakes searching for their den."

"Stop, please stop," she sobbed. "Don't do this. Please, please. I don't deserve this."

"Shut up. I told you I am not going to hurt you. If I wanted to fuck you, I would have taken down your panties and done it."

"Don't hurt me, please."

"Shut up, or I'll hit you."

As she flung her arms about, her hand came upon an X-Acto knife at the back of the drafting table. She grabbed it and slashed wildly at his face and arm.

He let out a scream and brought his hands to his face. He howled in pain. She felt the hot spurt of blood on her face. At once she slipped out from under him, and with the determination of a survivor raced toward the door and out.

"Bitch," he cried. "Come back here. I wasn't going to hurt you. I promise."

How she got through the other doors, down the stairs and into the street she didn't know. She ran and then hailed a cab.

"Where?" the driver wanted to know. "The Omni William Penn? It's only a few blocks from here. You want a cab?" Then he looked back. "Jesus, lady, you okay? You got blood on your face and blouse."

"Just go. Quickly, please go. I'm okay."

He reached back and handed her a soiled McDonald's napkin. "Sorry, lady, it's all I got."

"Thank you."

She put twenty dollars in his hand and walked quickly past the doorman and to the elevator bank. She made it to her room unobserved. She had to get out of there. He might know her hotel. He could kill her. She washed, threw her things into her bag, called down to check out by phone, and asked for a cab to the airport. She would figure out where to stay once she was out of downtown.

She was surprised when the cab came for her. The driver was an old Black man—*too old to be driving after dark*, she thought. In the cab she realized she could not go to one of the hotels that served the airport. It was too dangerous. This guy was smart. He'd figure it out.

"I'm flying out in the morning," she said, "but I'm trying to avoid my boyfriend. Things got a bit rough. Is there some out-of-the-way motel you can take me to? Some place he won't look? I can't stay at the regular hotels. He could find me, and it would be bad."

"I don't want to pry, but did he hit you?"

"Something like that. I just need to keep out of his way."

"If you really mean it, I can take you to Mabel Anderson's. She a friend and runs a small boarding house for Blacks, but you would be welcome. It's probably not what you meant, but it will be clean. And no way he's gonna find you. We're invisible a lot of the time, if you know what I mean."

"Thank you. That's very kind. I need this. He's big and has a mean streak."

"Forgive me, I'm old and you may not want to listen, but at some point you will be tempted to go back. I've been driving thirty years. I've seen a lot, and they all want to go back. They are afraid to be alone or think they can save the guy. Or it's all they know. Don't do it. It never works. You'll only get beat up again, maybe worse."

"Don't worry. I'm firm on this. I never want to see him again."

Her room at Mabel Anderson's was small and clean with floral wallpaper and a dark wood floor. A braided rug at the foot of the bed added to the warmth. She was shaken. She sat on a small straight back chair, clasping her arms to her body and rocking slowly. She sobbed. After a time she regained her strength and dried her eyes. She re-booked her flight on her cell phone and spent a fitful night imagining he would find her at the airport before she got through security. She cringed. He knew her name and that she taught at Harvard. Anytime he wanted he could come after her. She imagined him with another scar from her wound. Maybe over his eye like the first. She had marked him for sure—branded him with a scarlet letter and enraged him. She was afraid of that rage. Rage in a man so large and evil could only mean trouble.

Back in Boston, she taught her fiction workshop that Friday. Well, she went through the motions. Pittsburgh and Edvaldo's hands so filled her with fear that she barely focused on her students' stories. Mostly she offered vague, open-ended suggestions.

She reasoned that if Edvaldo were coming for her, he would take a few days to heal and think through a plan. What to do? Call the police in Pittsburgh and report it? Go to a rape crisis center for support? Talk to her friend Adriana for advice?

She felt dirty and abused, almost as if it had been her fault. It was certainly an assault, a sexual assault if not rape. She hoped the police would take her seriously if she called. But she would expose herself to intense scrutiny, be held up to ridicule, be demeaned by the process necessary for justice to move forward. The personal price would be high.

In the end she simply lacked the courage and resolve to come forward. She had been frightened, traumatized, but she had not been physically harmed. He had not slapped her or beat her or physically attacked her. He had deeply humiliated her. But there was some recompense in her slashing him. In some ways she imagined that he had been more the victim than she had. He must have gone to an emergency room and lied about his wound. He would have stitches, a scar, maybe something worse like a nerve palsy or loss of vision in an eye. Instinctively she knew that if he had a good lawyer, a tough woman lawyer, he might claim she had consented and then panicked.

She decided that he was a creep. He could easily have raped and killed her if he had wanted. No, he was sick and needed help. He was not a rapist. He was a pervert. And a pervert, she hoped, would not pursue her in Boston.

Healing, that's what she needed, to become whole again. She had been violated and she was ashamed. It was *he* who had done something, and *she* was ashamed. *He* was guilty and *she* felt at fault. He had stained her soul. If he felt remorse, and she did not believe he did, he could not now reach out and help her. Revenge on her part or due process before the law would not help. She needed a way to heal herself.

When she had lunch with Adriana a week or so later, she said nothing. Adriana had asked about her trip, and Olympia was vague. She said it was a good trip, and she had plenty of background for a first draft. There was no way Olympia could tell her what had happened, not yet at least. She was knotted into a fist of pain and fear. Maybe sometime in the future but not now.

She settled into a routine of sorts—teaching,

writing during her free afternoons, and performing all the small tasks of living—shopping, taking clothes to the dry cleaners, working out, paying the bills.

She struggled with her novel. She tried to sketch out its arc, but Sarah Leswicki, her investigative journalist, and the maritime lawyer, whom she decided to call Hunter Meredith, were not cooperating. Sarah rebelled against living in Pittsburgh. Every duplex Olympia tried to find for Sarah, she rejected. Men did not seem to want to be in a relationship with her. Hunter was gunning for partner in his law firm. He had no interest in bending the rules or working with sleaze. He turned out to be a deacon in his church. In fact, when he was not billing hours, Olympia could barely tear him away from the large flat panel TV in the family room. Olympia did not like rejection, especially from her own characters.

One day there was a letter—a plain business envelope with no return address and her name and address printed in crude block letters as if by a child who had not yet learned cursive. It contained a single white sheet of printer paper with a message assembled from letters cut from magazines and newspapers:

DON'T WORRY. PITTSBURGH IS SAFE FOR YOU.

Now she worried. Was Boston safe for her? He had her address, and she was once more in his sights. She was glad for her new dog, a dachshund, but he could scarcely protect her against a sex offender, and especially one of Edvaldo's size and strength. She cast about for a strategy and came up with the same options. Go to the police. Find a support group. Talk to a friend, to Adriana.

Again she set aside all of these and did what any reasonable person would have counseled against. In what can only be called a macabre and self-destructive act, she pulled out his business card and called him.

"Leave me alone. Please leave me alone. I have suffered enough."

"Olympia? Is that you?"

"Don't call. Don't write. Don't contact me."

"I had to send you the note. I want you to know that it is okay. I won't hurt you."

"You have stained me, and that stain has seeped all the way through to my soul."

"I couldn't help it. I have a problem. I know I do. I'm sorry."

"Edvaldo, look, you do have a problem. There is no way I can help you. Please leave me out of this."

"You can absolve me."

"I, absolve you? You can't be serious. You're a, a," she repressed the word "pervert." . . ."You're sick. You need help."

"I know that. But first I need your blessing, your absolution."

"You get yourself in a treatment program. Then you can call me back and we'll see. I don't want to hear from you again until you do." And she hung up.

A few minutes later when the phone rang and a 412 area code came up, she didn't answer.

She was a good person and look what had happened. A sex offender had violated her integrity and scarred her, and now he was asking her to take care of him, to absolve him. How did that work? It was all she could do to try to heal herself. How could she take care of him? Let him get himself into a program, and if he made progress, maybe then . . . The phone rang again. Pittsburgh's area code. You must not answer, she cautioned herself.

She sat in her living room, limp and indecisive. She needed support, but she had no idea how to get it. And worst of all, she couldn't write. There was absolutely no energy in Sarah and Hunter. She could not build tension between them. They might as well have lived together in Biloxi. Pittsburgh was not the right place for them. And the reason was clear—Edvaldo Eichenbaum dominated the landscape, scorched it so that nothing would grow there. Nothing. Nothing but the stain he had cast over her. That was something she had to deal with before she could go forward with her life or her novel.

She was stained by him, made impure, and she saw no way out. The huge Argentine with the massive hands and the scar was choking off her life. She would suffocate.

Then it struck her that the act that was choking off her life was choking off his. He was a prisoner of his own impulses and ghosts. And her ghosts held her apart from life as well. That was the other side of the story, wasn't it? She paused. It was a story, she realized. It was not only her story; it was his too. And surely more compelling and necessary to tell than Sarah and Hunter's non-story. Leave them in Biloxi. Let them gamble at the casino there. The story she had to tell was Olympia and Edvaldo's.

She had never written a memoir—she wouldn't know how to begin. But what about a novel that told the tale? Surely that could be set in Pittsburgh. And if the villain couldn't be a city planner, could he not be an architect? That would be close enough. A way forward had opened up. All she had to do was write her story. It would help cleanse her while she waited to see what would happen with Edvaldo. Teach your classes, eat, and focus, focus, focus on your writing. And don't take any calls from area code 412.

She worked demonically. The words flowed. She had no need to plot the novel or invent characters. She wrote what she lived. Nothing impeded her. It was easy to imagine an occasional change of venue—a hotel or a restaurant—and to substitute an architectural firm for a planning firm in Pittsburgh.

And she held to her resolve not to answer phone calls from Pittsburgh. She wondered why he had sent her no emails. Certainly he was clever enough to find hers. Then she realized that he needed circumspection as well, even plausible denial. He wanted no electronic record.

One day the mail came, and in it was a letter with a Pittsburgh postmark. This time the letter was typed.

"I took your advice and I am in a program. I'll let you know how it goes. E.E."

In a few months she had a creditable draft, not

a finished product, but a solid draft. She had never worked so quickly, not during the school year anyway.

Then she got cold feet. What if she were found out, if people realized that this was her story, that she was the woman pinned like an insect on the drafting table? What would happen then? Her shame would be compounded and deepened by her fraudulent behavior, her deceit. It would be accompanied by disgrace. She decided she could not go forward. This was not the kind of story she wanted to be known for.

She was clearly at a crossroads. Maybe the act of writing alone was healing. Maybe she didn't need to publish or even show a draft to someone. Simply to have given voice to her violation and her fears, maybe that was enough. As she struggled with whether she was comfortable publishing the manuscript, she thought about her student Henrietta Markham. There was something to be learned from her, she realized.

The student had written a vivid and chilling novel about murder and depravity in five generations of a Maine family. It had been her honors thesis. Henrietta claimed it was the truth about her family, and Olympia and the other faculty readers were content to allow a student this conceit. It was a terrific piece, easily worthy of honors and publication.

What Olympia now remembered was that when she checked, Henrietta appeared to be from the Boston area, not Maine. That left in limbo any speculation about the veracity of her claim that the novel was almost a memoir. It was clear that in fact the novel was not "true" in that it did not recount actual events in Henrietta's life. But something must have gone on in that household. There must have been something that sparked the novel, and in that sense the novel was "emotionally true," if not a log of actual events.

Henrietta's daring was a challenge to Olympia. If an undergraduate had the courage to tell her story albeit fictionally, could Olympia not summon the same courage? At that moment she decided to publish and let the chips fall where they may.

*   *   *

Her agent loved the manuscript and assured her that it would be well received. During the months of revision and editing, she did not hear from Edvaldo. Did she need his permission to publish the book? *No, she thought, the identities were so heavily fictionalized that he had no claim, legal or emotional.* Besides he had dropped from sight. So, everything seemed to be moving forward.

"It will be a triumph," her agent predicted.

The book went to press, and during the printing, Olympia began to dread the idea of exposing herself. Of course she did not call the protagonist "Olympia," but she worried that her heavy use of actual events would come out. There was denial and authorial distance. But was that enough? Was Philip Roth the author or the protagonist? How did personal history and fiction intertwine? Was Dante the author or the protagonist? It didn't matter, she decided. No one cared if it was a good book. And hers, she was sure, was a good book.

Why then was she so tense? It was like an unconfessed sin. How could being the victim of an assault be a sin? What was to be confessed? Nothing, she realized. The assault was about shame and humiliation. The sin was not being forthright. Not stepping forward for other women and for herself. Hiding behind the cloak of fiction, pretending that it might be about Edvaldo's pain. How many others had he molested? What about their pain? What about, what about, what about? She simply didn't know. There were no answers, or rather there were too many—and all of them conflicting.

She was bursting with shame and guilt and grief. And there was no way to unburden herself. She was surprised, but none of her fears went away with her writing. They still hung over her, and at any moment a great funnel of wind could descend and carry her off.

Then the book was out and a success, and she felt a failure.

*   *   *

A letter came from Pittsburgh "I saw the book. Very nice. I am looking for a new program. E.E."

Oh, my God, who knew he was a reader? What would happen now? Would he come for her? Did he feel that his privacy had been violated, that he had been exposed and outed? It was crazy. It was his crime, and she worried about him and at the same time feared him. Why was he no longer in his program? Without it, he was like a psychotic off his meds. She imagined his coming to Boston with that X-Acto knife.

She emailed Adriana. "I am in terrible straits. I need your help right away. Something awful has happened. You're my oldest friend. I'm coming apart. I need to talk right away. Can we talk? The sooner the better. Olympia"

Adriana wrote back on her phone almost at once. "I'm at UMass Worcester giving a seminar. At 6 my place? A."

"Yes, I'll be there," Olympia responded.

Olympia got back from teaching at four and found an email with an attachment in her inbox from Edvaldo:

"You have marked me as I have marked you. I found a new program. E.E." She opened the attachment. She looked in disbelief. It was horrible. A photo of a human ear, Edvaldo's. Most of its lower lobe had been severed away.

When she arrived at Adriana's, Olympia was shaking.

"Come in at once. Oh, Olympia, what's wrong? You look terrible. Come in and tell me."

Olympia sank limp into an armchair. "I hardly know where to begin. First, I'm being stalked by a man, a giant. A sex offender. And I'm guilty. It's about the novel. I'm so ashamed. It's all so scary and demeaning. Nothing like this has ever happened before."

"Tell me what's going on. A sex offender, here in

Cambridge? Did you call the police? Is he known to them? There must be something they can do. When did this begin?"

"In Pittsburgh."

"And he's here in Boston now? He's after you?"

"No, he's in Pittsburgh."

"Then how is he stalking you?"

"He will."

"He will, what?" Adriana asked.

"He will come."

"Olympia, it will be better if we talk this through. Tell me everything from the beginning, and we'll figure out what to do."

"Are you sure?"

"Yes, for God's sake, I can't help you if I don't know what's going on."

"You know I went to Pittsburgh a while back to do research on the novel?"

"Of course, we talked about it, twice if you remember."

"Well, I didn't tell you the whole story after I came back. I was ashamed of what had happened to me and fearful as well."

"You'd better tell me now."

And Olympia told her the whole story, every detail of the trip, from first seeing the Golden Triangle, to Edvaldo's groping her and her slashing him, to her night in hiding and the flight out. She sobbed like a child who had had a terrifying dream and was in need of her mother's comfort.

"I'm so sorry, Olympia, this has happened to you and you kept it bottled up all this time. Now I understand about the book. It's lightly fictionalized autobiography, isn't it?"

Olympia nodded.

"Oh, poor baby. You are in a state. You can stay here with me for as long as you need to. It will be a little like old times in the dorm. You need company and love. But first, you must talk to the police here in Cambridge and maybe Boston. They can be on the lookout and maybe check with Pittsburgh."

"But it will expose me. I'll be stripped naked in

front of everyone. People will realize my novel is a fraud."

"Don't be silly. If you handle it properly, people will see you as courageous. They will understand the risk you took in publishing it—in speaking up. You will be viewed as a hero. And if you're worried about sales, don't. From what you tell me, they are already through the roof. And now more people than ever will buy it." She paused. "Why are you looking so sad?"

"Because he's a victim too."

"Who, this guy who held you down and groped you? What are you talking about?"

"He can't help himself. He's miswired. He's got some disease. He's sick."

"And you think by cowering in the corner here in Boston you can help him? You have to go to the police for your own protection and for others."

"But what about him? I can help him."

"You can't, Olympia. Maybe a trained psychologist can, but you're a novelist, an English professor . . . ."

"I hurt him."

"Don't be ridiculous, Olympia. He's a criminal."

"I did. Look at this," and she called up the picture on her iPhone.

Adriana looked at Edvaldo's ear. "You may have wounded him, but you had to protect yourself. He was attacking you."

"He said he wouldn't hurt me, and he didn't strike me or beat me. And I cut him with a knife."

"For God's sake, you're the victim, not the criminal."

"It's more complicated, more . . . nuanced than you realize. I know how he feels—he too was attacked. By me, by me. You can look at me as a perpetrator."

"Nonsense, Olympia, how many times do I have to tell you that you are the victim?"

"Not really, not entirely. I did this to him. And I was attacked. I understand. But I can help him."

"Olympia, get ahold of yourself. You're not thinking clearly."

"I keep thinking I must take the chance and

reach out to him. I can't stop obsessing about him, that there is no one else to help him and he needs me."

"He needs professional help," Adriana said.

Olympia straightened herself up in the chair and blew her nose. A resolve came over her face. "Thank you for offering to let me stay here. You are very kind, but for the present I'm okay on my own. I think I need to go home. You were generous to listen, but I can't crumble on your doorstep."

"Please, stay. You need someone to be with you."

"I'm fine. I really am fine. I'll call you tomorrow to let you know."

When Olympia got home, she sat in the dark trying to summon her courage, the courage that Adriana assured her she had. Eventually she felt a little better. She poured herself a glass of water, put a Lean Cuisine in the microwave, and took an apple from the fridge.

Adriana was right, she thought. She had to own up to deceit publicly, to admit that her book was a lightly fictionalized narrative of her own terrifying experience in Pittsburgh. She thought Adriana was probably also right about sales. And if she herself were criticized for deceiving her readers, well, thoughtful people would understand—especially if she did it now. If it came out in a few years, if she were discovered to have lied, she would be discredited. Would some view the new disclosure as a publicity stunt? Maybe, but she would have to take that chance. Best face the issue as soon as possible.

Olympia went to her laptop and sent an email to her agent saying that there was a new slant to her story, something important, that they must discuss as soon as possible.

Then she turned her attention to Pittsburgh and looked for flights and departure times. Staring at the information, she stopped. She had no understanding of why, but she closed the laptop. Something did not feel right. Yes, Edvaldo needed help, but why did she feel that she should provide it, that she alone understood what he had gone through? Where had that come from? What was she thinking?

Slowly it came to her. She was too close to her characters. They had become real. She reasoned that it was like Henrietta Markham and her novel. The student had conflated her own life with that of her characters. The Maine of Henrietta's novel was not the Boston of Henrietta's life. Olympia recognized that she had done the same. The real-life Edvaldo, who needed therapy, was not the fictionalized Edvaldo whom the narrator of *Under My Skin* felt she could save.

Yet she was still left shaken and fearful. Yes, publicly owning her deceit would help. Yes, recognizing that she could not help Edvaldo was important. But neither was enough. She still felt alone and vulnerable.

She called Adriana back. "Is the offer still open? Can I come to over for a day or two? Maybe talk to you some. I need your help seeing my way out of all this. I emailed my agent about publicly owning what I have done, and I think I've got going to Pittsburgh out of my system. But I feel as if the world could dissolve around me."

"Of course, come. Just pack a bag—and bring your laptop in case you want to write here while I am at the lab."

"Thank you. I am very grateful. I'm probably not ready to write though. I have to get myself sorted out first. I'll be right over. And another thing, you have been too polite to say it, but I think I need someone, someone professional to talk to. You're right. I can't be responsible for Edvaldo. I have to heal myself, and I need help."

VII. Abigail's Private Cache

It has always amazed me how behavior patterns are passed down the generations, sometimes skipping one, but often reemerging in the next. At eighty-seven I have enough perspective to see these things. I look at my daughter Adriana and see some of myself, but with Agnes, my granddaughter, I see a soul mate—a transporting of my twentieth-century self to a young woman of the twenty-first century. She is truly flesh of my flesh.

If this were a literary tale, if I were as well educated as my dear, deceased husband Hans, I might be able to point to examples in literature or the arts—perhaps the Darwins or the Huxleys, or even the Bachs—that could substantiate my speculation. Before you get the wrong idea, let me say that my tale owes more to the prurience of Henry Miller and D.H. Lawrence than to the more proper interests of those eminent families.

Agnes and I share a delight in the salacious. To be sure, there is a deeply spiritual side to her. But our common interests are much earthier. Do not be surprised that at my advanced age I think about these things. I do, women do, perhaps not twenty-four hours a day like younger people, but often enough.

You know about Agnes's journey of exploration: that at this moment she is having simultaneous affairs with her boyfriend Maynard and Maynard's ex-girlfriend, her friend Diana—and this *ménage-à-trois* has given her mother Adriana apoplexy. You may know too that Agnes's friend Diana is also having a winter-spring romance with Norman Penderevski, a faculty colleague of Adriana's, for whom Adriana longs. What you do not know about is what I will call for now "My Private Cache."

My name is Abigail Lubeck, although it was not always. Before I was married, I had a famous Boston last name, not Leveret or Saltonstall or Cabot or Lowell, but a similar one. One you would know. Part of my family helped settle the Massachusetts Bay Colony before the founding of Harvard College in sixteen thirty-six. I have ancestors buried in the graveyard next to the Unitarian-Universalist Church in Harvard Square. Lubeck is the surname of my dear Hans.

From my given name, Abigail—I do not want to say "Christian name" since I am the descendent of those Unitarians, who, although Christians, would probably not want to emphasize the Christ aspect of God—you might wonder if my original family name was Quincy or Adams. It goes so well with Abigail. An interesting thought, but no. And you will search the rest of the names of the Harvard residential houses in vain for this name.

Presently you will see why I am reluctant to disclose my maiden name and expose this branch of the family to public embarrassment.

That Hans and I met at all speaks more to my pluck or perhaps to my naïveté than to the prevailing mores of the last century. That the daughter of Boston Brahmins met and married a dark foreigner of murky origins was more than a rarity. It bordered on the scandalous.

My parents were inadvertently responsible. They colluded with the fancy boarding school I attended to steer me toward Wellesley. I had wanted to go to Radcliffe, but my mother and father were afraid of what they termed "the Harvard distraction," meaning boys. And importantly Wellesley met the standards of their class; it was socially acceptable. I didn't mind Wellesley. I was in Cambridge every weekend anyway, which is where I met Hans.

He was raised in Essen, Germany near the Dutch border. His mother was Lutheran, but his father was Jewish of German-Dutch extraction. In the mid-nineteen thirties Hans was forced from the university before he could complete a literature degree. A few days after Kristallnacht in nineteen thirty-eight, he fled to the Netherlands and then to the U.S. He served in the war and was discharged to Boston.

I met him on one of my Saturday escapes from the Wellesley nunnery not long after he opened Lubeck's Foreign Books in Harvard Square. I was twenty-one and viewed myself as a sophisticate. This pretension led me many weekends to the Grolier—which later became Grolier Poetry Book Shop—where I would leaf through Pound and Eliot pretending to make sense of what was totally incomprehensible to me. One day I happened around the corner to Lubeck's Foreign Books, and for some unaccountable reason I found myself pushing open the heavy wooden door.

He was speaking in German to an older gentleman, who I assumed was a professor somewhere. I knew no German, and except for a worn brief case I had no evidence of anything. When the man left, I came forward, and he said, *"Guten Tag,* how can I help you?" I made him out to be in his early thirties with dark hair and dark features. I remember thinking that if he had had a mustache, he could have been Hitler's cousin.

"I don't know," I said. "I am just looking."

"What is it you are interested in?"

"Well, poetry, I guess." Remember, I was in my pretentious stage.

"My personal favorites are Rilke and Holderlin, but Holderlin is much too difficult for a young person. May I suggest this?" And he put a volume of Rilke in my hands. It was in German with no translation.

"What am I to do with this? I do not speak German."

"I will translate." And as I remember, he translated what I later learned was the beginning of one of the Duino Elegies right there, without notes or a dictionary. To hear him animate this amazing new poet Rilke in this fashion was captivating. Then it didn't dawn on me that he had probably looked at the passage many times and wondered how it would sound in English. I tried to buy the book, but he said, "What for? Buy an en face translation at Grolier or the Harvard Book Store."

Of course I took his direction. And that is how it began—a chance meeting between a romantic Wellesley junior and a German-Jewish-Dutch bookseller. One day he said he would like to invite me to tea, but he had no one to mind the store. I volunteered to go for tea and brought back two steaming, disintegrating cardboard cups. We chatted. It was very sweet. That afternoon and many others we talked and talked, oh, my, how we talked. The only interruption was an occasional superannuated customer who would appear and begin in German or Dutch, though often they would switch to English.

As I listened to these conversations, I realized that to survive as a specialist in European literature, Hans needed to have a broad selection of books in translation. He could not rely on foreigners with arcane interests to survive. At first he was dubious.

"But my language is not good enough to converse intelligently about these books in English," he said.

"Your customer base is too small in German and Dutch. People like me will read en face editions or translations. And you shouldn't confine yourself to German and Dutch. People are interested in French and Russian literature. And you can add a small section of Polish and Czech books, maybe Cervantes and a few Spanish books. But the key is translation." He liked the idea. After we were married, I coordinated the store's transition. And later, as you will see, enlarged our stock to appeal to a very discerning audience.

Of course our relationship did not remain platonic. At five he would flip the open-closed cardboard sign on the door and turn off the lights. Then we would slip behind a large bookcase and, hidden from the street, make out. We were both young and hungry. I struggled with the burden of my virginity. Its loss seemed monumental to an upper class woman of that time. Remember it was only a few years after World War II, and it was Boston. I worried about what my very proper, prominent family would think if they found out.

In the interests of taste, I will only say that I succumbed to his needs and my own. I loved it—out of proportion to what women in those days were supposed to feel. I will not deny it: most Saturdays I could not wait for five o'clock to arrive.

It is hard for me to believe—even though these events occurred almost seventy years ago—that the Boston Brahmin in me, the girl who led a privileged and sheltered life on Beacon Hill and then attended Wellesley, was making love on the floor of a bookstore with an immigrant polymath. For that's what he was. He was an authentic genius. I don't want to derail the story with examples. But his intellectual gifts are what have made my daughter Adriana a world-renowned biology professor and my granddaughter Agnes a gifted MIT neuroscience graduate student.

You probably have anticipated the resistance, that's the most polite world I can think of, from my parents when I decided to marry Hans. People of my background didn't do such things. It was unthinkable enough to imagine marrying into a Boston Irish or Italian family, but a penniless foreigner, a mongrel— as my mother undiplomatically phrased it—who was uneducated to boot, meaning he completed his baccalaureate degree at Northeastern. It was as if I were marrying a Neanderthal.

My family fairly stumbled over their objections trying to get their criticisms out. He was German, no, he was Jewish, no, he was stateless. Of course, he spoke German, what a useless, guttural language. Educated people speak French, and Italian is so beautiful. He's so dark. It's practically like marrying a mulatto. He's a shop owner, what a coarse occupation. You need to look for someone better—a lawyer or a businessman, a physician or a professor. Of course, it's not the money, dear. I'm sure he's very decent, but that does not make him appropriate for someone of your background.

And now you understand in part why I have withheld my family name. The major reason though has to do with the valuable cache I accumulated in the process of modernizing the bookstore.

The trick was to give Lubeck's more appeal without losing the old world charm. The first issue was the name "Lubeck's Foreign Books." This moniker was fine for collectors and scholars looking for specialty items, but we needed something for the serious, general reader. Finally Hans and I settled on a simple name, "Lubeck's Books," and in smaller letters "The World's Best Literature in Translation." We greatly reduced the stock of foreign language books and replaced them with en face editions of poetry and translations of novels and non-fiction. With many items—the books of Thomas Mann, Rilke, Tolstoy, and so on—we competed head to head with other bookstores. But we also stocked items like the mysteries of Georges Simenon and the work of Harry Mulish, Witold Gombrowicz, and Bruno Schultz.

Then, almost as an afterthought, I added a few art books, mostly French Impressionists, and usually in bilingual editions from Europe. I watched surreptitiously as the customers paged through the books. I realized that while many were genuinely interested in the art, they seemed to dwell especially on the nudes. Pictures like those of Renoir, Cézanne, Monet, and so forth. Most of our customers were educated men, and I thought, *dumb me, there is a market here for erotica that pushed the boundaries of pornography*. Before I could figure out how to capitalize on this idea, *Playboy* appeared, and with a little care these men could buy enticing pictures of Marilyn Monroe and other playmates without detection. My balloon was punctured before I could launch it.

That's when I had to take the next logical step. Erotica was easy to find, good pornography was not. When I laid my idea out for Hans, he was momentarily resistant. We were turning a small profit at Lubeck's

Books, but we could not live on what we were making. It was my trust fund that kept us afloat.

"Go ahead," he said, "tell me what you are thinking."

I suggested that we use our European contacts to buy good French pornography—photographs—vintage material if possible, which was not easy to find in the U.S. at the time. We could import it, hidden in our crates of European books, and sell it discreetly in the store. We began with a few, select trusted customers. We had some large scrapbooks with mounted photos, and after five we would invite them in. Behind locked doors they could leaf through the albums and make their selections.

Soon, a few percent of our sales had boosted our profits by thirty percent. And it was an all-cash, off-the-books business. Next an amazing thing happened. As our stock increased, there was more variety, and sometimes Hans and I would lock the door at five and look through the scrapbooks ourselves. We had a healthy sex life, but now life with Hans sizzled beyond anything either of us had ever imagined.

I convinced Hans to take a gamble. We took a mortgage—guaranteed by the income from my trust fund—and bought a larger building. We built a windowless backroom with its own exit and moved Lubeck's Books. Now our pornography sale hours were not limited, and our customers had complete privacy. There could be no advertising, but we marketed cautiously to our clientele. Word of mouth might have helped, but the natural reticence of our customers limited its usefulness. If someone looked suspicious, we turned him away by politely explaining that he was misinformed. We sold only books. These difficult conversations were my job, and since by background and breeding I was very much a lady—no one ever challenged me.

Now that we had a secure backroom, we added books—forbidden titles that could not be legally purchased in their unexpurgated versions in the U.S.—books like *Lady Chatterley's Lover, Tropic of Cancer,* and *Fanny Hill.* Some of these were collector's items, first editions in mint condition. We made a decision not to sell pornographic films or magazines. We did not want to risk additional visibility.

After the early sixties and the loosening of restrictions, pornographic novels became more widely available. So the profit margin on standard editions shrank. But we were able to obtain some examples that contained interesting inscriptions and marginalia—sometimes from well know authors or personalities. And mint condition "first edition" copies from the small presses that challenged the pornography laws commanded a premium. Even various pirated editions had value. Among a certain class of collectors, there was a good market for this material.

One of us was always there with the customer. At first it was Hans. We reasoned that men would be uncomfortable buying pornographic photos from a woman. But we experimented, and it turned out that I was much better than he was at selling. Perhaps his formal European manner was a little off-putting. I approached sales as if I were selling lingerie or perfume to a man for his wife or girlfriend. I was polite and tactful, but I got the point across. "If she is as special as I think she is, she will appreciate these photos from Paris or Rouen." "It has been our experience that men and women especially like this set from Toulouse." "If you have not read such and such, I think you will find it very satisfactory." The utmost care was required. I never asked customers what their preferences were or what they used the photos or the books for.

I listened carefully to our clientele and picked up a few hints that there was a market for photos of men having sex with men and women with women, and we increased our stock of same-sex pornography. The women with woman collections were especially good sellers.

With the money came two problems. One was a supply problem and the other was the police. The police were the simpler problem. We knew that we could not escape detection forever. And so we were prepared to buy them off, to bribe them to look the other way. What we didn't anticipate was how cheap it would be. They didn't want cash. They wanted pictures. And so we paid them off in wholesale dollars! It was a great business deal.

Business was really humming. One day a young man in a dark suit and a buzz cut came in. Instinctively I knew it was trouble. He said that he was so and so and worked for the federal government. *Oh, no,* I thought, *who will raise Adriana if I go to prison?* He said that he was an administrative assistant to a certain congressmen. He must have read my face because he told me to relax that he had shown me his federal identification to establish his credibility. He would like to do some discreet shopping for the congressman. I ushered him into the backroom. *Very clever,* I thought, *if someone gets caught, this guy takes the fall.* Plausible denial.

It was another gift. Who was going to bust us if we were serving the U.S. congress?

The supply problem was solved by good fortune. As our business expanded, we were chronically short of inventory. For a time we ended up importing crates of ordinary books just for the photos we could hide in them. We donated the books to libraries. We worried that someone would look at the size of our store, the volume of our imports, and our sales records and find us out.

Then I had a brainstorm. We needed a new approach. Of course, we knew we were not going to hire models and shoot our own photographs, but we could make high quality copies of what we had and sell them. There were no copyright or ownership issues in the porn business. The key was our sales data. We had always kept good records of who had bought which items. So we were able to sell the material many times over to our existing customers without duplicating what they owned or having to risk detection. At first we worried that customers would trade photographs with one another. We soon realized that the customers didn't know one another, and even if they did, we reasoned that with our uptight clientele they were unlikely to get together and swap material.

The problem was production. Who was going to do the darkroom work and where? We had no one to rely on but ourselves. We built out a darkroom in some unfinished space on the second floor. Hans and I learned the craft of photography. We each spent a fair number of nights and weekends replenishing our stock and filling special requests.

We were making more money from a little bookstore than the income my trust provided. A new problem arose, Adriana. Of course, we had to keep this a secret from the child. If we went down that path, there would be no turning back. The problem was that having a secret erected a barrier between mother and daughter. It was almost imperceptible, but it was real. A certain indefinable estrangement grew between us. I loved her and did all the things good parents do, but we could never be as close as either of us wanted. She must have sensed something. Children are very intuitive that way.

From the moment my granddaughter Agnes was born, I was determined not to let circumstance erect a similar barrier. Of course it was easier than with her mother. By the time she was born we were already winding down our involvement with porn. I have always bent over backwards to be open with her—not to judge her, but to listen. And it has paid off. We are very close. So close that some days I feel as if she is my own child.

Eventually interest in the books and photos we sold waned. Changes in attitudes toward sex and sexuality, better cameras and video equipment, and then the internet saw to that, but by then we had made a lot of money and saved a lot. And the value of my trust fund had increased substantially with time.

When Hans died in the mid-nineties, I was heartbroken. He was the center of my life. We were very close and depended almost entirely on each other. I had a circle of women friends. They were a comfort but not a replacement. As for my family, with them I had only polite relations. I felt very much alone. I was left with a decision—what to do with the bookstore. At age seventy did I want to run a bookstore without Hans? Did I want to consider a partner?

I dallied, but about six months later, I closed the store. The books, the legitimate stock, that is, I sold for a song. I wanted out as soon as possible. And I didn't need the money. I had the trust fund. Hans and I had made money, and over the years the building had increased in value. In that location it was worth a small fortune.

The rub was what to do with the pornography. It was old, and a lot of it was black and white. Much of it—the photos and the books—was tame by modern standards. And honestly, even if it had value, I couldn't take the chance of selling it. I worried about my reputation. People would correctly wonder where I had gotten it and how long I had been at it. In the end I boxed it up myself and had it delivered to my house. I was living alone in large, comfortable house. I simply put all of it in a spare bedroom and locked it. All the boxes were sealed, but I didn't even let the cleaning lady in.

Occasionally, I would open a box for old times sake and indulge both my nostalgia and my prurient instincts. Each time I would fastidiously reseal the boxes. I came to have favorites, and although I purposely kept no inventory, I had a good idea what was in each of the many boxes.

There they sat until about two years ago. As Agnes grew up and visited, she would sometimes ask about the room. I told her it was filled with her grandfather's personal papers, and I was working on organizing them for publication as a book. I planned to write an accompanying memoir. She was satisfied. As for my daughter Adriana, she had the same question, and I told her the same thing. But when there was no draft, she became skeptical. Perhaps she thought I was losing it. Finally I had to tell her point blank that it was personal and none of her business. Out of frustration, I suppose, she stopped asking.

* * *

Sometime back I invited Agnes over for tea, and we sat in the living room catching up. As we chatted, she talked a bit about her social life. She mentioned that she had invited a friend named Maynard, who was a graduate student in Adriana's lab, and his girlfriend Diana over one Saturday night. She knew Diana a little, she explained, because they were both in Adams House together.

"Granny Abigail, he's a very interesting guy. I worked with him all summer collecting specimens, insects, in a nearby bog. It's a long story, but we were studying their DNA sequences. I was going to use the data for my honors thesis. I didn't know Diana well, but she wrote this really interesting play called *Disraeli's Apricot Tree*. I invited them over to get to know her a little better and maybe to cement relations with Maynard. We had a really great time."

"Agnes, dear, tell an old woman what 'a really great time' means. I know it means that you hung out together. But what made it a really great time?"

"So, we've always been honest with each other. I'm going to tell you what went on, but I haven't told anyone else. Please don't say anything to Adriana. She wouldn't understand. First, to put your mind at ease, there were no drugs, not even marijuana. I treated them to a little psychodrama around science and religion. We did drink a fair amount of Benedictine and Brandy, but no one was really drunk."

"What does 'a psychodrama around science and religion' mean? I hope you will forgive someone my age, but, and I know this is silly, the only thing that comes to mind is something like a reenactment of the Scopes Monkey Trial. Have you ever heard of the play *Inherit the Wind?*"

"Not really. What I did was to invite them without giving them a clue about what was going to happen. When they arrived, the apartment was lit only by candles, and I wore a white caftan and this little cross. You know, the one I always wear.

I blessed them and welcomed both the Jewish and Christian spirits with an extemporaneous speech that was half-meditation and half prayer. Then we went to my bedroom."

"You did what? A ritual and then the bedroom. It sounds almost satanic. What were three half-drunk young adults doing in a bedroom together? I can understand two but not three."

"Well, that's just the point. They were bewildered too. I opened my closet door, and on the floor I had a small diorama of the bog where Maynard and I had worked all summer. I invoked Our Lady of the Bogs and Pitcher Plants and asked for her intercession on our behalf."

"Young people actually do such things today?"

"Well, Granny Abigail, I don't know about all young people, but your granddaughter does."

"Sounds very new-agey to me, dear."

"Anyway, I had been angling for a way to get closer to both Maynard and Diana and this was it."

"To Diana too? In what way?"

"You are very perceptive, Granny. I ended up kissing Diana passionately in the bedroom in front of Maynard."

"And that was okay with him?"

"I'm not sure, but I think so. Anyway, Diana said we had a lot to talk about, that she was thinking of using an idea of mine as the basis for a new play. I could tell she liked the kiss. She said she wanted to get to know me better."

That's when I had a brainstorm. Agnes could help. I knew what to do with my cache of pornographic photos and books. I realized that she was fully an adult, not only intellectually, but sexually too. And she was twenty-one. I took a chance. "Agnes, I want to change the subject slightly. Hear me out before you say anything."

"What's up, Granny Abigail?"

"Please listen for a minute or two," and I told her the whole story of how Hans and I got into pornography."

"Granny, that's like crazy amazing. I knew

you were a liberal and forward thinking, but I never would have guessed. Way to go, I mean, really."

"Agnes, how would you like to go into business with me?"

"You mean it? That sounds way cool. Exactly what kind of business?"

"Selling pornography." I couldn't believe that I was saying this to my own granddaughter, but we had always thought alike. So why not?

"You're kidding."

"I am dead serious."

We talked things through. I said that I knew the pictures, many of them in black and white, were tame by today's standards, but there might be some young people who were interested. They were collectors' items for a very special type of person. Think of these vintage photographs like vinyl records—vinyl has interesting material and occupies a different space, psychologically, from MTVs, internet downloads, streaming, and what have you. I mentioned that I had some gay and lesbian photo sets as well. She thought there would be a great deal of interest in the lesbian sets—mostly women and maybe a few men. I suggested that she take an envelope full and keep them in a drawer in her apartment. I imagined students buying them. I left the pricing to her and said that we would split the proceeds fifty-fifty.

Well, it was a modest success. Some of the young people were interested, and we made a few thousand dollars. More importantly, the business solidified our bond. Wisely, when a professor or two hinted at seeing some of the material, she disclaimed any knowledge. I didn't ask who bought them or how Agnes located potential buyers. I assumed they were students and friends.

It turns out that Agnes is a very clever marketer. She did something I wouldn't have imagined could work. With some of her clients she gave them a free photo and asked them to take it home and experience it—and share it with a select few other students. Then if they were interested in purchasing some "at startlingly reduced prices," they should come back and talk to her. My share of the take as of then was almost $1200—*not bad*, I thought.

Agnes and I had no secrets, at least as far as I knew, and sometime later when she and Adriana had a huge blow up in a restaurant at lunch, she came by and told me all about it. She also mentioned that she was now living in Brookline with both Maynard and Diana. I pretended to be unfazed, but it is upsetting when you find that your unmarried granddaughter is living with both a man and a woman at the same time. After a while I got used to it. *What is so terrible about that?* I thought. With all the meanness and heartache and psychopathic behavior in the world, if this is the worst thing that happens to my granddaughter, both she and I should count ourselves lucky.

I did have one small worry, so petty that I'm ashamed to admit it. I asked her where she stored our photos if she was living with two other people.

"Don't worry, Granny Abigail, they are safe. I have kept the apartment in Cambridge just in case things don't work out, and the photos are there."

Immediately I relaxed. I was imagining a *Boston Globe* story featuring an heiress with roots in Beacon Hill who was using her granddaughter to sell pornographic pictures.

Sometime after the blowup with her mother Adriana, she asked if she could bring her special friend Diana over, and she reminded me that Diana was the author of the new play that was part of the ruckus with Adriana at the restaurant. "Remember, Granny, it's called *Bach Among the Pitcher Plants*." I pretended I did, but in any case I was always pleased to meet Agnes's friends, and in this case Diana was more than a friend.

When they came by, I put out tea and petit fours, and we chatted amiably. I was struck by what a beauty Diana was. I am ashamed to admit it, but I could see why Agnes fell for her. Any experimentation of this sort would have been unthinkable in Boston in the late forties and early fifties, but I wondered what I might do if I were young today.

As we sat there, I felt Agnes had some agenda, so I waited patiently.

Finally she said, "Granny Abigail, Diana would like to talk business with you."

Not a good sign, I thought, but I smiled and told her to tell me what she was thinking.

Diana explained that Agnes had given her a particularly attractive French photograph. "It was a lovely picture of two women in love," she said.

I looked at Agnes, and she nodded as if to say that Diana was one of the people to whom she marketed our photos with a freebee. Of course, it had to be more that that. They were living together.

"Mrs. Lubeck, I would like to help broker a deal between you and Agnes and an older gentleman friend of mine."

I cut her off immediately. I said I was not interested in large-scale transactions with older adults. I was not in the wholesale business. This business that Agnes and I are doing together, I explained, was a pleasant collaboration between the two of us. "Our own American Cosa Nostra," I said.

She persisted, "How much inventory do you have?"

I gently explained that it was not "inventory" and that I really didn't want my life to go in that direction. To her credit she was gracious and said that Agnes was very lucky to have a special person like me as her grandmother.

She said she understood my position and added, "May I tell you a story, Mrs. Lubeck?"

Now I felt on safer ground, so I said, "Why of course."

She told me the whole story of how her play *Bach Among the Pitcher Plants* came to be, beginning with the evening in which she and Maynard had come over to Agnes's Harvard Square apartment and ending with the story of how the extended allusion to a vibrator that she called the Michelangelo came to be included in the play.

I was impressed. What a fine imagination she had. And I said so. I didn't add that the play sounded a bit jumbled to me. There was no need to be impolite.

She thanked me and said she had a small gift for me. I am sure that Agnes had put her up to it. She handed me a simple brown box with a ribbon. When I opened it, I found a Michelangelo. I thanked her and asked her why she thought I had any use for a vibrator at my age. She pointed out that I was still interested enough in pornography "to traffic in it." I never felt I was trafficking in pornography. I tried not to let my face show how startled I was. The other reason she thought I might like the Michelangelo is that I was Agnes's grandmother. I did not let on, but she had me dead to rights. From there on, the conversation ran down, and they soon left.

"What did you think?" Agnes wanted to know when she called me that night.

I said that she was a very nice young woman and I saw why she liked her. I described Diana's gift as "sweet." Then I let down my guard a bit and said, "It is useful as well." That was the only tactful way I could acknowledge to my granddaughter that even at eighty-seven I was not sexually dead. I reiterated that I liked Diana, but I did not think we should proceed with any business dealings with a gentleman friend whom we did not know. Agnes was disappointed. She wanted to help Diana, and maybe make a little money as well.

And that's where things stood until a few weeks ago. I got a call from a Professor Norman Penderevski, who said he was a colleague of my daughter Adriana's in the biology department. Might he come by for a chat? Why, yes, of course. And a few days later I again set out tea and petit fours. I wondered what could be on the mind of one of Adriana's colleagues. Were they going to honor her in some way and wanted my participation? Or was she in some kind of emotional or financial trouble? I had no idea except I was sure moral turpitude was not involved.

Professor Penderevski was a chunky, shortish man in late-middle age, who looked like a caricature of a professor. He should have had on a Harris Tweed sports coat with elbow patches. In fact he wore beige slacks and a plaid shirt and slung a herringbone sports coat over his shoulder. He had come to Harvard from St. Louis a few years ago, and so on. We made polite small talk until he worked his way round to the reason for the visit. He explained that he was raised in Philadelphia and still had a brother there—Jan, as he referred to him—and they were very close. Jan was in the novelties business. When I asked what that meant, I got a mix of vagaries I could make no sense of.

"Let me tell you why I am here. I am a friend of Diana's."

"What kind of friend?"

"A friend." He swallowed. Did he sense my disapprobation? "Diana and I are close. And to come to the point, she shared with me some of the photos that your granddaughter Agnes gave her."

"Really." That was all I could think to say. "And what did you think?"

"I'm a professor. I'm no judge of such things."

"Ah, Professor, I'm an old woman, but I ran a bookstore for many years, and sometimes the meekest of men are the best judges. So please tell me what you think."

"Well, the few I saw were, ah, actually, they were very, ah, appealing."

"Good. Now that we have established that, why are you here?"

"My brother Jan. I called him, and he may have an interest in your photos and other material— classic books and movies, or perhaps magazines—if you've got any. This is my brother's area of expertise, not mine. But he thinks there is a market for vintage material like yours in Philadelphia."

I was a bit snippy. "I hear there is a market for almost anything in Philadelphia, but, Professor, he can't sell enough of what I have in Philadelphia to make it worth his while."

"I am wondering if Jan might come up and take a look."

I hesitated just long enough to set the hook. "No, even supposing I had what he is looking for, I don't do deals like that. Thank him for his interest. And thank you for coming. It was very nice to meet one of Adriana's colleagues."

Agnes called. I suppose Diana had lobbied her because she said, "Granny Abigail, trust me. I get the feeling Jan is a player. At least let's hear what he has to say. We would do Diana and her friend Norman a good turn. I like her very much. She is a close friend."

I pretended to humor her. I told her I had no real interest in dealing with this man, but as a favor to Diana and her I was willing to meet with Jan.

"Great, Granny, leave it to me. I'll set things up."

Saturday morning a white truck pulled up. "Penderevski Ventures" was painted in purple letters on the cab door. Norman and a thinner, less finished version of him got out and stood talking. A moment later Diana and Agnes arrived.

"Please come in. You must be Jan. So nice to meet you. Agnes, show everyone to the living room. I'll get coffee. I won't be a moment."

"A cup of joe would be great, Mrs. Lubeck," Jan said. *A cup of joe, indeed*, I thought.

I poured coffee. "Now, gentlemen, tell what you are thinking. You must imagine I have a large trove to drive a truck all the way from Philadelphia."

"Always like to be prepared. You never know what you are going to find once you get into the middle of things."

"Mr. Penderevski, so far you aren't in the middle of anything. What is it you are looking for?"

"Anything you've got. After what Norman showed me, I'm guessing you've got the goods. I'd love first editions and especially first printings of any classic books you've got from Marquis de Sade to Henry Miller. Vintage magazines if they are in mint condition. Movies and tapes, especially classic French movies and tapes. Negatives of classic European porn or attributable prints. I'll take copies, but of course they are not worth much."

"And you think I have such stuff."

"I'm betting you have some of it. You may not be able to fill my truck, but I'll take what you've got if the price is right."

"You can't possibly sell all this material in Philadelphia. What is your business model?"

"You surprise me, Mrs. L., but Norman said you were sharp. If the material is good, I'll sell most of it to collectors in the Middle East and Japan. Maybe a little in New York. L.A. is a good market with the film industry there. Yeah, I don't know if you have ever been to Philly, but I can't do much in South Philly. And you go to North Philly with stuff like this, and you take your life in your hands. So that's it. Now are we going to talk or not?"

I turned toward Agnes pretending to look for a sign. "Perhaps," I said. "Why don't you come with me and we'll take a look at my cache? The room's too small for all of us."

Jan and I went through the boxes. It was exhausting. It must have taken several hours. My collection was not everything he wanted. We had never stocked film or tapes, and we were not into the magazine market. But he liked the photo collection and the books.

"Very nice. Good stuff. How did you find this stuff?"

"I bought a lot of it in the fifties and early sixties. They were a value then."

"Let's you and me talk. Norman's hunch was right. He really has a nose for this work. I'm trying to convince him to give up his researching and join me. So what do you want for everything? I'll pay you in cash, today."

"Let's go out and talk. I want my partner Agnes to participate."

"What? The skinny one with the braid?"

"'The skinny one with the braid,' as you put it,

cleans up really well, and she's a whole lot quicker than you are, my friend."

We went in the living room and joined the others. "Mr. Penderevski has an interest in our material, Agnes. He's wants to make us an offer, but I want you to participate."

"I said to your grandmother that she should tell me what she wants for the collection. So what do you want, Mrs. L.?"

"We want $100,000, but if you pay now and take everything as is, we'll discount five percent," Agnes said.

"Very nice, little lady, but you're way outside the worth of your material."

"Fine, my grandmother and I have no real need to sell. It's okay with us if we quit now.

"Hold on, I didn't say I wasn't interested, only that the ask is crazy. I'm willing to offer $5,000 in cash, right now."

"You're a moron," Agnes said.

"Hold on, dear. Give me a moment. Mr. Penderevski, you don't really think we would go into this without an independent appraisal. Once we realized you were coming, we asked a local dealer and a dear friend Saleh Wadi Wadi to look at the collection. He offered us $60,000 or $50,000 and 10% of the profits." I looked at Agnes. I couldn't tell if she was surprised or worried.

"Your guy can't be for real. No way this stuff is worth anywhere near that kind of money."

"That's okay, if you change your mind, you or Norman should get ahold of us. I've asked Saleh if we can have thirty days to think about his offer."

"Mrs. Lubeck, I'm sure you were very good at retail. But I've been down this road a thousand times. Give it up. You want to do business with Jan Penderevski, then you gotta cut the horse feathers. It's worth maybe six, seven thousand to me, but I know how it is between Norman and Diana, so I'm gonna come up a little. My offer is nine thousand."

I cleared my throat and looked at Agnes. "If you give us ten, it's a deal."

"I like your spunk, Mrs. L., but it's over. I'm not going to haggle. You want nine thousand in cash today, you got it. That's it. No ten or anything else. I am only doing nine because of Norman."

"Cash today, and you will never come back to me asking for authentication or documents, right?"

"I wouldn't think of it. My clients will take care of that."

I looked at Agnes. She nodded.

"Okay, Mr. Penderevski. We have a deal."

He went out to the truck and brought back a large shopping bag. And right there in front of us, he counted out $9,000 in twenty dollar bills. At first I worried that they could be counterfeit, but I had Norman as a sort of informal hostage. I figured we could get a graduate student friend of Agnes's to spit in his test tubes if the money was fake. When we were done, the four of them carried the boxes to the truck, and the men drove off.

I sat in the living room with my granddaughter and Diana. After loading the truck, they looked like two migrant workers in from a day in the sun.

"Thank you, Diana," I said. "I didn't think this would amount to anything, but clearly you sized Norman up correctly."

"I have a small favor to ask." Agnes said. "I normally wouldn't do it in front of Granny, but we're all here. And it's clear there is very little that will shock her. Maybe she can help."

"I'll do my best, darling."

"It's about my mother. Adriana, and I don't know how to put it, has an old fashioned crush on Norman. She hardly knows him, but she admires him, and although she has never said so, I think she finds him sexy."

"The Norman who was just here? The professor who knows pornography?"

"Granny, in a word, 'yes.'"

"But I thought there was something between Norman and Diana," I said. "And I'm a little confused too. Aren't you and Diana and Maynard living together?"

"Mrs. Lubeck, don't worry. It will all work out."
Diana turned to Agnes, "So what are you asking?"

"How serious is this thing between you and
Norman?" Agnes said.

"I'm not the problem. I'm willing to share. It's
Beverly Ardmore. Sometimes Norman comes over or
we go out, but he thinks of himself as in a relationship
with Beverly. So unless your mother plans to learn
Spanish and sing in a Mexican band, she's going to
be a cowgirl with the blues."

"Beverly Ardmore? A Mexican Band? I had no
idea Norman was so, well, so capable."

"Hold on Granny. It's a little incestuous, but it's
all right. Let me explain. Diana, my mom's in a funk.
She has no idea how to get Norman's attention. You
know Norman well. You have any ideas? And by the
way, I would never say anything to Adriana about
you and Norman. What you and Norman do or don't
do stops with me."

"Me too," I said. "After you gave me the
Michelangelo, my lips are sealed, more or less."

"Granny!"

"Granny, what, child? Innuendo is wasted on
the young."

"Here's an idea," Diana said. "You are going to
have to trust me and maybe bolster your mother's
courage, but it will work." She reached into the back
pocket of her jeans and pulled out an antique picture
of a man and woman engaged in fellatio. "Tell your
mother to put this in a plain envelope, seal it, and put
it in Norman's faculty mailbox. Tell her to include a
note that says, 'If you would like to meet, leave a note
in your mailbox—meaning his mailbox—that says,
"Contact me" and I will check your mailbox and give
you a time and place in a return note.'"

"Adriana could never do such a thing. She is
much too straight for that. I guess she has had affairs
over the years. In fact I am sure she has. But your
approach is too brazen," Agnes said.

"I doubt that. Look at you and your grandmother.
She is sandwiched between the two of you. That's not
the problem. She will come round. The problem is

once she meets him socially for coffee or a drink, can she carry it off?"

"Well, that's true. She is a bit shy and ill-at-ease in situations like that."

"Come on, Agnes, we're all adults," Diana said. "We know how this has to work. She needs to flatter him and let him talk about himself. And then flatter him some more and allow him to talk even more about himself. Then she needs to feed him. I hope she's a good cook. And if she's any good in bed at all, she's got him."

"With Adriana, this scenario is far from a sure thing," Agnes said.

"When Norman gets the photo, he will talk to me about it. I'm sure. I'm his muse. I'll guide him a little. You and I can compare notes, you know, help bring the process to fruition."

"Children, this is incredible. Actually it's very funny. I'm happy for my daughter, and I'm glad to see my cache helping our family. I never imagined when Hans and I started that our collection would be a tonic to an unborn daughter's love life. I know I'm an old lady, but she is my daughter, and I still worry about her. Oh, let's be truthful here. Keep me in the loop as you kids say. I still have a strong prurient streak in me. And daughter or not, the photo will set a great caper in motion. Come back for tea and tell me every blessed detail."

VIII. She Stoops to Conquer

Professor Adriana Lubeck's desk was cluttered with stacks of unread journals and drafts of in-progress manuscripts. There was hardly space for her computer. A bookcase behind her was heavy with scientific tomes and rows of her former graduate students' dissertations, all neatly bound in what could pass for Harvard crimson. Her daughter Agnes had pulled a chair around the desk so that she had a clear sightline and was letting her mother have it.

"Give it up, Adriana. Come clean," Agnes said. Her smile was impish and sympathetic as she perched pixie-like on her chair.

"It's absolute nonsense. I don't have a 'thing,' as you put it, for Norman Penderevski. He's a colleague, that's all. As far as I'm concerned, he's just another professor in the department."

"Let's call it what it is. I know it and you know it. So just own it."

"There is nothing to own," Adriana said.

"Okay, you're a scientist. Why don't we let science be the judge?"

"What is that supposed to mean?"

"Why don't you come over to MIT and let Dr. Crowley and me do an fMRI on you. I'll bet you anything that when I say 'Norman Penderevski,' your brain will light up like the fireworks at a Fourth of July Pops concert."

"Okay, so what if I am a little interested? Anyway, he's seeing someone, this woman, Beverly, Beverly Ardmore."

Agnes was not about to let up, not with her mother's love life at stake. "I'd say that you're more than a little interested. You're a whole lot interested. Maybe even sizzling. And you know what? The business about seeing someone—how lame is that? If he were a research project, you wouldn't say, it's someone else's area. You would figure out a new angle and go for it. So what are you waiting for?"

"Agnes, you know I'm not very good at these things. I have no idea what to do."

"Want some advice?"

"I'm not sure. Maybe. It depends. Damn it anyway. I've got a lot of frayed nerve endings over this. I can't throw myself at him. I'm not built that way."

"I didn't say you should throw yourself at him, just maybe try a fresh approach."

"Okay, Agnes, what's your advice?"

"One more question. Didn't you tell me that you and Norman were collaborating on some problem in protein structure?"

"Yes, but that's different."

"Nonsense. It's not different. Work is sexy."

"Work is work."

"Look, Adriana, you were the one who set me up to work with Maynard for the summer, and you know where that has led. So don't give me that work-is-work BS."

"All right. Let's hear it."

Agnes got up and pushed the door securely closed. She sat back down and squinched up her large brown eyes, which gave her a slightly conspiratorial demeanor. "You're the professor of biology, so I'm going to ask you to trust your biology and Norman's to get things going. You know more about courtship displays in the animals than I ever will. So think about a rhesus monkey in heat. When she wants to attract a mate, she shows him her swollen hind parts to get his attention."

"Jesus, Agnes, whatever else you may think about your mother, she is not a rhesus monkey in heat. That's degrading."

Agnes ignored her. "We both know these same neurobiological pathways still exist within us. We are primates too."

"So what do you want me to do, take him to the primate house at the zoo?"

Agnes was surprisingly composed as she gave her mother, the professor, a lesson in the birds and the bees. No, she didn't expect her mother to present her hindquarters to Professor Norman Penderevski for inspection, but she was thinking of something similar. Without comment, she give her mother an antique black and white photo of a woman performing fellatio on a man, who was dressed in nothing but a beret. Her mother winced.

"Agnes, are you crazy? What am I to do with this? This must have come from Diana and that artsy crowd she runs around with. I'm sick and tired of the deviance she is teaching you. After I saw *Bach Among the Pitcher Plants*, I knew that she would never be a playwright, and now I know she'll never be a decent human being."

"You're jumping to conclusions. This is about you, not Diana. You haven't even heard what I want to suggest, and you're throwing up all sorts of barriers."

"You're a loose canon. That's what you are. What kind of daughter have I raised?"

"A pragmatic one, just like you. And one who wants to help her mother. Once more—do you remember how resistant I was when you told me to quit my summer job in Vladimir Rajewsky's lab and work with Maynard for the summer? You calmed me down and told me to listen. And I did. Now, I'm asking you to do the same thing."

"All right, I owe you that courtesy. But this is disgusting."

As Agnes explained her plan, her mother pushed her chair back from the photo on the desk as if it were coated with Ebola virus.

"Put the photo in a plain envelope and leave it in his mailbox with a note that says something like, 'If you would like to meet me, leave a note in your box that says, "Yes." I will come by and check. I'll leave you a note telling you when and where.' And Adriana, don't forget to seal the envelope."

"A thing like this could never work. I love you

for worrying about me, but I need another approach. This is stooping so low that, that, if I were found out, I would be deeply humiliated. I could lose my job." Adriana got up, kissed her daughter, and gently urged her toward the door.

Adriana sat back down at her desk. Perhaps she would never get up. She would sink into peaceful oblivion and forgetfulness. Then she realized the photo was there face up on her desk. She picked it up and was about to put it in a drawer, but she studied it. What was it about the photo? Something. She was not nearly as prudish as she pretended in front of her daughter, but what kind of man would want a long-term relationship with a woman whose opening gambit was a pornographic photo? As she continued to look, she liked the photo. It was true that it was a woman pleasuring a man, but would there not be reciprocity? Was this not foreplay?

What came immediately to mind was Monica Lewinsky. Yet when she stripped away the lying, the concerns about national security, all the moralizing and hand ringing, and the irreparable hurts that the affair caused the Clintons, she was left with two consenting adults for whom the relationship worked. In Adriana's view what went on between Monica and Bill Clinton had nothing to do with how he functioned as president.

Where did all this leave her? Exactly nowhere. She got up and locked her office door. The photograph. What was it about the photograph? She swallowed hard, stood up, and not knowing what to do with herself, sat back down. Finally she had to admit that it excited her. It wasn't supposed to. For someone like her, it was supposed to be a curiosity from another era or perhaps a bit repulsive, but not arousing. What was it about the photograph? She gave a shrug of incomprehension. No, wait. "Jesus, that's it." The man in the photograph was wearing a beret. And which middle-aged male professor in the biology department wore a beret? She pursed her lips and exhaled a long pheeeeeeew. "Norman," she said slowly as if she had unroofed a hive of bees and sought to replace the cover carefully. Was this a coincidence or was Agnes diabolically clever?

She walked back and forth in her office holding the glossy side of the photo against her chest. The phone rang and startled her. She let it ring. Whoever it was could wait. She couldn't very well go back to her daughter and ask about the beret. She looked at the photo again. No, it was not a new photo that had been antiqued, or at least she didn't think so. Could her daughter and Norman be in collusion and this was a photo of him? She looked again. No, the man seemed younger and taller. Not as pudgy.

She thought to call her friend Olympia and ask her advice. Adriana was trying to imagine how she would explain the photo and her daughter's plan to her oldest friend. Even someone as close to her as Olympia might ridicule her if she explained that she found the photo stimulating and was tempted to go forward.

And besides, Olympia was still a little frail from the trauma of Pittsburgh. She was seeing a therapist she had confided, and it seemed to Adriana that she was making good progress. But why push it? She put the photo under some papers in a desk drawer and locked it.

That evening she picked at dinner and then sat on her couch and tried to read. Her mind was whirring. Finally out of desperation for something to distract her, she changed the sheets and put in a load of laundry. About ten thirty she drove to her office, typed up the note Agnes had suggested, and was about to put it and the photograph in an envelope. Should she sign it? Of course not, not with her name anyway. The approach seemed both tacky and half-hearted—a burlesque of a come on. Perhaps a little humor would help. She picked up a pen and printed "FRENCHIE" in block capitals beneath the typescript.

She almost tiptoed to the faculty mailroom. Good, all the lights were out. She let herself in and placed the envelope in Penderevski's mailbox. Her next impulse was to leaf through his mail to see what she could learn. Just get yourself out before you have to explain why you are rummaging through a colleague's mailbox at this time of night. Quickly she turned off the lights and slipped down the stairs to her car. Each night she came by between ten and midnight. Nothing. Her original envelope was still in his mailbox.

She got cold feet and went by to retrieve the envelope. As she put her key in the lock and heard the tumblers click, she was startled from behind by O'Ryan Smythe, the bat physiologist. She flinched. "Hello, Adriana. What brings you to your mailbox so late?"

She paused and smiled. "I've been working, and thought I would check my mail before I left."

"Me too." And he walked in behind her.

A close call, she thought. What if she had been going through Norman's mail? Now she could not go near his mailbox. Instead, she went to hers and pulled out a series of seminar flyers, advertisements, and, wait, what was this, a small, powder blue envelope addressed to "Prof. A. Lubeck"? A woman's hand, surely. She looked over at Smythe who was engrossed in the latest issue of some scholarly journal.

The note read, "Forget the old adage 'Be careful what you wish for.' For you, Professor, it should be, 'Pursue carefully what you wish for.'" It was unsigned. No one could know about her envelope in Norman's box but Agnes. And this was not her handwriting. Did someone see her and steam the envelope? Impossible. She retreated to her office and sat. After a while she figured that Smythe would be gone, and she went back to Penderevski's box. The envelope was still there, and it looked untampered. Not sure what to do, she held it for a moment, bit her lip and grimaced as if she had jammed her fingers in a door. She sighed and put it back.

I'm in the middle of it now, she thought. *The die is cast.* Then picking up the gallows humor of the note, she smiled sardonically. "Someone in the cast is going to die."

The next morning she tested the waters by

sending Norman a bland email asking for some detail of their joint protein structure project. She got back an out of office reply. So that was it.

She waited and finally the envelope was gone. In its place was another addressed to Dr. I. E. French. This must be it. He got the joke. In her office she opened it. He had kept the picture. Either he liked it or thought it too risky to shuttle it back and forth in his mailbox. There was a single sheet of white legal size paper with "Okay" typed in large font. Adriana was shaking. She couldn't think of what to write or where to meet. She fled and drove home without leaving a reply. Her identity was still safe. She gripped the steering wheel as if she were about to be lost to outer space and it was her only mooring. She didn't have to go through with it. She didn't have to respond. She could be in control, she could. Damn it, she could. She recognized she was in a state. She needed to talk, to work things out with someone safe.

She dialed Olympia's cell phone.

"Adriana? It's midnight. What's wrong?"

"How did you know it was me? Oh, caller ID. I've got myself in a terrible pickle. You're my oldest friend. I need to talk something through. Do you think we could have breakfast tomorrow? I'm coming apart a bit."

"Give me some hint. What wrong?"

"I've got myself in a tough spot with someone, someone in my department. It's really terrible."

"I'll come over now. I'll throw on some clothes and be there in fifteen minutes."

"No. I'm too wound to talk. I need to get control before I can sit down with you. It's bad."

"You sure, Adriana? I'm coming."

"No, please don't. I need to get my thoughts in order. How about breakfast?"

"I'll be there. If you put on the coffee, I'll stop for Danish on the way."

Adriana sat on the couch, wrung tight by the tension of indecision. What should she do? She played the conversation with Agnes over and over in her head. And the drama of the drop in Norman

Penderevski's mailbox. What really unnerved her though was the message on powder blue notepaper. How could anyone know? It threw a wrench in the works. And then there was the problem of what to say to Norman after she explained that *she* had left the fellatio photo in his mailbox. Damn it all. Maybe it would be easier to be a rhesus monkey in heat. At least the decision would be clear-cut.

Olympia was almost cheery as she set the bag of pastries on the kitchen table. She was dressed for class. Then over coffee and Danish Adriana put her elbows on the table and her chin in both palms. "I want to discuss something with you that's upsetting me, but now I'm having second thoughts. I mean I worry that you are not quite strong enou . . . not quite ready for this. I'm in a bind and it's a sexual thing."

"It's okay. Actually I'm doing better. I'm getting some help as you know. Whatever it is, it can't be worse than Edvaldo Eichenbaum and Pittsburgh. So out with it. Go ahead, from the beginning."

"Thank you. I hardly know where to begin. You're not going to believe this. I'm so ashamed. The whole thing is so crazy."

Olympia waited.

Adriana turned to a second Danish for comfort and told her the story leaving out no detail: Agnes's recognition that she still carried the torch for Norman. The bizarre idea of sending him a pornographic photograph. "Not just any photograph, a picture of a woman performing fellatio on a man with a beret. And Norman, you remember, sometimes wears a beret." The intrigue of leaving the photo in his inbox with mysterious instructions to him. The attempted humor of "FRENCHIE." And then the confounding note on powder blue notepaper. His adroit response, Dr. I.E. French. "What in the world am I going to do, Olympia?"

"Seems to me there are three possibilities. And come on, you know this as well as I do. It's not, as my brother Chandler would say, rocket science. One, you can walk away from the photo and the mailbox and develop a completely new strategy for attracting

Norman's attention. That would be a good mix of prudence and desire. Two, you can walk away from the whole idea and look for someone else. Or you can play out this hand. What is it you want?"

"I have no idea."

"Of course you do. Your infatuation with this guy is a chronic condition. I remember the way you looked at him when we ran into him and the tall woman in the lime green blazer at Diana's play, at *Bach Among the Pitcher Plants*."

"Her name is Beverly Ardmore."

"Thanks, but really, she's not the issue. You're infatuated with this guy. No, you are . . . and I'm looking for the right word here, something like the female equivalent of 'pussy whipped,' maybe 'dick dazzled.' You are dick dazzled. Don't look so offended. If this were one of my novels, I wouldn't hesitate to use the term. Because this, well, this escapade of yours is like a novel. At the very least you are enthralled or infatuated. It goes way beyond interested or even smitten. You have a condition. Some force is holding you captive. So out of hand let's dismiss the idea that you are going to forget about Norman. It isn't going to happen."

"Okay, you're right. I am interested. I am. But I am not any of the other things—enthralled, infatuated, and, God, dick dazzled. None of it."

"Adriana, you're the one who sent him the picture of fellatio. You didn't have to send him anything, or you could have asked Agnes for another picture. Let me ask you something while we're on the subject. When was the last time you had the serious attention of a man—other than the Michelangelo, I mean?"

She hesitated and put her tongue in her cheek and looked down. "It's been a while."

"Stop looking so ashamed. There is nothing shameful in wanting a relationship and the sex that goes with it. For God's sake, you're the biologist. So you are going to go forward. That's a given. The only question is how. Do you have any ideas?"

"If I did, I would have tried them. I can't think of anything. Nothing, absolutely nothing. I'm stuck."

"Well, you've got that joint scientific project with him that you were telling me about. Can you work a dinner invitation into the conversation?"

"It's not so easy to recast a relationship once it has developed. And much of the time it is, as the joke goes, his people are talking to my people. Besides, you know very well I'm starting with a handicap. He and Beverly Ardmore are in a relationship."

"Why don't you simply call him and ask him to have a cup of coffee with you?"

"I can't, that's why. Call it shyness or lack of nerve or reticence or whatever, but I can't."

"Well, then it's solved."

"What do you mean, 'It's solved'?"

"You don't have a conventional approach to getting to know Norman better, or if you do, you don't want to use it. You have had a thousand opportunities to suggest coffee or lunch or a movie, and you haven't done anything. Either you won't or can't, or you are paralyzed. So that leaves you with the unconventional approach. It's that simple. I know the whole idea is bizarre, but it's where your unconscious is leading you. If it isn't, then you would have dismissed the pornographic picture idea out of hand."

"I'm not sure this is a good idea."

"Remember, I'm the novelist. I make stuff like this up all the time. But if you don't like *your* idea, you can go after Beverly like Tonia Harding and try to kneecap her or stalk her like the woman astronaut in Florida. You get the picture."

"Suppose you are right, how would I do it?"

"You don't need me for this. Put a note in his box with the suggestion to meet you somewhere. And when you meet, don't mention the photo. Let the conversation develop normally. See what happens." Olympia looked at her watch. "Sorry, I have run. I have to take care of some things before class. You can do this, Adriana. You can."

"Thanks for listening. You've been a big help. I don't know what I'm going to do, but thank you." She put her arms around Olympia and hugged her. "Really, thank you."

*   *   *

Once Olympia was out the door, Adriana thought, *of course you know what you are going to do, but first what about the powder blue note?* She was fuming. It could only be Agnes. How could she?

She picked up her cell and called her daughter. Without so much as a hello she launched into a full-scale assault with armor-piercing shrapnel. "What the hell do you think you're doing? How dare you send me such a note. I've raised you to be better than this. Your brazen effrontery astounds me. I hope you have an explanation."

"Adriana, Mother, what in the world are you talking about?"

"I'll tell you what I'm talking about, though you know perfectly well. The note, that's what."

"Note? What note? I don't have the foggiest what you mean."

"We must discuss this now. Come right over."

"I can't. I've got a cat in the MRI. I'm tracking things. I'll call you back in about thirty minutes. Got to run."

Silence. Adriana looked at the phone in disbelief. She wanted to hurl it against the wall, but instead she shook it as if she were trying to extract information from a terrorist. "Damn it."

When Agnes called back, she begin, "Okay, Adriana, what happened?"

"You know perfectly well what happened. You or one of your henchmen sent me that note."

"No way. Again, what note?"

"The one with the smartass rewriting of the proverb. The unsigned one on power blue paper. The one that says . . . hold on, I'll read it to you." She fished the note out of her briefcase. "Forget the old adage 'Be careful what you wish for.' For you, Professor, it should be, 'Pursue carefully what you wish for.'"

"I have no idea about any of this. I'm clueless."

"Who knew about this besides you?"

"Just a sec. I think I better step out of the lab. Call you right back," and the phone went dead.

"Damn it, damn it, damn it. I have raised a discourteous simpleton."

"Okay, I can talk now. So I've got no idea what's going on. None. Really."

"Well, where did you get the photo?"

"I'd rather not say."

"I don't want to hear it. Where?"

"A friend."

"What friend?"

"Diana, okay?"

"No, it's not okay. I need to know everything before I, well, I've already started the process, before I go any further with your little plan. There is some risk that when I respond, I will be humiliated. And surprise, surprise, it would feel really bad. So I want to know about the note."

"Adriana, I don't want to discuss this over the phone. Can I come by after I'm done here, maybe five-thirty or six, and talk about it?"

"Okay, fine, but today. He has sent me a note back, and I want to put one with directions in his box late tonight sometime."

"Way to go, Adriana! The heart won't be such a lonely hunter."

"So now you know why I think you are the mastermind behind the note to me. There's the proverb BS again. I'll tell you what. The hunter is a lonely hart. That's H-A-R-T. See what I mean? See why I think it's you?"

"I'll be over later. But think about it, think about turning around a proverb. You don't need to think about me. I did make a little joke about the heart being a lonely hunter, but then *you* turned it around. Anybody, almost anybody, anyway, can do that. It doesn't have to be me. See you about five-thirty."

They sat in Adriana's kitchen. In the same spots that early that morning Olympia and Adriana had occupied, mother and daughter, both hoisting mugs of tea with their left hands and the same mannerisms. They looked alike and they thought alike if you allowed for the generational difference, and that was one reason there was so much conflict between them.

"Let's have it, young lady."

"I told you all I know. I didn't write the note or dictate the note, and I got the photo from Diana."

"And where did she get it?"

"I have no idea. But it doesn't matter."

"Did she know what you wanted me to do with the photo?" Adriana said.

"Yes and no."

"Which? Yes or no?"

"A little. We discussed it a little."

"How could you betray my confidence, Agnes?"

"It wasn't betraying a confidence. It was trying to get a little help to get you the best possible plan."

"So she knows everything?" Adriana said.

"Sort of, yes. She knows."

"Does she know Norman?"

"I don't know. I don't think so. No."

Adriana looked over the rim of her mug, half focusing on Agnes's eyes and half hiding her face. "I want an apology from her and a pledge of secrecy."

"Trust me, Adriana, play the hand out and see where it goes. I promise it will work. That's all I'm going to say on the subject."

"This is like one of Olympia's novels. I can't believe this is happening to me. No, it is not happening to me. I am doing it."

"Yes, Adriana, just do it."

As Agnes got up to leave, Adriana put her arms around her daughter and said, "I love you, Agnes, but some days you try me."

Adriana slipped into the faculty mailroom in the early hours of the morning—no one, not even batman, was around—and placed her note in Norman's box: "I'll look for you today, Thursday, at Corrigan's about four-thirty. Take a back table. If you are not there, I'll try Friday. Or it's over. FRENCHIE."

The surprise came when she checked her own

mailbox. There was another powder blue envelope waiting for her. It read, "'Mum's the word' in both the American and English senses." And of course, no signature. Was it Agnes after all? No, she would have owned up when they talked. But "Mum," who would write that? Diana could do that. She was the writer, the playwright, and playwrights were ventriloquists, impersonators whose gift allowed them to live in other people's skins. That she had a flare for drama went without saying. Yes, definitely Diana. She and Agnes were colluding. In a way Adriana was relieved. If Diana had written the notes and she and her daughter were in cahoots, her discretion could be counted on. Or at least Adriana thought so.

That afternoon as she walked into Corrigan's, she saw Norman at once in the rear of the coffee shop with his back toward the door, his face hidden from colleagues or students who might wander in. He held something, a journal or a scientific paper, which he seemed to be reading. She guessed it was a ruse. For Adriana there was no doubt who it was. How many pudgy, older, professorial types would be wearing berets in Corrigan's at this hour? An irrelevant, but delicious thought sprang to mind: Che Guevara was still alive and had aged well. She walked around in front of him and let out a slight cough. He looked up with a start.

An eternity elapsed while he composed himself. "Ah, I, hello . . . I am, ah, nice to see you. I am expecting someone. What are you doing here, Adriana?"

"I'm not sure I understand the question."

"Well, I am supposed to meet someone here at four-thirty, and you surprised me. Do you come here often?"

"Oh, half a dozen times a year. And I'm the person you've come to meet."

It was as if someone had zapped him with a stun gun. His mouth moved, but no sounds came out. He swallowed. "It, it can't be. I can't be meeting you. I, no, you cannot have sent me that, ah, well, that, let's just say communication."

"Then how do you explain that I am standing in front of you in a hot pink blouse open at the throat?" He was still dazed. "Are you sure, Adriana?" "Of course, I'm sure. Do you want me to prove it by describing the communication in an overloud voice?"

Before he could answer, a waitress came by. She ordered a mint tea and sat down.

"Really," Norman said, "you sent it? Well, what an amazing thing. I never would have guessed in . . . no, a million years doesn't begin to cover it. Well, I'll be. Whatever possessed you to, well, send it?"

"Whatever possessed you to respond?" She didn't wait for an answer. "I wanted to get your attention."

"Well, you certainly did. But there are easier ways like giving me a call or sending an email or even dropping by my office. I don't live in Tasmania. Why the intrigue?"

"I was a little hesitant and, oh screw it all, a little shy."

"Well, you certainly have an unusual way of expressing reticence."

"I'm just not very good at such things, but I wanted to meet you."

"It seems to me that you are very good at these things. You got my attention." He softened his tone and smiled. "You look very nice this afternoon. That's a great color on you."

The waitress put down the mint tea and refilled Norman's coffee.

"Forgive me," he said. "I know you only as a talented researcher, but is this your normal modus operandi?" His tone was gentle as if he wanted to understand. "I'm still reeling from the approach. You know we have a scheduled monthly meeting with our postdoctoral fellows about the protein chemistry collaboration. You could have excused them at the end and said, 'let's have coffee.' I'm truly speechless . . . but not in a bad way."

By unspoken mutual consent they moved away from the photo and all it implied or promised or foretold and talked about themselves. For her part she talked about Abigail and Hans Lubeck and Lubeck's Books ("My upbringing was very exotic"), about being an undergraduate at Radcliffe ("Let's just say it was a time of experimentation and personal growth"), her marriage ("I wish it had worked"), and graduate school and her professional life ("I've had more than my share of good fortune"). For his part, growing up poor in South Philadelphia with a scholarship to Friends Central ("One was grit and the other was grind"), college and graduate school ("I got a scholarship to Brown and did my Ph.D. at the med center in San Francisco"), marriage and children ("Harriet and I wanted different things—the divorce was painful, very painful"), and scientific advancement ("Hard work, but some lucky breaks too").

"Funny," she said, "how two people can have such different backgrounds and be so similar."

"Incredibly similar, unless you get too granular, and then nothing seems alike."

It was a very comfortable afternoon—as long as they avoided the depth charge she had placed in his mailbox and kept it personal without being confessional. Adriana wondered why it had taken her so long to meet him socially. He seemed very nice, just the way she imagined from his seminar and her interactions with him in their collaboration.

"So, I have two questions," he said.

"You have taken a line from my script. My students call me the question lady, and my daughter Agnes is even worse."

"No matter, the first is, are you free next Saturday evening, not the day after tomorrow, next Saturday evening. I would invite you out to dinner, but I have another idea. The restaurants are so noisy we won't be able to hear one another. How about if I cook for the two of us at my place? Will that work?"

"Yes, I would love to come," she said. "Can I bring anything?"

"Your smile, your charm, your . . ." he paused for effect, "mystery."

This guy is good, she thought. *Who knew*

molecular biologists had such good lines? And he cooks.

"So what's your second question?"

He ignored her. "I'll give you a call, and we can firm things up."

She sensed him take in her smile and glance at her breasts. Behind his polite control she could see the slightest hints of arousal. His lips pursed a bit, and then there was the slightest brush of his tongue across them. He body relaxed and his palms, which had been facedown on the table, were now turned up slightly. A wisp of a smile crossed his face. They stood and looked at each other, neither sure what the proper form of disengagement should be. They could not shake hands (too formal), they could not hug (too committed), they could not kiss (too intimate). Finally he laughed and said, "Until Saturday a week or tomorrow morning at the faculty mailboxes."

She watched him head down the street with his worn briefcase. *It was an odd encounter,* she thought—what was not said was as important as what was. Not a word about Beverly. Maybe he had forgotten that she and Olympia had run into him and Beverly at Diana's Play. No, it was an awkward enough encounter that he could not have forgotten. Perhaps he was not seeing Beverly any more, or the relationship was more casual than it had seemed at the time. Maybe he was simply polite or oblivious or self-assured. Maybe he was a jockey and wanted a whole string of fillies. She hated the image of herself as just another woman he would ride, but after her opening fellatio gambit (damn it to hell) and his adroit avoidance of the photo, she allowed that anything was possible. There was no way to gauge his behavior, though it did give her pause. After all, he had not ignored the photo or reported it to the authorities. He had pursued it. Where did that leave her? she wondered. She smiled, maybe she and Norman really did belong in some sylvan landscape with the rhesus monkeys.

Or maybe he is what he appears—polite, quiet and professorial. This conclusion suited her perfectly, for that is what she imagined she was looking for. Not some fancy champagne and caviar type. *Really, she thought, what is so wrong with a professor of biology wanting champagne and caviar too? Not a damn thing. Then what is so wrong with a professor of biology wearing a beret and wanting fellatio?* Scientific accomplishment was judged by what went on in the lab. What went on in candlelight and later had nothing to do with it. Who knew what scientists were up to in their secret lives? She thought about the scientific meetings she had attended over the years—healthy men and women with shared research interests attending a meeting in a neutral city away from spouses and lovers. Did nothing ever happen between those thousands men and women?

Besides, she had had her own intermittent flings as well. She could no more fault him than she could fault herself.

What bothered her most was his response or lack of it to the photo. He avoided the issue entirely. How could he be so cool when a colleague and a collaborator sent him a picture of a woman going down on a man, unless he was truly dense (unlikely) or lived and played in that world (could such a thing be possible?)—or was embarrassed by the photo too but wanted a relationship with her? In a different state of mind she might have been put off by obtuseness or prurience, but this afternoon she was titillated.

The next morning Agnes called. "How'd it go yesterday?"

"It went just fine. We had a very nice time."

"And what else?"

"What do you mean, 'What else?' We chatted."

"What is this? Adriana. Is this on a need to know basis?"

"No, we're going to have dinner a week from Saturday."

"Where? Did he say?"

"Dinner." *No need to tell Agnes everything,* she thought.

"What about the photo? How did you handle it?"

"Agnes, I'm not going to send you a transcript.

Everything is okay. I'm going to see how it goes. There is nothing more to tell."

"But he likes you?"

"Enough to invest an evening. There is nothing more to tell, honestly. We had coffee at Corrigan's."

"Well what did you wear?"

"That hot pink silk shirt of mine. I thought it looked pretty good on me to tell you the truth."

"Sounds like he did too. Way to go, Adriana."

"Now that things are moving forward, do you want to tell me about the notes in my mailbox?

"Honestly, I've told you all I know. I'm not sending you notes if that's what you're asking. We've been through this."

"All right, for now let's let it go. Thanks for calling. I love you. I especially love you for worrying about your mother."

That evening Adriana called Olympia and shared even the smallest detail.

"And he didn't say anything about the photo?"

"Nothing, as we were getting ready to leave, though, he said he had two questions, one was if I would like to have dinner with him a week from Saturday, and the other he ducked. Maybe that's what was on his mind, the photo, I mean."

"You can be sure it's on his mind. How could it not be?" Olympia said. "Turn things around for a second and suppose he sent you a picture of a man with a beret performing cunnilingus."

"Jesus, Olympia, you're worse than my daughter."

"Well, what would you do?"

"I'd duck, and I might run for cover too."

"Of course you would, but you would be intrigued. So what do you think?" Olympia said.

"What do I think? I think I'll go out with him. Actually as I've told you, we're not going out. He is going to cook for me at his place. It might be a come-on, but . . ."

"But, nothing. Isn't that what you want?"

"But he mentioned the restaurants are so noisy we wouldn't be able to talk."

"Okay, a suggestion or two from the novelist who has women going out with men all the time. Make a hair appointment for next Saturday. Young people may think it's chic to let their roots show, but not at our age. You want to look elegant, in a word 'expensive.' Wear the diamond studs your mother gave you and your simple black dress—it's slimming on you—and low heels. He's short and you're going to be at home. And a jazzy pin of some sort, something that says I'm expensive but fun, a bit zany. I'm not sure what. And nice underwear—black. I know you don't think it should go that far, but just in case."

"Thanks, Olympia, I'm not sure about the pin, but I'll figure something out."

Adriana was happy to be invited to his place. She was not entirely sure whether it really was about the noise or a way to impress her with his cooking or a contrivance to allow her to see his personal side or an adroit prelude or all of these things. They all appealed to her. And there was no denying that going to his house would allow her to do some sleuthing too. Just what was his relationship with Beverly Ardmore? Adriana could practice a little forensic science while at Norman's. She contemplated the likelihood of finding a cosmetic case with mascara in a bathroom closet or perhaps only a comb. That would tell her something. Maybe there was a woman's umbrella in the front coat closet.

That Saturday when she and Norman climbed the steps of his brownstone and he opened the door, she got a surprise. She had been imagining an updated Victorian motif—something stodgy with dark floors and woodwork, heavy woven rugs in deep browns or maybe frayed orientals. But the house was full of light. The floors were steamed beech and the walls a soft white, the ceilings coffered. In the living room the fireplace was marble with a mottled bluish cast. The sofa and chairs were delicious, the sofa done in a chocolate corduroy and the chairs upholstered in fun patterns and black leather. The color came from the wall art—a stunning collection of colorful prints that might be Joseph Albers, and a maroon rug under the coffee table.

"Norman, where did this come from?"

"Biotech. I was part of a startup that got bought for our intellectual property before we went public."

"What was it?"

"You wouldn't have heard of it. I developed some novel approaches to protein anticoagulants. And well, I grew up poor as I mentioned, I mean not so poor that we didn't eat or I had no shoes but poor enough that it was rare for us to do anything. The only way I got to see the Eagles play was by selling hotdogs. And when I made some money, I decided to spend a little."

"More than the money. How did you learn to do this? They don't teach this in graduate school, at least not where I went."

"It's like anything else, you learn."

"I didn't think I was coming to James Bond's for dinner." Then she regretted saying it. It reminded her of Pussy Galore.

"Here, let me take your coat."

They settled in the kitchen. She sat on a stool at a center island while Norman uncorked a bottle of champagne. The loudness of the pop started them both. "It's in keeping with the French theme." He laughed. "The whole thing is so preposterous that the only thing to do is to go with it. Just a second." He put on an Edith Piaf CD. "Okay, it's a little corny, but there's also Brie and a baguette for appetizers. And stuffed mushroom caps."

"And you know how to do this?" she asked

"Go to the store and buy champagne and put it in the fridge? Pick up Brie and make stuffed mushroom caps? Yeah, I do. It's not as hard as it seems. You get in your car and turn on the ignition . . ."

She started to laugh. "Stop, or I'll have champagne coming out of my ears. Okay, I get it."

He looked at her and raised his glass. "To merriment."

And they both took a long swallow.

Dinner was to be simple, Halibut with rosemary,

grilled asparagus, rice with almond slivers, and a salad—already made and chilling in the refrigerator. As he worked, they chatted.

"You're very good at domesticity, even the fresh daffodils in the vase by the front door." "You have to be if you live alone, and I have for a long time. Harriet and I have been divorced for almost twenty years."

"And you have never lived with anybody?"

"I've had relationships, of course, but we always had separate households and spent time at one place or the other. It seems to have worked. And you?"

"About the same. After Agnes's father and I divorced, we sold the house, and I bought the place I'm in now—and lived alone. But well, I, ah, enough said. I had my own place. And the pictures over there, who are they?" She carried her champagne flute across the room and looked at a collection of framed pictures on the counter.

"Well, one's of me and my brother Jan when we were a lot younger."

"Yes, you can see the resemblance."

"And my parents, they have both passed away."

"What did your dad do?"

"When he worked, that is when he wasn't drinking, he was a merchant seaman. We didn't see a lot of him. Mostly my mother supported us. She was a licensed practical nurse."

"Sorry, I'm curious, and these two here?" She held up two frames.

"The one with the young man and woman with backpacks is my older son Norm and his girlfriend. He's a resident on the west coast. And the other is Mark and his girlfriend in Cancun."

Norman turned to preparing the halibut, and for a moment she was lost in her thoughts. Seems pretty normal to me. Smart, good taste, divorced, a sense of humor, two grown kids and an endowed chair here at Harvard. Oh, there was the problem of Beverly, but maybe Olympia was right: she could just knee cap her if she got in the way. Hard working and honest. And kinky enough or lacking in judgment enough not to toss a fellatio photo that showed up anonymously in his mailbox. It didn't add up. *Maybe,* she thought, *life never added up.* When you thought you understood something, maybe that was the time to realize things can't be as straight forward as they seem.

"Can I freshen your champagne? Dinner should be ready in five or ten minutes."

Without waiting for an answer, he refilled her glass.

"You're trying to ply me with drink."

"I'll bet you are many things, but you have never struck me as pliable."

"And the gift for words and puns, were does that come from?"

"A gene I cloned some years ago," he said. "It was unintentional, a spin-off from another project. Don't look so puzzled, Adriana. You already know about it."

"Ah, I do? Well, refresh my memory."

"It's the merriment gene."

There was noise at the window. A mix of small hail and corn snow was pelting the glass.

"A good night to be in," he said. "Look, we have a decision to make."

She looked at him. What was he driving at? A good night to be in. Was this the come-on? Was this how he did it?

"What's that?"

He caught the wariness in her voice.

"We've come to the end of the bottle. Should I open another bottle of champagne for dinner or the Sancerre I have chilling."

Her face filled with relief.

"I think the wine. Any more fizz and I'll start banging against the windows."

She excused herself to go to the powder room. She reapplied her lipstick, a shade of peach that worked well with her complexion and eyes, and straitened and smoothed her dress. A last look in the mirror, a last pressing of her lips to even her lipstick, a last assessment—not bad all things considered. She paused. *A little espionage,* she thought. She checked the medicine cabinet and the vanity drawers. Nothing. Of course, not. If Beverly had left anything at his place, it would be in the master bath or his closet, not the power room. Adriana would save that for a future visit.

Then she was sitting at the dining room table, looking across at his warm face with its slight droop anticipating jowls and its crinkled laugh lines at the eyes.

"You know," she said, "you are very polite and attentive, in fact almost courtly. You haven't mentioned the photo I sent you. It felt so out of character for me. I shouldn't have done it. I'm a bit embarrassed. No, more than a bit."

"I didn't know what to say, so I thought to wait and see how things played out. When it came, my first thought was to throw it out. One gets lots of junk in the mail, crank calls, emails from all manner of people. But something grabbed my gut and told me to respond. Maybe it was curiosity or prurience or some unconscious wish to be embarrassed or humiliated. I can't say. I thought, if the person—for really at that point I didn't even know it was a woman—if the person wants to meet in broad daylight in a public place, why not? If it seems risky or there is the possibility of entrapment—and this assumes that I would have been wise enough to recognize entrapment—I would back off. I told you I had a private school education and went to Brown, but the streets of South Philly are in my bones. I figured I could handle it."

"But what about the beret? Did you feel targeted or stalked?"

"I thought maybe it was someone who knew me and was sending a message of some sort. I didn't believe it was coincidence. It was definitely not chance. I realized that the photo might have been sent maliciously, but I didn't think so. I can't tell you exactly why." She watched him lean forward. He had the earnest, inquisitive look of a schoolboy. "So was I targeted? Where did you get the photo? Before you answer, I want to say part of me, a large part of me, is happy that you sent it. When one works with colleagues, often one sees only a monochromatic picture, grays and halftones really. Not the brightness of those daffodils you mentioned in the kitchen. The photo is helping to dispel that."

"I shouldn't have sent the photo, but I'm glad I did . . . ." Adriana fell silent. She looked toward the window, which was noisy with drumming snow. Somehow she hoped it would help her with a way forward. Then she scanned the dining room, again hoping for a sign. In a decisive gesture, she brought her lips together, and pressed peach on peach.

"It is only complicated," she continued, "if we make it so. It is true that I have a lot to ask you about who you are and about you and Beverly Ardmore, whether you are still seeing her. And I am sure you have a lot to ask me. We hardly know each other beyond molecular biology and protein chemistry. So I am going make a suggestion, actually I going to ask a favor of you, one that will feel odd in the modern world in which we try not to have double standards for men and women. I am going to ask your indulgence. Let's roll the scene back a hundred years, maybe more, to a time when a woman had secrets she didn't necessarily share with her admirers or her lovers, when there was more mystery as you say, when liaisons were more clandestine. So I am going to ask for your indulgence around the photo, that on a night when the world is being assaulted by the elements and we are here in this warm, bright room, in each other's company, that you suspend the present and allow me to invoke the privilege of a lady."

IX. When Shall These Three Meet Again

Florentino had plunked his bar down in the Montrose section of Houston and called it Bar Antofagasta after his hometown, and if the drenching humidity of August had nothing to do with the bone dry landscape of the Chilcan city, it did not matter. Air conditioning wrung out the water, and bright posters caught the bare hills that sloped through the cool desert city and down to the Pacific. The bar could have been anywhere, a purely synthetic creation that the proprietor, here as elsewhere in the modern world, confected to evoke another place and time.

And in that regard Bar Antofagasta was the perfect spot for me as I thought back on my perplexing trip to Boston with Henrietta. I took a swallow of my pisco sour and pushed it aside. What had happened there? Months later I still had no idea. The three young women—Henrietta, Diana, and Agnes—had shorted out my emotional circuitry. A few days in their presence and my motherboard was toast.

Henrietta, I understood well enough, or at least I thought I did. But maybe it was only because a while back she had wandered into the bar and sought me out under circumstances that had seemed possible if improbable. And having lived with her here in Houston for a time, I mistook familiarity for understanding.

The chemistry between us was instant and overwhelming. By what seemed pure chance, I had acquired a good-looking, intelligent young woman as my live-in muse. I'll be the first to admit my writing improved at once. I jettisoned my extravagant descriptions. My sentences toughened. I took chances and explored my ghosts.

When I met Henrietta, I was working on a book-length poem. The impetus was an unpleasant incident that occurred in here one night when a biker came in spoiling for a fight. He was a mean son of a bitch almost the size of an NFL tackle. He called himself Achilles Peleuson. I should have held my tongue, but I said, "That can't possibly be your real name." A crazed look came over him. He pulled me from my chair and shoved me against the bar. Somehow I was able to back him down—but at the cost of begging for mercy.

I swore to get even. My absurd idea of revenge was to write about the incident, and with a preposterous sense of retribution I chose to compose an epic poem. Surely iambic pentameter would put a bully with the gall to call himself Achilles Peleuson in his place. I was surprised how well the poem idea worked, but as I read over a draft, I saw that what I had written had the punch of a fading bantamweight. Parts of it were awful.

Henrietta watched me struggle, and one day as we walked to Café Apollo, she said, "A.E., stop. Let's go back and get it."

"Get what?"

"Your manuscript, the thing you're calling *Achilles in Houston* or maybe *The Houstiliad*. Maybe I can help. We'll look at it over coffee."

And that's how it began. Soon we were reading it aloud together, sometimes at Café Apollo, but mostly here in a corner of Bar Antofagasta. The odd part is that beyond reading aloud, she said very little. Her mere presence informed my work. I made good progress. New sections got written rapidly with a fluency I had never had before. I could hear her composing entire sections in my head. It seemed as if I were transcribing her dictation. Whatever I heard was always stunningly better than anything I could have written on my own. From then on I was under her spell. Whatever my outward appearance, inside I groveled at her feet.

I felt compelled to show my appreciation by dedicating the poem to her in mock heroic verse:

Most of the ritual, most of the slaughter
I owe the narrator of *The Lobsterman's Daughter.*
I take no credit as the deft inventor
of this story propelled by muse and mentor.
The author's debt must surely harken
back to the pith of Henrietta Markham.

Doubtless these lines will improve once she has read them.

Henrietta's undergraduate advisor had invited her back to Harvard to participate in a daylong symposium on emerging women writers. We were welcome to stay with Olympia, and the night before she planned a small dinner for us to meet two young women. Her note said, "The dinner is for you and your friend A.E. to meet Diana Endecott and Agnes Lubeck, whose acquaintances I believe you will come to value. Diana is a playwright and Agnes a neuroscience graduate student at MIT, her best friend and the daughter of my best friend Adriana. I am sending videos of Diana's two plays, *Disraeli's Apricot Tree* and *Bach Among the Pitcher Plants*, by way of further introduction. I hope you find them as exciting as I did."

I did, but not in the sense Olympia meant. Watching Diana's plays with Henrietta stirred a gust of desire that blew out of the recesses of my unconscious and into my life. And when I met Diana and Agnes over dinner at Olympia's, the gust turned into a category five storm that raged and battered my imagination—and, in the end, almost swept me out to sea.

Disraeli's Apricot Tree captivated me. I sat with Henrietta watching and thinking, My God, what an imaginative young woman Diana must be. She had put the most provocative questions in the mouths of three young women in apricot colored body suits. What did the proper, stuffy prime minister think about Dostoyevsky's *The Brothers Karamazov*? That was the premise of the play. The answer is plenty. Try to imagine a nineteenth-century Victorian politician and novelist dealing with the depravity and competing lusts of Fyodor and his son Dmitri for a marvelous femme fatale. Then try to imagine a young woman imagining it, and you will immediately see why I was enthralled. Full disclosure here, in high school I was as taken with Grushenka as Fyodor and Dmitri were. I was wired into the plot of the play. It was as if the three young women who writhed—and believe me, that is the correct word—on stage in body suits were calling specifically to me.

And who was the master puppeteer who made young women dance her message? Of course I became obsessed by Diana. There was a droll aspect to the play as well. It was a sheer act of imaginative chutzpa to ask Disraeli to speculate on a book which he could not have read since it appeared in Russian in the last few months of his life. How could I not be intrigued?

I won't try your patience by summarizing *Bach Among the Pitcher Plants* in detail. But perhaps a few vignettes. The video begins with an introduction by Diana—she appears sitting on a high stool in a black turtleneck and hoop earrings, legs crossed provocatively, offering a wry smile. Her acknowledgment caught my attention: "I owe much of the material in this play to my best friend Agnes Lubeck. She is a biologist and a very spiritual person who spent a summer collecting insects in a bog filled with pitcher plants. It was she who imagined that pitcher plants could be Bach's pipe organ. So this play is hers as much as mine. I dedicate it to her."

Now Agnes was in the picture. What kind of young woman scientist feels the spirituality of Bach in nature? Someone I also wanted to know, that's who. It's not difficult to sense the spiritual in nature. The romantic poets are filled with such conceits. But the specificity of the vision and the imaginative way in which Diana developed it were a world apart from the God-in-nature crowd.

About halfway through the play there is a brief, mostly deleted scene that shot my testosterone levels past Pluto and into outer space. The scene opens with four male and four female actors dressed completely in black in minimal lighting. As we watch, suddenly

Diana herself dances into the scene. She is completely naked. The video shows just an instant of her and then cuts to the next scene. It is expertly edited to show her lithe, supple body moving gracefully among the actors. What can I say? Men are prisoners of their hormones. I sat next to Henrietta, my arm around her, feeling the length of her leg against mine and longing for Diana. One has to have a sense of humor about such things. Who says men are poor multitaskers?

The video had another salacious, if puzzling, aspect. Toward the end there was an incongruous bit filled with sexual innuendo about Michelangelo. I didn't understand how it related to the play, but it clearly had something to do with the well-known observation that the sculptor's statue of David left him underendowed.

Henrietta had a more troubling side that I did not give much credence to initially. One morning a few days after we met and she moved in, we were having coffee. She gave me what was then her current draft of *The Lobsterman's Daughter*. I found the novel remarkable, especially from someone so young. It was also very dark. I was not prepared for a story of murder and deceit coursing through five generations of a Maine family—one that the protagonist claimed was her own. The approach was unsettling because Henrietta Markham, the author, all but effaced the line between author and narrator by calling her "Henrietta Markham." I worried, yet we continued to get along well and work together on my Achilles project.

Then a set of improbable deaths rattled our neighborhood. One morning my next-door neighbor found her two cats dead in her yard. They seemed unmarked and uninjured. I felt sorry for Rowena but passed it off as coincidence. A few days later the Swanson's tabby died. Again, no marks, no sign of foul play. *Worrisome*, I thought. I tried unsuccessfully to puzzle through the problem. The conundrum hit home when a feral cat showed up dead in my front yard. The mysterious deaths of four cats and the possibility of satanic rituals got the police involved.

They tracked the deaths to antifreeze-laced cat foot set out in small plastic cups. They had no leads. Normally I would have done nothing, but reading Henrietta's novel had raised my concern. I went out back to my work shed and checked my own container of antifreeze. It was full, but the seal was broken. I had no recollection of opening it. Maybe my memory was faulty. Or perhaps someone had removed antifreeze and replaced it with water. It was certainly possible, but I wasn't worried enough to fill out a police report and submit my container for analysis.

I could not shake my intuition that Henrietta, for all her vibrancy, had a dark side. Only later—after I had been to Boston—when my mind was released from house arrest, did I fully grasp that she and the other two young women had incarcerated my judgment.

All I could do was hope that if her evil filtered into me, my own darkness would be an imaginative darkness, one that I could confine to my fiction. Hers, I worried, might spill over into her life and bring with it the possibility of rage, mayhem, dismemberment, or even murder. Had she or could she infect me with an infernal virus that could sap my strength and allow the blackness to reach up from below and drag me into the swamps? I thought not, but then I had no idea.

Something happened that should have left no doubt. One afternoon we found ourselves in a convenience store, and she whispered to me to slip a package of double A batteries into my pocket. I looked at her and told her she was crazy. She said, "Do it." And you know what—I did it. I was so totally under her spell that I would shoplift something of little value that I had no need of.

Still, I stayed with her. I loved her, and I was dependent on her. I had a craving that overrode any fear for my physical self. I was addicted—the smoker who could not stop, the alcoholic who must have another drink, the uscr dependent forever on his fix. In the final analysis it was chemistry—neurochemistry and emotional chemistry—that bonded us. And I was wholly devoted to her. Those lovely brown eyes, flickering and laughing, obscured the darkness. We sat at Café Apollo or Bar Antofagasta and talked about poetry and books, love—and Lord knows what else. If Achilles Peleuson had swaggered over to our table, I would have stood and faced him down.

Then Florentino came by. He was in a chatty mood. "Want company?" he said. "I'm buying. I've got to tell you about the strangest thing that happened last night. You're not going to believe it."

"Can I take a rain check, amigo? I'm in the middle of something."

"It doesn't look like it. You didn't bring your laptop."

"Well, I am. I'm trying to think through the next part of my book," I lied.

"Maybe tomorrow?"

"Sure. We'll see how it goes."

Anyway, Henrietta and I flew to Logan for the symposium. I looked forward to meeting Olympia but especially Diana and Agnes. At Olympia's, I paid the driver, and we carried our roll-ons up the wooden steps of her porch.

The place was almost what I had pictured—an old wood-frame house, slightly tumbling, with a large front porch and third floor gables, all of it in need of paint—the cream-colored wood siding and the navy trim. And Olympia looked much as she did on the dust jacket of *Under My Skin*. She was handsome more than pretty, with clean features and intelligent blue eyes—a penetrating almost husky blue, partially bred out by a lighter, kinder essence. For someone her age she had kept her figure. Not a bad package, especially when you tossed in her well-regarded novels.

"Ooooh, careful, Henrietta, you'll squeeze the life out of me with a hug like that," Olympia said.

Suddenly we heard barking and looked down.

There, squirming at our shoes, was a frisky, young dachshund.

"Oh, Pepin, quiet. Hang on a second," and she shooed the dachshund to the back door. "How was the flight?"

"Okay, except the plane was a little late leaving Houston. A.E., I'd like you to meet Olympia, my teacher and mentor. Olympia, this is my special friend, A.E."

"Nice to meet you. I've heard so much about you from Henrietta. And thanks for putting us up. Thanks too for the videos. They helped me get a flavor of Diana's talent. They are quite accomplished for a beginning playwright."

Olympia had put us in a room at the top of the stairs. I excused myself and carried the roll-ons up the bare treads. It was spacious, wallpapered in a cobalt blue hyacinth pattern and overlooking the street. I flopped down on the four-poster bed—*doesn't squeak, that's good*, I thought. I came down and sat with them over pinot grigio and listened to them reminisce.

"You know that a while back when you sent me the revisions of your novel from Barcelona with no way to contact you," Olympia said, "I thought you might have done something drastic."

"Didn't we talk about this at Thanksgiving? I went to a retreat house, part of a monastery, to meditate. A mistake. I am too much a woman of action for silence. Then I traveled, ended up in Texas on my way to Mexico, and met A.E. You know the rest. I decided to stay. I've added a bit to the novel. It's a short coda about my time with A.E. in Texas. You've seen it. I think the piece really works. It ties the book together."

"I'm thinking you probably ran it by A.E."

"She did and I liked it. The ending forces the reader to think about the creative process, where fiction comes from."

Olympia guessed correctly that we were famished and ushered us to the kitchen table where she had laid out a deli lunch. As we ate, she summarized the program for tomorrow. The morning would be devoted to short readings of juried fiction and poetry by Harvard women undergraduates, many of whom were in her writing workshops. She had hoped that President Faust would speak at the luncheon, but she had had to back out at the last moment because of other commitments. Lydia Zenhauser, principal of the Zenhauser Literary Agency in New York, had agreed to step in. The afternoon was Henrietta, the poet Nancy Delgado, and the playwright Sally Goodman Cohen, followed by a panel discussion.

"After watching the videos with A.E., I'm wondering why you didn't select Diana to read. And she's so glamorous."

"Well, the plays are not published," Olympia said. "I didn't think I could go with someone who didn't have anything published or staged by a major company. I could justify you because when I planned the symposium, *The Lobsterman's Daughter* had been accepted for publication. And I couldn't choose two of my own students."

"Is Diana upset that she's not included? I know I might be," Henrietta said.

"No, I think she understands. Besides, I've heard she's working on something more substantial. Maybe she'll tell us more at dinner. Anyway, I thought you might like a little time alone with her. I've got her cell if you want to grab coffee with her before dinner."

"Yeah, that would be great."

Olympia pointed her cell phone screen toward Henrietta, who tapped the number in and sent a text.

Henrietta paused and asked if it was all right for her to leave Olympia and me alone. Then, somewhat embarrassed by her phrasing, she added that she didn't want to abandon us. I told her not to worry, that we could take care of ourselves.

"One more thing," Olympia said, "after the conference people are invited back here for wine and heavy hors d'oeuvres."

"So, just to clarify, the program features emerging women writers, but everyone is invited, right?" I said.

"Yes, of course, men, if that's what you mean. I've already reserved a seat for you right up front."

Henrietta got a text from Diana inviting her to meet at Café Algiers. She was bringing her friend Agnes.

"Ah, there is one more thing I need to warn you to about," Olympia said. "Actually, it's silly. It's not at all necessary, but, well, you should know that Diana and Agnes, in addition to being interested in men, are, well, the best way to put it is interested in each other."

"Hey, no problem, I'm totally cool with that," and she headed out the door.

I confess to being titillated. My French is weak. What comes after *ménage-à-trois*? I wondered.

Olympia and I sat in her comfortable living room over another glass of pinot grigio. We chatted about her new book. I had read *Under My Skin* and praised her narrative style and her intrepid honesty in telling the backstory. The conversation went on politely—her other books, my books, Italy, and especially Rome—and eventually found its way to Henrietta.

I talked about our relationship and recounted her help with my Achilles poem. "I have met few young people with her combination of maturity and brilliance . . . ."

"And? As you spoke, I saw something else in your face. Tell me."

"Now I know why you write so well. So let me see if I can say this without sounding overly critical or judgmental. I sometimes worry there is a dark side to Henrietta, to be frank, an unappealing side." I watched her eyes—the mix of husky loyalty and resolve and their kindness. "I guess I worry about what she might be capable of."

Olympia gave me a look that I interpreted as sympathetic. "Go on. What happened?"

"Nothing really. Well . . ." and the story spilled out—the poisoned cats, my suspicion that someone had removed antifreeze from my shed, my complete lack of evidence tying Henrietta to the deaths. I mentioned the double A batteries and the shoplifting.

Olympia was ashen. She gulped down the rest of her pinot grigio, got up, brought the bottle to the coffee table, and refilled her glass. I didn't have to ask her why she was so shaken.

"I need to tell you what happened last Thanksgiving," she said. All her friends knew about the incident, but she had not been very public about her concerns. I didn't quite follow. She said that the day after Thanksgiving her poodle Charlemagne, whom she dearly loved, died under mysterious circumstances. And like me, she couldn't put aside her concern that Henrietta might be involved.

Now I was stoned faced. Without asking, she refilled my wineglass.

At Thanksgiving she had had a group of friends over. It was nothing unusual—just friends, some visiting Brits, and her bother Chandler who was in from Tucson. A few days before, perhaps on that Monday, Olympia got a call from Henrietta saying that she was in town to visit family over the holidays. Could they have coffee? The week was complicated, Olympia explained, but she was welcome to come to Thanksgiving dinner. Henrietta jumped at the chance. When Olympia realized what she had done, she asked why if Henrietta was in town to visit family, she was free that evening. Her answer bothered Olympia. "She said something like, 'My father isn't around, and my mother is a mess. Besides, my twin brothers are dumber than sin. I can't bear the thought of sitting around the dinner table with them. I've got to escape.' And of course, if you think about it," Olympia added, "the description roughly parallels the story of *The Lobsterman's Daughter*."

I agreed. The similarity was striking.

Olympia filled me in. Henrietta ended up coming to dinner. Nothing out of the ordinary happened, at least not at first. For some reason people struggled a bit to make conversation. But it seemed to work. At the end Olympia asked everyone to pitch in to help clean up. During the evening Henrietta had seemed fond of Charlemagne, so she asked her to take the dog out in the backyard to do his business and for a little exercise. When Charlemagne came back in, he seemed too tired for the amount of run around. Olympia worried but thought he would be all right in the morning.

In fact, he wasn't. Olympia awoke to find him dead at the foot of her bed. It was awful. Her brother helped her take Charlemagne to the vet, who did a necropsy. He was almost apologetic: "I can tell you how your dog died, but I can't tell you why."

I asked her what that meant. She enumerated all the things that were not the cause of death. The vet found that Charlemagne died of abdominal hemorrhage, but he couldn't find a cause. There were no ruptured vessels, no tears or puncture wounds, nothing. It was possible that the dog had been accidentally poisoned, but the toxicology was negative. The vet asked about rat poison and said that it can sometimes cause bleeding, but he added that the distribution of the bleeding would have been different. So the rat poison was another blind ally.

Olympia was distraught. "At the time, I was looking for answers. You know how it goes. If you watch detective stories on TV, the inspector always says to someone that they are a suspect because they were the last person to see the victim alive. So I wondered about Henrietta, but honestly until you told me about the cats, I thought it was my own grief speaking. There was no evidence, and no reason to blame her. All evening she had seemed so affectionate with Charlemagne. It was devastating, and I still don't really understand what happened."

"So, Olympia, this is impolitic in the extreme, but it's clear you were deeply suspicious of her. Why did you invite her back for the symposium? Why didn't you cut your losses and move on?"

"Honestly, I really couldn't believe she could do such a thing. And the vet offered no evidence to substantiate her involvement. I couldn't let what felt like irrational fear stand in the way of helping one of my most promising students."

"Now that I have been impolitic," I said, "let me be intrusive as well. Maybe after these few days, the two of us should gently guide her out of our lives."

She let the suggestion slide. I wondered if I could do such a thing.

"Well, if you'll excuse me, I've got to tend to dinner," she said, and I went upstairs to continue working my way through Pope's translation of *The Iliad.*

I heard the doorbell and a moment later the boisterous camaraderie of the three young women. I knew even before I slipped on my shoes and went downstairs that coffee had been a success. Olympia made the introductions.

Diana looked as she did in the video, again the gold hoop earrings and a brown pageboy. What I hadn't appreciated was her quick smile.

"Hello, nice to meet you," she said, "Henrietta has been telling us all about you."

"And?"

"And it's all good. She says that you're a writer too. She mentioned your long poem. We're very curious, Agnes and I." She looked at Agnes with an inquisitive affection, as if to ask approval for being so direct. "We both want to hear about *The Houstiliad.* Is it true that you think of it as "An Iliad for Houston"?

"Well, yes. I know it sounds a little campy, but I do."

"Will you share a few lines with us? The idea doesn't seem campy at all, more like inventive."

"Thanks, maybe in a while, maybe after dinner."

"So, I'm Agnes," and she extended a hand in a gesture that felt both egalitarian and regal. In that instant her presence became very large, so large that no one else was in the room with us. I wasn't sure whether to shake her hand or kiss it. "I'm the odd person out. Four writers and a neuroscientist. It's okay, somebody's got to tend to the circuitry."

"It sounds interesting to me," I said.

"It is. It's really cool," Henrietta said. "She told me all about it at Algiers. She says she uses microelectrodes to record the activity of individual neurons in the brain. Can you even imagine that?"

I said that I couldn't, but then there were a lot of things about Agnes, and Diana too, that I couldn't imagine.

Agnes was nice-looking with lustrous black hair, which she wore pulled back, and inquisitive, intelligent eyes. I wondered if she missed anything. There was a mischievous quality to her face that dared others to best her in her jests and imaginative forays.

Her comment about being the odd person out clearly applied to me as well. I was the only man surrounded by four, successful, attractive women— warriors, in league with one another, I imagined, modern amazons fighting an undefined battle. I felt like a modern sultan, as if I had a seraglio of beautiful, agreeable women to dote on me. Of course, I had nothing of the sort. The women were all their own people, who were only interested in serving me when it served their needs. But for a moment I did feel privileged. And amazed.

I was in an odd state, as if some god were flushing and reflushing my radiator with different fluids that were alternatingly scalding and freezing. I was left with the feeling that nothing made sense and everything did.

Olympia passed round a tray of drinks. I looked at her and took a sip. "High octane, I would say."

"It is. Long Island ice tea seemed a good way to start," she said. "You know, in case there is any ice to be broken."

"Olympia, you'll blow our brains out," Agnes said.

"Just don't tell your mother that here in staid Cambridge I've thrown propriety to the wind. Honestly, wine seemed a bit fussy."

"No, no, it's good," Agnes said.

"Yeah, it's all good," Diana confirmed, and she enslaved me with her gaze. There was no escape.

At the table Olympia sat at the head, Agnes and Diana on one side, and Henrietta and I on the other. It was as if Olympia had three daughters, and

I was a perspective suitor. One daughter was more beautiful than the next. What was I to do? I had no idea, so I mostly listened. The conversation was oddly gracious without cattiness or ribaldry. Yet I was slightly disappointed—honestly, it felt too sanitized as if someone had written a script for a junior high civics class.

Olympia, perhaps as a precautionary measure, had rusticated her dachshund to the backyard. And it seemed that Diana and Agnes were on notice: best behavior for our guests. There were no adoring glances or holding hands. And no one overdid the booze. On the surface everyone was cloyingly polite. Yet Diana sent me signifying glances every now and then. And Agnes had a captivating, prank-threatening smile. Henrietta missed nothing. Under the table she put her hand on my thigh as if to steady me against the invaders.

I felt like Paris before the start of the Trojan War. Was I to judge whether Henrietta, Diana or Agnes would be awarded the Golden Apple? Certainly not, I hoped.

"A.E., I want to call the question," Diana said. I had a momentary start—perhaps I would be called on to render an impossible judgment. "You have seen the video of my plays and read Henrietta's novel, and, of course, Olympia's latest, for sure. But we don't know your work at all."

I relaxed.

"Yeah," chimed in Agnes. "She's right, give us the bit of *The Houstiliad* you promised."

"Okay, but only a taste," and I went upstairs to get the manuscript.

I could hear tittering as I left. Was it their turn to have sport with me?

Diana shouted after me, "Hey, A.E., we've showed you ours, now you show us yours."

I returned a minute later. "So it's actually a novel in verse, an *Iliad* for Houston."

"Does Houston really need its own *Iliad*?" Agnes asked.

"Well, I don't know, but it's going to get one."

Everyone laughed.
"Here is the opening action of Chapter I which is called 'Mayhem in the Park.'"

Achilles, haunched by his bike and sidecar,
the white macaw, Patroclus, on his shoulder—
two omnivores intent on prey—the man,
his bird now scan the scene for strollers, drunks.
Their hopes for booty fade as darkness nears,
but twilight's maw disgorges easy marks.
"Say, Mister, can you take a shot of us?"
His wife obliges, hands her iPhone to him.
"Do it. Do it," and Patroclus whistles.
The hauncher straightens, "Cheese, eternity
should remember happy, smiling faces."

Complete silence. It felt like forever.
Finally Diana said, "Wow, A.E. it's good, but who would have guessed your darkness? I don't even want to think about what happens to this guy and his wife. You seemed so normal, so straightforward, so positively Midwestern. And Patroclus is his bird, very clever."

"I don't think Homer would mind being ripped off with stuff like this," Agnes said.

Yet everyone seemed uncomfortable, as if I were some sort of mass murderer who had been invited to dinner by mistake, as if I might drag one of them down the backstairs and into the yard. I smiled, what else could I do?

"Like all of you," I said, "I write what I have to. But if you doubt me, ask Henrietta. It's only on the page, and what's on the page, stays on the page."

"Amen, to that," said Henrietta.

"I guess, I have to be the voice of experience here," Olympia said. "Sometimes real life intervenes, and as you know, it can be very ugly."

I was not prepared that evening for the young women who had embedded themselves in my unconscious to analyze me. I had thought fantasy was a one-way street: you imagined something and got to keep what your unconscious concocted. Who knew that a phantom could spring from your head and critique you? Damn, I said to myself, who knew that these phantoms could be judgmental and stingy in their regard for their charge?

After tea and coffee, Diana and Agnes got up to leave. For an instant the three of us were alone. Henrietta had gone to the powder room and Olympia to the kitchen. What happened next should only be written by someone using a pseudonym. Agnes came up behind me and Diana in front of me. They came together and squeezed me between their bodies. Simultaneously Agnes whispered in one ear and Diana in the other, "You are ours for eternity." Then they laughed, shouted goodbye to the others, and instantly vanished out the front door.

When Olympia and Henrietta reappeared, I said nothing. I steered the conversation toward small talk and thanked Olympia for putting the dinner together. I mentioned how polite and cordial she and Diana and Agnes had been. No, more than cordial, welcoming. I stood in the front hall trying to appear placid and contained, but after my moment alone with Diana and Agnes, my insides heaved like a knot of churning snakes. I feared Olympia or Henrietta could sense the quivering pit in my gut and intuit my captivity. I wondered what Olympia was thinking after hearing the beginning of *The Houstiliad*. Did she feel that she had confided her fears about Henrietta to someone who might be Henrietta's fellow traveler—Lynette Squeaky Fromme and Charles Manson do Cambridge?

Henrietta and I went up to bed and lay talking in the dark.

"It was hard to miss," she said. "I don't know if you were more taken with Diana or Agnes."

"Diana."

"Now what?"

"Now what, what?" I said.

"Now what are we going to do with Agnes?"

"What are we going to do with Diana is an equally good question."

"Well, A.E., I am calling the shots, and I vote for keeping them both."

I was glad it was dark. I didn't want to try to read her face or have her read mine. So I said, "Just what are you proposing?"

"I'm not proposing anything. That's the point. I am Henrietta Markham, period. I have no special powers. It's not as if I were Eris, the goddess of discord, who threw the golden apple into the wedding and made Paris chose among Athena, Aphrodite, and Hera."

I ignored the inconsistency—some days I worried that she could be the goddess of discord. I was perplexed, but I knew I would not get an answer I could comprehend for any question I could imagine asking. So I did what any reasonable, reasoning man would have done. I segued.

"Speaking of the judgment of Paris," I said, "I want to read you a short passage I came across this afternoon in Book III of Pope's translation." I snapped on the light. "Listen to this:"

Thus having spoke, th' enamour'd Phrygian boy
Rush'd to the bed, impatient for the joy.
Him Helen follow'd slow with bashful charms,
And clasp'd the blooming hero in her arms.

"The Phrygian boy," I explained, "is Paris. It's quite beautiful, don't you think? Venus, Aphrodite, delivered Helen to Paris as the prize for his awarding her the Golden Apple. The lines are from just after Venus saves him from Helen's husband Menelaus. She arranges a tryst for Paris with Helen. I know what I'm about to say is pure sentimentality, but in some ways I feel that the gods have delivered you to me. I am grateful for that."

"Turn off the light, and let me show you how much I love you. We'll see if Helen has anything on me. Let's make that old Trojan tart jealous of us."

Later after Henrietta was asleep, I lay awake in the dark struggling to make sense of the three young women—what they were doing in my thoughts and in my life. It was no use. They were so entangled within me it was impossible to dislodge them. And I had no idea what Henrietta meant by "I am calling the shots," and, worse, no way of finding out. I had no choice but to wait for tomorrow and see what would happen.

At lunch the next day after the morning session, I listened to Lydia Zenhauser's talk. Her remarks must have been sobering to the young writers. The literary world is a tough place to live, she said, and even if one is lucky enough to find a good agent, however important that is, it's only a beginning. Be prepared for rejection, she added. If they were serious about being writers, they should work on their craft and persevere.

We reassembled in the auditorium for the afternoon session. Although Olympia had, in fact, saved me a place up front, I preferred to be in the back. I sat in the last row between Diana and Agnes. I supposed they were silently chortling to each other that they again had me wedged between them. I was certain Henrietta's reading would be superb, but my attention was elsewhere. My overwhelming memory of that moment is how much I was distracted by the energy radiating off the bodies of the other two women.

Olympia introduced Nancy Delgado and later Sally Goodman Cohen. After their readings and a few questions, Olympia turned to Henrietta. She was an exciting young writer whose first novel *The Lobsterman's Daughter* had just appeared. Henrietta got up and smiled. She looked attractive and appropriate for the occasion in a white blouse, open at the neck, and a modest long black skirt that was not too formfitting.

Henrietta stood confidently before the audience. "I want to thank the organizers and especially Professor Olympia Breathwaite for inviting me to read this afternoon. It's been a lovely day, and I have the challenge of keeping you awake after a full morning and afternoon of readings."

I looked around. Yes, Zenhauser had stayed and seemed to be paying attention.

"So I want to say a few words about the book and then read a short section. First, I need to be up

front about something. No matter what you read in
this book—whether it is the individual sections of
the main narrative or the parts that take place in
Barcelona or Houston at the end—it is all fiction. I
do not have a Maine family. It is a pure creation of
my imagination."

In the back I winced. I certainly hoped so.

She explained that she had learned from
Professor Breathwaite's classes that almost any point
of view or any conceit can be useful, provided it moves
the narrative forward and holds the reader's attention.
That was how she came to "Henrietta Markham" as
the protagonist of the novel. It seemed the best way
to give the story immediacy. She emphasized that she
was not the character, Henrietta Markham, any more
than Dante, the poet, was Dante, the protagonist, in
The Divine Comedy. She was raised in greater Boston,
she said, and added that she was not a violent person.
"The fashion today is to blur the line between fact
and fiction, but that is not the case with this novel.
It is all fiction."

Then she read a brief passage in one of the voices
she conjures in the novel—that of the protagonist's
father, Hiram Markham.

Hiram Markham

I don't know when exactly I came to consciousness. It
must have been gradual, the seeping in of awareness
that with time congealed to clarity. At first the only
certainty was the blackness. Slowly I realized I
was on my back, wedged into a box with a wicked
strut digging into my spine that made movement
unthinkable. It didn't matter. I couldn't turn left or
right. There was a slight flex to my legs, which forced
my knees against the top of the container. I pushed
forward hard with the toes of my sneakers, but they
met an unyielding solidity. I ran my fingers along the
side—wood, wooden slats. Some sort of crate. It was
becoming clearer. The distinctive blend of smells—
diesel, sawdust and crustacean—confirmed what I

have known for some years: my sons are what my grandfather, the first Hiram Markham, would have called *mumsers*, bastards, rotten bastards. They crated me in our work shed. Caged me. Strange what comparisons roil the puzzling mind. I thought of the chain-linked madness of Hephaestus and the score he settled. Poor lame bastard. How justified was his net. Aphrodite and Ares were getting it on, cuckolding him, and he settled a score. Enough said. But me—I have done nothing to those twins, nothing but nurture them.

They must have slipped something into my beer at dinner and carried me out here. I was in one of the big ones that we had built specially for the new lobster boat some years back. Oversized with oversized struts to withstand the heavy seas. With the fall in prices we hadn't used them recently. These pots were stacked in the back of the shed. Or at any rate all of them had been until, I guessed, last night. They had stuffed me in like an oversized lobster and left me. I could feel where one of the slats was splintered and wearing. One of the newer traps, I imagined. What else could it be? They were the only ones big enough. It was still pitch black. But of course it would be in the shed. Its few windows were grimed over and obscured by gear. Morning would come late here. What were they thinking? I have never even raised my voice. Dinner had seemed okay. No one said much—not my sons, not the one wife who was there. We sat and ate in silence and half-listened to the jabber of the TV. I remember the beginning of a movie. A high-speed chase, the cops trading shots with some guys in a pickup. And that's it. And now, at whatever time it is, I am their prisoner.

No, no way they could have put me into one of the traps. There's no lid, only the netted hole in the side for the lobsters to climb through. Can't be. They must have built one special, put me in and nailed it shut. Used old wood. Thrifty bastards. Premeditating sons of bitches. Why would they do that? They planned it. Right under my nose they planned it. Built it. No, they could have pried the slats off the top last

night and put me in. Am I a pagan in my own house,
no better than Queequeg, encoffined by my idiot sons?
Worse, Queequeg's coffin was measured and cut, mine
a slap-dash, ill-fitting affair. Stupid bastards.

There was genuine applause. People seemed to
enjoy it. I glanced at Zenhauser. She was nodding.
Olympia asked if there were any questions.

A largish woman in a black hoody and nose
piercing raised her hand. "Well, it's more of a
comment than a question. This piece of yours doesn't
feel like literary fiction at all. I don't know what it is.
We haven't heard enough, but it feels more like a
mystery or noir genre fiction. For all I know, Dracula
will show up any minute. It didn't do much for me
personally, but maybe I'm a hardliner."

Diana squirmed beside me and then put her
hand on mine. I could feel the tension in her grip.

Henrietta was poised. She thanked the speaker
for her comment and said, "I take your point, and
I agree that in a short segment you can't see the
sweep of the whole work. But think about *The Iliad*,
for example."

People seemed surprised. Most were not thinking
about Homer that afternoon.

"We would all agree that it is literature," she
continued, "but it is filled with brutality, more than
any noir thriller of today. Homer makes Cormac
McCarthy sound sweet. Last night I was reading Book
III in the Pope translation. There is this wonderful
section where Venus has saved Paris from Menelaus's
sword and has delivered him to his own bed. Then
Helen appears in the bedroom. There is spicy talk
about making love. I'm sorry I can't quote it verbatim
for you, but Homer says something about Helen's
bashful charms and that she clasps the blooming
hero in her arms. No one would call *The Iliad* chick
lit, but there it is. Forgive me, life happens."

"Yes, in the back," Olympia said.

Diana was on her feet with a hand-held
microphone. "I think Ms. Markham has been much
too polite. Frankly, the woman's comment is inane.

I'm a playwright, and as she was talking, I was thinking about *Macbeth.* I suppose you could classify it as horror, but that misses the point. Or *Othello* or *Julius Caesar.* Give me a break."

She sat down, and I leaned over and whispered a thank you. I was enveloped by the scent of freshly washed hair and a fragrance I could not identify. *Oh, my,* I thought.

"It's the least I can do for a fellow writer and, I guess, a new friend," she said, bringing her lips so close to my ear I could feel her breath.

I was paralyzed. The scent, which I now identified as lavender, had taken over my brain. I said something that in retrospect seems so ill-phrased and embarrassing that I am ashamed to admit it, "Diana, that was charming, intellectually lithe, almost sisterly."

She said the oddest thing in return. It felt as if she were talking to my unconscious. "I am here for you—that's what I'm here for."

Mercifully, the panel discussion was short. No more than twenty minutes or so. It had been a long day. People were tired, and as so often happens, the authors were better at writing than describing how they wrote.

Hunger. As I watched Olympia's reception unfold, I was surprised. I had expected more gentility in Cambridge, but young and old, undergraduates and superannuated academics participated in a rapacious dismemberment of Olympia's repast. With great vigor the guests forked away most of a sliced ham and a spread of smoked salmon and freely shaved Jarlsberg from a large, rapidly diminishing slab. I smiled to myself. I had thought the literary world inhabited by piranhas, but I had no idea it was literally true.

The students flocked to Henrietta and Diana who stood at opposite ends of the room. Remarkable. They were already role models for the undergraduates. I watched one curly-headed guy wearing a T-shirt that read "Write the Wrongs of the World" chatting earnestly with Henrietta. In a moment of unfair accusation I wondered if she were the best person for him to be talking to. The only thing I was certain of was that she was a brilliant, young writer.

The young people were equally solicitous of Diana, because of her plays, I imagined. A group of men and women were gathered about her, rapt by her every word, but I was too far away to hear. I imagined their fantasies were of two types—the men's were mainly sexual with a minor literary component, and the women's were mostly literary with a latent sexual component. But as I said, I was too far away to hear the conversation. And, by the way, projection is the storyteller's friend.

Olympia was busy entertaining the professors. Who knew? Swapping favors or speaking engagements. Maybe blurbs for upcoming books. I began to feel sorry for myself, disappointed that a network like this was unavailable to me in Houston. But it was all so self-congratulatory. At once I brightened. Did I really want to buy artichoke dip for forty at Whole Foods or listen to windy stories of literary conquest? Mostly imagined literary conquest, I was certain. *No*, I thought, *it was better to have the time to think and write than to pander.* Hustling books is no different from hustling drinks or sex or selling Bibles door to door. Honestly, most nights the conversation here in Bar Antofagasta is more genuine than the BS of the literati and the sycophantic sickos who hang out with them.

Part of me had come to Cambridge to understand its mystique, but at that moment I realized there was none. That is, the mystique was only what others perceived it to be. From the inside, or almost the inside, the cocktail party was as vapid as cocktail parties everywhere. And the symposium? Zenhauser's comments were interesting and Henrietta had read well, but the rest I could have heard in a dozen American cities.

I caught sight of Agnes staring out into the backyard. She seemed at loose ends. She lived in an entirely different world. I wandered over.

"So last night we didn't get a chance to talk. Tell me what you are working on at MIT.

"I'm doing MRI, brain imaging, and behavior. We're trying to track where certain emotions are experienced in the brain—where they live and how they work."

"Forgive me. I know this is naive. But what are some possibilities? I mean, where could emotions live?

"Good question. So think about the brain as a grocery store."

I tried to imagine a little Krogers in my head. She picked up the puzzlement in my face.

"Okay, you know how a grocery store is divided into different sections which serve different functions— say, the meat department or produce or frozen foods?"

I nodded.

"Well, that's just how the brain is. You probably know some of this—that vision is interpreted in the back of the brain and the frontal lobes are involved in executive functions that determine the appropriateness of our actions."

"Sure, at least I think I do."

"Well, we are trying to map the emotions in the same way. The only difference between what I just described and what we do is that our approach is much more fine grained and detailed."

"So I sort of get it. I'm impressed. Sounds interesting and complicated"

"It is, but it's a lot of fun. It's a very competitive field . . . . Look, I was thinking, would you and Henrietta like to come out for pizza and a beer with Diana and me tonight? Nothing fancy, just come and shoot the shit with us."

"Sounds good, but I think we should include Olympia, don't you?"

"You really want the truth? I bet she is dying to unwind a bit and grab a bite alone with my mother Adriana. And here's a guess—the two of you have probably exhausted topics of conversation. Anyway, you and Henrietta would be doing her a favor by giving her a little time off."

"You mean it?"

"Of course. Let me to check it out with her. Trust me."

I watched Agnes make her way across the room. Then the two stood at the dining room table talking, I guessed, about plans for the evening. What came to mind was totally unexpected. Agnes moved as if she were in a protective energy field, as if she existed outside space and time. Yet one more example of how I processed the events of those few days in Cambridge with my heart, not my brain.

Henrietta still had a few students around her. Somehow Olympia's dog had found his way onto a chair next to her. As they chatted, Henrietta stroked the dachshund and bent down occasionally to kiss its upturned belly. Of course, I thought of poor dead Charlemagne and the cats. I watched her for a moment and let it go. After last night, I was a fine one to point an accusing finger.

My three muses—I foolishly supposed the gods had assigned them to me—stood out in this room of talented people. Each radiated excitement and possibility. They were engaged, alive, electric. I was curious to see how our individual needs would unfurl. Or was there only one collective need? I had no idea if our little outing had been prearranged among them or orchestrated by one of them. It didn't matter. I was glad for any intervention that moved the evening in that direction.

People began to drift toward the door. I looked at my watch. Eight o'clock. A little later the four of us helped Olympia clear the table and collect plastic glasses and plates from the living room. I noted that Olympia herself let the dog out. Then we were off— Olympia to meet Adriana and the four of us for pizza.

On the way Agnes suggested we pick up pizza and go back to her place. "It will be quiet, and we can kick back and talk."

As we drove, the young women chatted about the reception, the undergraduates and their needy, eager attempts to understand how Henrietta and Diana had been so successful.

I began to drift. It had been a long day, and I was tired. I had eaten very little at the party, and I could practically taste the pizza Agnes promised. I remembered my student days visiting Rome and the small pizzerias hidden just off the squares. Then my thoughts wandered to the fountains in many of those squares.

I must have nodded off, for soon I could see the three young women dancing in the Trevi Fountain under the watchful eye of Neptune. They glided through the water with indescribable grace in diaphanous gowns that never seemed to wet. I was a prisoner of their allure, swept into the fountain with them. My mind was empty of everything but their primordial beauty. I longed to join hands with them, but as I reached out, they receded. I longed to talk to them, but I found I could say nothing. The three became one as they danced, then three again—as if there were no distinction, as if they were part of one whole. And still I longed for them, to flow into them. I longed to merge with them, to alloy my Self with their Selves.

The fountain grew to a sea—a vast encompassing, unstructured sea—and I was immersed in it, rocked gently by some greater force, which also animated them, yet kept us apart. Diana, Agnes, and Henrietta, so much a part of me, so distant, so unreachable. Then the water became choppy, and a storm seemed to gather on the horizon. They danced toward the thunderheads and I followed.

A loud shrieking, a siren of a different sort, jarred me back to consciousness. A police car passed. We had been driving a while. We were out of Cambridge, on Hanover Street in Boston's North End. I listened as the three of them weighed the merits of thin crust versus thick, more or less tomato sauce, cheese, toppings, ambiance, price. More than the choices, the process interested me. The easy give and take, the collaboration, the melding of personalities, as if the three were a single organism.

Everything is provisional, I thought, *even decisions about where to go for pizza.*

We did not go back to Agnes's. A better plan emerged. We ate pizza on white tablecloths and drank

Chianti in an immaculate trattoria. As I sat looking at them, my dream seemed like a prelude to reality. That evening with the warmth of the restaurant, the posters of Italy, the smell of oregano, rosemary and garlic, I was overcome with the feeling that the women were a part of me, the expression of my feminine, my muses, that they were inexplicably integral to the process of how I was present in the world.

I listened wistfully as the young women planned their futures, which at that moment must have seemed unlimited. And what could I plan? The present. I understood that no one planned the future, all the more so when the final curtain could descend at any moment. The tension between two possibilities was overwhelming and binary—either you had a good day and hoped for one tomorrow, and not much more, or you dissolved into despair, one step closer to death.

I cannot explain any of what happened in Boston. All I can say is that I believed the three had given me what the poet called a moment of glad grace, a magnificent moment, really. How I had the presence to know that they had cast a spell, held me prisoner, and lured me out to sea, I cannot say. In an instant the healing waters they promised could boil with destruction. A seething maelstrom could drag me under. I had held on far too long. I was weak with yearning. I wanted them.

I looked around the bar. It was late, and besides Florentino only a few sleepy patrons remained. I could not tell them these things. I could tell no one.

Guide for Readers and Book Clubs

1. Why is the novel set in and around Harvard Square? Would the plot and the flavor of the relationships change if it were set in New York? Or Ann Arbor? Or Houston?

2. One of the structural cores of the novel is the relationships between the women—Agnes and Diana, Olympia and Adriana, Adriana and Beverly. What is the function of this device? How do these relationships differ from each other?

3. Each chapter tells a unique story. How does the author maintain continuity in the face of disparate themes?

4. What role do the male characters—Maynard, Norman, Chandler, and A.E.—play in advancing the plot?

5. Why do Agnes and Abigail keep secrets from Adriana?

6. What is the basis for the relationship between A.E. and the three young women—Agnes, Diana, and Henrietta—whom he encounters at the close of the novel?

7. Many chapter titles allude to history, religion or literature. What function do these allusions play in advancing the storyline and putting the novel in perspective?

8. Which of the characters do you find most interesting and why?